Contents

Roman Treachery

Book 11 in the Sword of Cartimandua Series
By
Griff Hosker

Published by Sword Books 2014

Copyright © Griff Hosker First Edition

A CIP catalogue record for this title is available from the British Library.

Dedication

To Scout, the Border Collie! You are Wolf and you made the book so hard to write! Thank God you are trained now!

Prologue

The warrior saw the small turret at the end of the Roman wall; it looked strange and unlike the others which were part of a continuous defence. There were no wooden stakes and the stone was not mortared. The wall itself just ended although he could see the foundations and the prepared stone. They had built quickly since his last visit. The top of the sentry's helmet was barely visible, occasionally peeping over the top of the ramparts and the occasional shaft of moonlight reflected from his spear point. He knew that they were Gauls; he had crossed here often enough to know that but the smell they exuded marked them as different from the legionaries and the hated horse warriors. Had it been the legion he would have found it more difficult to evade detection but the Gauls, fierce warriors though they were, did not like to perform sentry duties. They preferred huddling beneath their cloaks trying to keep out the perfidious cold which seeped into their bodies.

He crawled cautiously towards the gap when the clouds passed before the moon, a little further forward towards the land of the Selgovae. In times past, the time of his father, he would not have dared this journey without arms and allies but, the coming of the Romans had made allies of enemies. The enemy of my enemy is my friend seemed an appropriate phrase to use. As he drew closer to the wall he heard them talking. He could understand their words for without them, south of the wall, the world was harder and harsher; it paid to learn how to speak like a Roman. The Gauls were bemoaning the climate. The thought flickered through his mind that they would all be better off if they returned to their own homes and leave the people of Britannia to govern themselves. Perhaps this meeting, the last of many, would see that day come a little closer.

With a sigh of relief he rolled down the heather covered bank away from the wall. Even if they saw him now they could not catch him; they wore armour and he did not and the forest was but eight hundred paces from him. He got to his feet and, keeping a low profile, ran down the trail and up the rocky slope to reach his destination; the rock of the wolf. It had been named by all the tribes for it resembled, from a certain angle, a howling wolf. As a feature in the landscape it stood out from all the other strange rock formations. Once there he was safe and he settled down with his back to the rock to await his guide.

Far to the south, at the other extreme of the province, a woman lay dying. Aula Luculla was a bitter woman. She had deserted her husband,

2

the Governor at the time, to flee with his nephew, her lover. Deserted by Decius Sallustius she had raised the two children he left in her when he fled Britannia, alone. Whilst not penniless she had been forced to hide both her name and the names of her two lovers. Both men had been deemed to be enemies of Rome. Her husband had been executed whilst his nephew had been hunted and killed by his own brother in Gaul. She had spent the long years alone afraid of detection and nurturing an unnatural hatred for her lover's brother.

Now her children were gathered at her bedside for a final journey, a journey she would take alone. Her illness had been long and painful. Gone was the beautiful woman who had intoxicated men and made them willing to sacrifice their honour for her; now she was emaciated and gaunt. Her red hair was now riven with grey and falling out in hanks. Her fingers and arms were skeletal. Her sunken cheeks made her look far older than her real age. Each child held a hand. She had been a good mother to them both, bringing them up alone in Londinium; teaching them to be survivors.

"I am dying." Neither child showed any emotion; their mother had taught them well. "Apart from this home and a few coins I have little to leave you. But I can offer you gold." There was the slightest flicker from their eyes. Gold had been the downfall of both their mother and their father but that did not stop it from being their own addictive drug. "Your father sent me a letter." She held it up to them. "When he fled to Gaul with the Druid's gold he secreted one box, just in case he returned. It is buried at the bend of the river where he took ship. You need to ask questions of the men of Marcus' Horse and discover where that was. When you find them then you must also kill the one who wields the Sword of Cartimandua; I know not who it is but I know that the sword helped bring about the downfall of your father and an end to my hopes of joy." She gave a wan smile. "I have taught you well enough for you to be discreet. You will need to hide your family name for it is known in that part of the world. That is my inheritance but I also charge you with a mission. I want you to promise that you will kill your father's brother, your uncle, Livius Lucullus Sallustius, Prefect of the ala called Marcus' Horse. He is the reason your father was killed and the ala was responsible for our poverty. Promise me that you will exact revenge on them all."

"We promise." Their voices, like their minds were as one.

She sighed and gave a brief, contented smile, "Good then I can die and meet your father in the afterlife knowing that we have had our revenge on all who brought harm to us."

3

They sat with their mother until she gave the last gasp of life and death took her. They looked at each other. "It is best we separate. We have more chance of success alone."

"I agree but we will both need to be at Eboracum."

"I will find this ala."

"And I will find the gold. I will see you in Eboracum."

They took the two rings from their mother's fingers; one from her husband and one from their father. They each placed a ring on the other's finger. "This will be our sign; the ring on the middle finger."

"Farewell."

When the breath had gone from her body, they held hands and both said a silent prayer for the only parent they had known. Finally, they took the letter and read it.

My Dearest Aula,

If you have received this letter then I am dead. For that I am sorry- I loved life but I am sorry that you did not share in my victory as much as I would have hoped.

I hope that I have killed my brother but if I have not, then swear that you will do so. In return I can offer you that which you prize the most, Gold!

Before I left Eboracum, I buried a box of gold. It is at the place that they ambushed us. It is buried beneath a dead elm tree which is ten paces from the river where the bend is the most acute. I hope you get the gold and, if you do, reward Marcus' Horse with the pain they deserve.

Your husband,

Decius Lucullus Sallustius

Chapter 1

Governor Aulus Platorius Nepos had had to visit the settlement devastated sixty years earlier in the Boudiccan revolt. The Temple of Claudius had been both cleaned and painted but even now, sixty years later, there was still the mental image of the women and children being burned alive. The colonia had been rebuilt; the veterans had returned but it was no longer the heart of the province. It felt, somehow, tainted. The Governor had paid his respects at the temple of the father of Britannia and the largest building in the province. He shook himself and turned to his aide. "And how far is it again to the wall of Hadrian?"

Appius Serjanus was an ambitious young patrician who had secured his appointment through his father's influence. They both knew of the incredible wealth of the province which was largely untapped. Now that the wall was almost complete, father and son saw the opportunity to profit from the Empire's investment. "It is over two hundred miles sir."

"Ye Gods! Please tell me there is accommodation along the way?"

"Yes Governor. There are forts and mansio at regular intervals although once we are beyond Eboracum they are a little basic in nature."

"So long as they have baths."

"I heard, Governor, that they have built a bath house, already, on the wall."

"Well that is good news at least. We have delayed long enough, Appius summon the decurion."

The cavalry escort was a turma from the Sixth Victrix legion which the Governor had brought to finish the building of the wall. The legionaries were hard at work in that cold northern outpost but Governor Nepos had wanted a tour of the safer southern lands before braving the harsh frontier. Now that Emperor Hadrian had left for Africa and the east, it was incumbent upon him to oversee the work. He saw it as a legacy for him, for all time. 'Nepos' Wall'; it had a good ring to it. This would be his opportunity to leave his mark for posterity.

Far to the north, Legate Julius Demetrius was feeling the northern clime more than most. Although he had served in Britannia for many years, his sojourn in Surrentum had made him prefer the warm nights which followed those, always, hot days of Italy rather than the chilling cold nights and wet days of the northern province. Here it was freezing nights after cold days.

He was pleased with the progress of the wall. Since they had established the line from the west and begun the line from the east he had been able to concentrate his patrols in the centre section. Of course that was, perforce, close to the highest part of the land but it could not be helped. The Votadini and the Selgovae were not taking the physical intrusion of a wall into their land well. The wall looked imposing close up but from a distance, as the Legate knew, it looked awesome. Faced with concrete and painted white it stood out above the green and grey of the grass and rocks. It had done as the Emperor Hadrian had intended and had shown the barbarians that the Romans were here to stay. What it had not done, as the Legate knew to his cost, was to tell the barbarians that this was the limit of Rome. The tribes north of the barrier seemed to regard it as an affront to their manhood that Rome had dared to tell them where they could and could not go.

He reined his horse in and the tent party of cavalrymen halted behind him. From his vantage point he could see the legionaries of the Sixth Victrix busily building the wall. Beyond them he could see the heather covered moor land stretching away to the forests in the north. He could not see them but he knew that the barbarians were there, just watching and waiting for a slip-up, a moment's distraction and the builders of Hadrian's Britannic monument would be slaughtered. The camp, just north of the Stanegate, had guards, despite the fact that it was south of the wall. Until both ends were joined the barbarians could slip through as the Sixth had found to their cost on numerous occasions. The sentries saluted the Legate as he rode through the two gates and headed for the workers. First Spear, Quintus Licinius Brocchus, was like his men, without his helmet as he toiled alongside them. Gone were the days when they could work without armour; too many men had been killed in surprise attacks and they worked with the chafing armour which did, at least, afford some protection.

"Ah Legate, come to give us a hand?"

Julius dismounted, "One of the few privileges of being a Legate and being a man of my years is that I get to watch young men like yourself working."

First Spear Broccus snorted, "You, old? Don't make me laugh. You can still keep up with some of these useless lumps of donkey shit here." The legionaries grinned at the insult.

"Is the patrol back yet?"

"No, not yet. They have been gone for just over a week and Marcus said that it would be a ten-day jaunt."

"How is he?"

Quintus stopped working to drink from the water skin hung on his spear. "He seems to have recovered, but he is a deep one."

Decurion Marcus Gaius Aurelius had been captured by slavers a couple of years earlier and had barely escaped with his newly acquired and heavily pregnant wife. The raiders had come to exact revenge and almost captured and killed his mother. Thanks to a rescued slave, Drugi, they had defeated the slavers but, as Julius knew, that always had an effect on a man's mind. The birth of his son, Macro, seemed to have given him a better perspective and, knowing that the man he rescued, Drugi, was watching over his family, helped.

"So long as he doesn't have the death wish his stepbrother had then I shall be happy. The Prefect seems satisfied but he is at Corio and Marcus spends more time across the border than he does here." Livius had known Marcus since he had been a boy and felt quite close to him as he had his father, Gaius.

Just then a sentry cried, "Stand to! Riders!"

Although riders normally meant Romans, here on the frontier it was more sensible to wait until you knew for certain. The barbarians had used captured armour and horses before now to make surprise attacks on unsuspecting auxiliaries.

Quintus peered north, "Stand down. It is our lads. Well, Legate, you can find out for yourself now." The horsemen were obviously Roman with their distinctive oval shields and spears, their red cloaks and, in this particular turma's case, the wolf standard following the decurion.

Marcus had grown up in the last five years and not just physically. The loss of Macro, his step brother had been a grievous blow following on, as it did, the death of his father. The enslavement had been a cathartic time for him as he learned to begin to discover how to live again. Alone and an ocean away from home he had had to rely on his skills as a warrior and his inner strength as a man. The slave woman Frann had helped him and, with the birth of his son, Macro, he had finally gained an inner peace. Promoted to decurion he was now, increasingly, taking on more of the role formerly performed by the Prefect at Rocky Point. The poor Prefect was embroiled in the logistics of moving from Coriosopitum to their new fort. Many of the comrades of both men had died in the recent conflicts. Both Marcus and Livius knew that it would only be a matter of time before Livius retired and began to enjoy the fruits of his labours but the threat was still there north of the wall. The both knew that it was Marcus' task to discourage the increasingly frequent raids.

"Hail Legate."

"Hail Marcus." Julius could not help but glance at the four turmae to look for empty saddles. He could see there were none. "Successful patrol then?"

"Chosen Man Gnaeus, take the turmae back to Rocky Point while I brief the Legate." Gnaeus threw him a quizzical look. "I think I am safe here Gnaeus and besides we have these cavalrymen from the Sixth who can bring me home and tuck me up." Gnaeus rode away shaking his head while the troopers laughed. "They are like old women, always watching over me."

"They just don't want to lose you again Marcus. They felt guilty the last time."

"I know. I am just glad that the Prefect has decided to promote Gnaeus; it was like having a mother with me all over again. You couldn't take a shit without him watching!"

"How was the patrol then?"

"We flushed a few warbands out. Having over a hundred mounted men helps to control them although they have learned to climb the high crags where we cannot follow." He shrugged. "At least if they are there then they cannot sabotage the wall but it is expensive on the horses." He idly stroked his horse's mane; the troopers were all very fond of their horses, many of them weeping like a child when they were injured.

"When are you out on patrol next?" Julius Demetrius' keen eyes carefully examined Marcus' face.

The Legate rarely asked superfluous questions and Marcus' interest was piqued. "Why? What have you in mind sir?"

"I think we need a prisoner or two to question. I hate just reacting to events. I would like a little more information and the best way to get that information is to interrogate prisoners."

"You need Explorates."

"I know but you, Metellus, Rufius and the Prefect are the last of the Explorates we could count on and we would really need native speakers. Still, if you could find a prisoner or two…"

"I will be back on patrol in fourteen days. That will give me the chance to check Julius' maps. He is very efficient at keeping them up to date." Julius Longinus was the ala clerk and also an unpaid intelligence officer. He had a sharp mind and kept immaculate records. "I think we need to get close to one of their settlements. The ones who are nearby are wary warriors. Closer to home they might feel safer."

"Come on then, I will ride with you to Rocky Point. I am supposed to be inspecting the defences after all." First Spear Broccus had gone back to work. "I'll be back along this way in a couple of days Quintus."

8

He pointed towards the east. "Then we will be about fifty paces that way sir!" He absentmindedly clipped one of the legionaries who had turned at the words. "He was talking to me you horrible little man! Get on with it!"

Rocky Point was nearing the end of its life. Built before the wall as a camp for the ala which protected the workers, it would soon be redundant. The fort of Cilurnum was nearing completion and, already, the clerks and farriers had moved from Corio to Rocky Point ready for the grand move. The auxiliary ala would have its first permanent base.

"I shall miss Rocky Point sir." The isolated wooden structure rose defiantly in the land which was still Selgovae and Marcus remembered the early days when the ala had been the only force keeping the barbarians away from the construction site of the wall. Many men had fallen defending its wooden walls and ditches.

"The new fort will have stone walls and a bath house Marcus. It will be more comfortable."

"True but I still think of this as a refuge. Remember the time we barely made it escorting those refugees the barbarians had captured?"

"Don't remind me. That was as close as I want to come to a Selgovae spear."

As they descended the primitive track which led to the fort Julius could not help notice the keen eyed sentries. This was not a safe posting; this was the edge of hell. Here the garrison was almost completely surrounded by the enemy. It was another reason for the move. When the wall finally reached this exposed northern ridge the fort that had been the cavalry's home would be beyond the frontier. The grim troopers faced death every day.

The first thing Julius noticed was that Livius now looked greyer and older. The frontier took its toll on its defenders and Livius had performed that duty longer than most. When he greeted them and smiled at two old friends, his face looked far younger. Marcus was so close to him, as had been his father and his namesake that Livius felt this was the son he would never have. His darkest times had been when he had been captured by Trygg, the Uite. Like Marcus he would be sorry to leave Rocky Point; it had been a bastion against the barbaric forces from the north. They suffered attacks on a weekly basis but not one enemy had managed to breach the walls. It was a record of which the Prefect was proud.

After greeting the Legate, he asked Marcus. "Good patrol?"

"We lost no-one; it was a good patrol but we did not find any enemies. The Legate here wishes me to capture prisoners next time."

9

Livius frowned. It was his task to detail the missions but he accepted that he was outranked. "Rufius is out at the moment with his turmae; he may have more success."

Marcus shook his head, "Sir, with respect, we defend first and think of prisoners second. When I try to get one it will not be through war but stealth."

"Stealth young Marcus? When were you ever stealthy?" The voice boomed from behind him.

Marcus turned to see the Decurion Princeps approaching. He had served under Metellus as an Explorate and had learned much from that most intelligent and thoughtful of officers. "Metellus! Good to hear you are still alive and your wife has not kept you south of the Dunum." Metellus and his wife, Nanna, ran a horse stud close to the farm where Marcus' mother still lived.

"Every time I am down there she nags me to stay home and it is tempting but, there is still so much to do and now that I am Decurion Princeps of the ala, I feel I have more responsibility. And how are your wife and your son?"

Marcus' face lit up. He would happily talk for hours about every slight change in his young son. Livius watched the two married men and felt pangs of jealousy. He would never enjoy a family life and he wondered if that was the curse of a Prefect in the auxiliaries. Marcus Maximunius, after whom the ala had been named had also never married; like Livius the ala was his family and the officers and troopers his children. "So Legate we need prisoners…"

Far to the north of the wall, in the safety of the Selgovae stronghold, Briac the Brigante, Randal the Votadini and Iucher the Selgovae were in deep discussion. Since their first meeting the representatives of the three main tribes in the region had hammered out their plan to rid the region of the Romans.

"The gap between the two walls becomes narrower each day and soon it will be closed." Iucher was becoming increasingly agitated. He had not believed how swiftly the Romans could build from stone. It was as though they defecated brick!

Briac smiled. "It matters not, for, when it is closed, I will be south of the wall and our plans will be in place. With our spy in the enemy ranks we will be able to communicate easily with you. You will know exactly what the Romans intend as soon as they do."

"Why have you not used this traitor before?" Randal was suspicious of the Brigante; old tribal differences were always just below the surface.

10

"He has only recently joined and it has taken time for him to become accepted. Another problem is that, at the moment, he is not yet at the frontier but he will be. The Romans have a great need for warriors and they replace them frequently. By the time I reach my home I will have made contact with him and arranged the signals we will use. Once I am home then we can begin to disrupt the Roman road. That is their weakness; they rely on the carts and the wagons which trundle up and down their stone ways. They cannot defend them all. We will slow down their supplies and then your tribes can destroy them on the wall. When they are weak then we will rise in the south and fall upon the garrisons. It may not be soon for we need to build up our army but we will rise and they will be destroyed."

Randal's interest was piqued. "What will you do then?"

"We will capture their wagons and kill their drivers. We will go into their forts and kill them while they sleep. We will poison their food and all the time we will smile, as though we are the grateful dog who feeds from their scraps. When we rebelled before we were open and hostile and they knew who we were. We live with those who love the Romans and we pretend that we love them too. How can they fight an enemy if they know not who the enemy is?"

Iucher nodded his approval. "And now that we are at peace with our Votadini brothers we can strike at many places along the wall." The two tribes had been mortal enemies until the Romans had come and now they had shelved their differences. Together they would be a formidable foe

"We have learned that the ones who build the wall, the legions will not be based upon the wall but further away. When the gap is closed it will not be the mighty legion you face but men from Gaul and other parts of the Empire. Those warriors, brothers, are their weakness. The legionaries stand and fight in lines with mighty weapons throwing stones and huge arrows. The others do not and we can beat them!"

The new Governor and his entourage finally arrived at Eboracum. His wife, Flavia was less than impressed with the frontier fortress. Thanks to the Emperors Trajan and Hadrian it was stronger and had better accommodation than in the early years of its life but the wife of the Governor was used to a more luxurious lifestyle. "And what of the slaves? Where do I acquire decent slaves, who can converse with me and understand my needs?"

Aulus Nepos sighed. His wife always felt that he lived below their station in life. He doubted that the slaves in this part of the province would meet her high standards. "Perhaps, rather than slaves, we should

11

hire well brought up citizens from the area. They could be your companions. There must be some intelligent young ladies who would like to enjoy the life style of the fort."

Flavia did not think for one moment that there would be any such citizens but, having seen and smelled the locals as they passed through the vicus, she knew that she did not want slaves. "I shall, of course, interview them and see if they meet my standard."

"Without a doubt my dear and now I shall set in motion the plans with the officials and officers of the fort. If you would care to inspect the quarters and make a list of any deficiencies then I will have them remedied rapidly." He knew that there would be many deficiencies but money was not a problem. He was, after all, Governor of the province of Britannia which had more potential riches than any other. The wheat alone, when controlled and managed effectively, would mean that they would not have to totally rely on the Egyptian harvest. "Appius!"

"Sir?" Appius was never far from the Governor and he tried to anticipate his every wish.

"We need some servants for my wife. Two should do for the moment. They should be literate and well presented. There should be some families hereabouts who would want their daughters to associate with the Governor of Britannia and his family. See to it. I will be with the senior officers to find out about the state of the construction of the wall and its attendant defences."

Appius knew that he had to make himself an invaluable asset if he were to succeed in his plan to gain power. Although finding servants was not the task he had anticipated it would enable him to gain power over someone close to the Governor's wife and that was not a bad thing. He headed for the forum; it was not as vibrant and bustling as the ones in Rome, or even in the southern half of the province, it did, at least, provide a place for the well to do to gather, talk and impress each other with their latest acquisitions; bath house, tutor, the list was endless. There were already merchants and their families gathered. Their Roman dress marked them out quite clearly as did the fact that the men, especially, looked uncomfortable in the newly acquired garb. He waited in the corner to observe them for a while. He identified at least four young women who looked as though they might be suitable; they certainly met the presentable category. The literate side was one he would have to gauge through conversation. He also noted the men for these would be the ones with money and power in this frontier region; they too would be worthy of his attention.

He took a deep breath and put on his most engaging smile. He stepped into the main area and was most pleased when the conversation dropped a little as they inspected this well-dressed stranger. The purple stripe on his toga told all but the most ignorant that this man had senatorial connections. Appius knew that he was good looking and was not surprised when both the matrons and the young ladies appraised him approvingly. He approached the family with the two most likely looking young ladies. "My apologies domina, for interrupting your conversation, but I am new in Eboracum having travelled from Rome with the new Governor. I am Appius Serjanus."

The portly gentleman who was the head of the family puffed himself up. He looked to Appius like a farmer who has made a little money and calls himself a merchant. He could almost see the dirt beneath his finger nails. "Delighted to meet you. I am Publius Bibula and this is my wife, Aula Bibula." Appius nodded to the wife who looked as fond of her food as her husband. She simpered and Appius assumed that she thought she was being coquettish.

"And who are these lovely young ladies domina? Your sisters?"

Aula Bibula giggled and her layers of fat shook in a most alarming manner. "Why no, this is my daughter Tita Bibula and her friend Vibia Dives."

"Delighted to meet with you." He took their hands and kissed the back of them. Tita was like her mother and giggled although, happily, without the rippling layers of fat. Vibia, in contrast, coolly met his stare with her own chillingly attractive look. "As I am new in the city I wondered if you might help me. The wife of the Governor is seeking two young ladies to help her settle in and to provide intelligent company for her. Do you know of any young ladies who might be willing to provide such service? There would, of course, be remuneration."

Aula shook her head. "I am afraid we could not consider letting Tita work as a servant, of any description. But Vibia is I believe seeking a position." If Vibia took those words as an insult she did not show it but merely carried on smiling like an enigmatic Sphinx.

Appius noticed that Tita did not agree with her mother but that Vibia did not look displeased. "I would be pleased to aid you Appius Serjanus and I believe that I know of another, Lucia Scaura." Her voice had a seductive quality to it and Appius could tell from her grammar that she was well brought up. She leaned in to speak more confidentially to him, "She has travelled from the southern part of the province and she has fallen on hard times."

Appius nodded, as though he cared, "How sad. If you could come to the Governor's residence later in the day then I will introduce you to

Governor Nepos and his wife, the Lady Flavia. Of course the selection of the successful candidates will be up to the Lady Flavia."

"Of course."

"Could I ask if you can read and write?"

Vibia gave a smile which could have been contemptuous but quickly became engaging, "Of course and I can speak and read Greek. Not that one has much opportunity here."

Appius could see that he had at least one potential servant and companion of a very high standard. Even if this Lucia was not as qualified it would not matter. "I look forward to speaking with you later on. Until this afternoon."

As he left he saw the look of hatred Tita gave to her mother. Although she had not provided a servant she might provide a bed companion. Appius resented paying for whores and Tita looked as though she might be willing to satisfy his needs. Eboracum was looking better by the moment.

Chapter 2

Marcus stood in Livius' office. "Now take no chances. I know the Legate asked for prisoners but I do not want to lose either you or Gnaeus. It will be his first patrol as decurion and he may try to impress you."

Marcus laughed. "He feels so guilty about almost losing his commander the other year that he will probably ensure that we all come back." He became more serious for, like his Prefect, Marcus cared about all the troopers. They had had few casualties in the last couple of years and they both intended it to stay that way. "The only dangerous part of this, sir, is that we will be further from the wall and have a longer journey home. I intend to leave two turmae halfway back as reinforcements should we need them. I promise you I will take no chances."

As they headed north through the gates in the wall Marcus hoped that the Selgovae were watching at the gap. It mattered little for this was just one of their regular patrols. He would take his four turmae north, into the huge forests and then swing to the east. The Votadini lived closer to the coast and felt largely safe from Roman incursions. He would have more chance of capturing a prisoner there. The eight spare horses they took with them were a normal precaution against accidents and injuries but this time they would be needed to transport the prisoners. Gnaeus rode next to him as they traversed the forest trails. Two of the better scouts were ranging far ahead to give them early warning of danger and it meant that Marcus could give Gnaeus advice on his new role.

"I know that you can command Gnaeus, it is why I recommended you for promotion but you will need to be able to take independent command. When I leave you with Titus and the Third Turma you will have to make the decision about the right time to return to Rocky Point."

"What do you mean return? You will be back will you not?"

"Hopefully I will but anything can happen and that is why I leave you in command. Titus has also been recently promoted but you and I have ridden together many years and I know you. That is what I mean when I say you are in command; it is a heavy burden you bear."

Gnaeus chewed on his lip; he did not like the thought of abandoning his leader again. "Which settlement will you try?"

"When we have crossed the old northern road, I will try the village of Tad. They are prosperous there and, as I recall, they are close to the

Votadini royal family. We need those who have knowledge of those with power at this moment. It is my intention to wait for dusk; we will then have the night to return to you."

"Where do you intend to leave us?"

"The old fort on the road; it is still defensible and yet you can remain hidden. If we are not returned in two days then inform the Prefect of my failure." He saw the terrified look on the young decurion's face. "I will return but my orders have to be quite clear Gnaeus."

Gnaeus did not look convinced but Marcus was his senior and he would obey albeit reluctantly. The fort had seen much action both during its lifetime as a northern outpost and since it had been abandoned. Many auxiliaries' bones lay beneath the sods and shrubs surrounding the burnt out and decaying wooden fort. Their sacrifice had been in vain for they had, inevitably, been pushed back, despite all the efforts of the soldiers who fought for Rome. Marcus looked towards the north-west remembering when he and his stepbrother had defended the eagle of the Ninth as the legion was finally eliminated as a fighting force. The survivors and Macro and Marcus had left the field with their heads held high for they took with them their eagle and left the field in good order. It was that memory which put steel into Marcus' resolve. He had lost many good comrades in that retreat and he owed it to them to help to hold on to the land they still owned.

After leaving Gnaeus and Titus at the fort, Marcus set off on his patrol with Publius. He was not a new decurion but he still looked up to Marcus who still carried the Sword of Cartimandua. The legendary blade had become an icon and symbol of luck. It was said that the first Roman to carry it, Ulpius Felix had been named Felix because he was lucky. That luck and good fortune still continued and Marcus knew that many men secretly touched the blade for luck before combat. He was not sure if it did them any good but he knew that, like his father before him, the blade gave him an edge in any combat. He realised that Livius would prefer the blade were left at home where men would not try to defend it to the last but Marcus would not dream of taking the field without it.

As the sun passed its zenith Marcus halted the turmae. They found a wood in the next valley to the settlement. Marcus chose the ten troopers he would take with him. They were from both turmae and they had been chosen for their ability to remain hidden. They took off their helmets and left their shields and javelins with Publius. Their cloaks would help them to escape observation but Marcus longed for the green cloaks and brown clothes he had worn as an Explorate. Those days were long gone.

16

"We will be back by dawn. If we have not returned by noon, then return to Gnaeus. We may have to leave in a hurry be prepared to cover our withdrawal."

The ten man patrol trotted off up the ridge. They dismounted just below the crest so that Marcus could belly up and spy out the land. He had been taught well by Gaelwyn, his mother's uncle and he sought every piece of cover he could. He peered from under the bush and saw the trail leading to the settlement some mile and a half away. He found what he was looking for, a wooded area through which the path to the settlement passed. He rolled back down the slope and, detailing two troopers to watch their horses, he led the others over the ridge and down to the woods. It was now a case of waiting and hoping to catch hunters as they returned, laden with game to their home. If there were none, then they would have to lie up overnight and catch early morning travellers.

The pheasants gave them warning of the approaching hunters as they flew noisily into the air. Using hand signals only, Marcus dispersed his men. They knew what they had to do. Four of them had cudgels and rope to bind their prisoners. They were, hopefully, far enough away from the village for any noise to bring help, for they were now far to the north of the wall and safety. Soon they heard the Votadini voices as they approached the woods. The hunters had had a good hunt and there were no enemies this close to their stockaded settlement. They were relaxed. Marcus breathed a sigh of relief as he saw that there were only six men. The one at the front would be a leader and he needed to be captured. The four men in the middle carried the dead deer and that left the one at the rear to deal with. Marcus nodded to the trooper next to him who bore the cudgel; at the same time he jammed the wooden branch at the man's feet making him stumble. As soon as he did so two of the troopers at the rear stabbed the Votadini rearguard and then the rest fell upon the last four. It was a noisy scuffle but the Votadini were tired and unprepared. All five were trussed, gagged and bound before the last warrior had expired.

"Quickly! Back to the horses." Marcus allowed his men to run up the hillside to the ridge while he watched for any other hunters returning to their village- there were none. The men were still unconscious when they were tied on the backs of the spare horses.

Publius watched the sun begin to dip behind him. Now the waiting would seem interminable; every sound would be magnified and every broken branch would be a barbarian with murderous intent. It was a relieved decurion who saw the line of troopers ride towards them. He turned to two of his troopers. "Ride ahead of us and make sure the trail is clear." As Marcus and his men donned their helmets and gathered their weapons Publius checked that the men were secure. "That was easy enough sir."

"Yes indeed Publius, now we have the hard part. Get them though the enemy lines."

"Bear Killer!" Iucher smiled as his old friend used the name he had first adopted as a warrior.

"Yes Colm. What is it?"

"Are you sure we can trust these Selgovae? My father still tells of the time they betrayed our king when we were close to capturing their eagle."

"Times change old friend and we must join together to fight our common enemy. Perhaps when the eagle has left this land we can once again fight the Selgovae." The two war chiefs were leading their hundreds close to the wall to begin their attacks on the auxiliaries. As they strode down the Roman road, neither man marked the irony of using the Roman's own road to fight them. It would take them another day to reach the land close to the Roman edifice and they would have left the road long before that.

Suddenly, one of the scouts came running back with something in his hand. He ran to Iucher who was his leader. "Horses. Roman horses." In his hand he held a piece of horse dung, still warm. It could be seen to be Roman from the grain within; Roman horses were well fed. "There were more than fifty of them and they were heading east."

Colm rolled the manure around in his hand. "Fifty may be just a patrol."

"Or it could be a raid. We will wait here for a while. It will do no harm to rest and, if we can capture some Romans then so much the better."

Marcus led the two turmae towards the fort. They had journeyed further south than their outward route in case they had been followed and it was for that reason that they escaped a total disaster. The last four Votadini scouts heard and then saw the Roman horses approach. One of them ran back to Iucher while the others watched. Marcus's horse, Hercules, had a sensitive nose and, smelling the barbarians, gave a whinny. Marcus knew what it meant. "Barbarians! To arms! Gallop!" His well-trained men needed no urging and their horses leapt forwards. They were riding in a column of fours with the captives towards the front.

18

The last two lines of Romans came under attack from the scouts and the Votadini as Iucher brought them to join the fray. What the barbarians lacked in skill and finesse they made up for with exuberance. They hurled themselves at the troopers, throwing spears, daggers, and loosing arrows in a vain attempt to bring them down. Three of the troopers fell to the enemy whilst a fourth had a spear lodge in his back. He kept his saddle and the riders galloped along and down the road. The horses of the dead troopers kept on galloping and it was only when they reached the deserted fort that they discovered their casualties. The two turmae who were waiting for them spread out behind them to watch for any pursuit. While the wounded man was dealt with Marcus rode back to see if he could see his lost troopers; the ala did not like to leave their men on the field. From the saddles of the dead men's horses he could read the tale and the blood which covered both animal and sheepskin were eloquent.

Publius walked over to Marcus shaking his head. "Appius has died."

"We will take him home. Gnaeus!" His former chosen man rode over. "We will return a different way. We will head towards the fort at Pons Aelius. They will expect us to travel west, especially if they follow our tracks." He looked over his shoulder as though willing the troopers to appear."

"Three men in exchange for the prisoners you have is a trade they would have all taken sir. They are soldiers and casualties happen."

Marcus shook his head. "No, it is not a fair trade but we have completed our mission and we will make sure that these men talk!"

Gnaeus thought he knew Marcus well but there was a chill in his voice which sent shivers down the decurion's spine.

The prisoners began to stir as they wearily approached the coast. The capsarius, Decius, and Gnaeus sat them upright on their horses. "One didn't make it sir. Someone cracked him a little too hard on the head."

Marcus was philosophical; at least they had four men to question. "Leave his body there and assign two troopers to each prisoner. We don't want to lose any more do we?" There was an edge to his voice which had not been there before his men were killed.

Once they passed through the fort at Pons Aelius they could relax. The wall was reasonably secure all the way to Coriosopitum but it would be a long twenty-five miles to reach it. Marcus glanced to his left at the busy port on the south bank. The Classis Britannica now had a presence there which made the coastline better defended and pirate raids from across the Mare Germania had dropped significantly. It was

19

now to the north where the danger lay. Marcus prayed for the day when the wall would be complete and the land to the south made safe. He worried every day about his mother, wife and child. There had been too many instances in the past when their lives had been in jeopardy; the completed wall would end all that and stop the barbarian slave raids.

The Legate and Livius were at Coriosopitum for the monthly briefing of senior leaders. Julius had initiated the meeting so that the officers all saw their colleagues face to face. If you knew the man then you fought much harder to protect him.

"Publius, see to the turmae. Well done lads. It was a good patrol. Gnaeus bring the prisoners with us."

The Tungrians who were based at the fort knew the ala well and the salutes were crisp and respectful as Marcus led the prisoners to the Principia. "Wait outside until I call for you."

The prisoners were still bound and gagged but their eyes burned fiercely with hatred for their captors. One of them spread his legs and urine hissed to the floor. The sentry reacted quickly and rammed his spear haft between the man's legs. "You dirty barbarian bastard!"

Marcus smiled at the man's courage. "Just sit him down in it soldier. It will soon clean up."

Julius was alone when Marcus entered. The relief on Julius Demetrius' face was palpable. The whole of the ala felt like family to the old Prefect of the ala but Marcus was special for there was a close history between Marcus' family and Julius'. "Successful outcome to the mission, Marcus?"

"We captured four prisoners but we lost some troopers sir. I would have preferred not to lose any and, from the look of the ones we captured, it will be hard to get anything from them."

"I think Prefect Sallustius and First Spear Broccus will manage; they can be very persuasive." Marcus smiled grimly; Quintus Broccus was a large and tough warrior. He was from the old school and learned his trade fighting Dacians. However, sometimes brute force didn't always work. It was as though the Legate was thinking the same thing. "And if the centurion's methods fail then Livius has a very persuasive tongue."

"Where do you want them then sir? One of them decided to piss on your porch."

"Feisty eh? Take them to the cell block. They can be its first customers." As one of the older forts on the frontier Coriosopitum had been improved as the years had gone by. The bath house and granaries had been completed the previous year and now a small set of cells built to house and discipline the soldiers of the wall, had been completed.

20

"You can take your men to your new fort. Rocky Point has been abandoned. Decurion Princeps Metellus is busy organising it."

"You mean Julius Longinus is organising it and Metellus is pulling his hair out?"

The Legate laughed, the ala clerk was a fussy little man who liked things done his way and the officers of the ala had to comply. It was a trade off for the clerk was highly efficient and made life easier for them in other ways. "Would you expect anything less?"

When the senior officers arrived they discussed the prisoners. "Marcus tells me they are Votadini and they are warriors."

"What do you want to know then sir?"

"Actually, Livius, we need to discover quite simple things. Who are the war chiefs? What is their strength? How prepared are they for war?"

"What about their plans?"

"That would be a bonus, Quintus, but we would have to be very lucky to have captured warriors who actually know the plans of the chiefs but I will take whatever I can get. We will use the cell block for the interrogation."

As they waited for their first warrior they took off their helmets, swords and cloaks. It was unlikely that the prisoners would be able to do anything but it made sense to keep temptation away from them. The first prisoner was brought out of his cell. His arms were tied around a log which was fixed behind his back and his feet were shackled. He came out like a wild animal and tried to ram the guard who tethered him with the log from behind his back. The guard just yanked on the rope and the barbarian crashed to the ground. The centurion picked him up and, pulling his fist back, hit him hard in the gut. The warrior doubled up trying to catch his breath. "Now that was just to get you to behave yourself."

The man didn't react and Livius said, "Well he doesn't speak our language. I will have to try his." He lifted the man's chin, gently and looked him in the eyes. "The centurion wants you to behave yourself. No more tricks eh?" The man shook his head but Livius knew he had understood. "Now tell me, what is your name?" The man spat at Livius who avoided the spittle. Broccus brought his fist back but Livius held up his hand. "Now if you do that again this man will hit you again and next time he will hurt you. What harm is there in telling me your name?"

He could see the man debating. Livius had no doubt that if the others were present he would say nothing but Quintus' fist had hurt him. "Lulach!"

21

"There, Lulach. That wasn't so hard was it? And your king is still Lugubelenus is it?" He looked defiant and Livius gave a slight nod to the centurion who hit him square on his face. The crack of bone told them all that his nose had been broken. He nodded. "The officer who captured you said you had been hunting. Was it a good hunt?"

He could see Lulach wondering at the question. The blow had hurt him and he wasn't sure if the information about hunting would help the enemy or not. He decided it wouldn't and if it avoided another blow then so much the better. He would need his strength when he escaped and killed the big Roman warrior. "Yes. We caught two big deer."

"And there were only six of you? Then you are mighty hunters."

The man, despite the pain, showed pride in his achievements. "I am the best hunter in the village."

"Well, that is good for there are many mouths to feed, especially with the new warriors arriving."

"The new warriors cannot hunt like Lulach!" There was an air of derision in his voice.

"And you will need them when you attack the ones on the wall."

"We do not need them." Now that he had begun to talk he could not stop the flow. "We need neither them, nor the Selgovae nor the Brigante. We could destroy the women who wait on the wall."

It soon became obvious that they had learned all that they could from him and he was taken back. With that information the next three were questioned using the knowledge they had gained for confirmation. They did not need to use force and they wondered how the Romans knew so much. Finally, the leader was brought out. Livius had seen the torc around his neck and he had left him deliberately until last.

"We have spoken with the others and know that you are mighty hunters and warriors. We know that your king, the powerful Lugubelenus has joined forces with the Selgovae and the Brigante to destroy the Emperor's wall. The only thing we do not know is your name, the warrior who leads them." He stubbornly remained silent. Quintus' knuckles were bloodied to the bone when he had finished his beating but the chief refused to say anything.

First Spear Broccus looked over to Julius and shook his head, admiring the courage of the Votadini warrior. "We'll get nothing from this one sir."

"Right then we will crucify him and see what effect it has on the others."

As he was picked up by the two sentries he spat out some teeth and snarled at Livius. "You will die Roman. You will all die. My chief, Iucher has promised me this." He grinned a bloody, lopsided grin, "And in the night when you think you are safe, watch for the knife in the night from one of your own." He gave a chilling laugh as he was taken away.

"Brave man."

"What did he say Livius?" Livius told them and First Spear looked puzzled but the Legate looked worried. "That sounds to me like they have a spy in our camp."

"Not just in our camp Legate, in our ranks and that is worrying."

Quintus looked confused. "Can't be one of my lads."

"No, I don't think it is. I think it will be amongst the auxiliaries. We are recruiting more from the Britannic tribes now. All we ask is that they fight for Rome. We do not check where they came from." He looked at Livius. "I will brief the other prefects, Livius, but you had better watch your men closely for any sign of deception."

The Prefect could not envisage any of his men being a spy but he had heard the words; unless, of course, the man was telling a lie to make them worried. Livius watched the man being dragged away. He was a warrior, he would not tell a lie and, chillingly, he had looked at Livius when he had spoken; the traitor was probably in Marcus' Horse.

Chapter 3

Governor Nepos and his entourage had finally left the safety of Eboracum. Despite having been there for a month he had resisted the journey to the frontier. Although it appeared to be quiet, he had heard, from his predecessor, that the tribes could take umbrage at a minute slight and pour south to slaughter all in their path. Flavia, who was even more nervous than her husband, had insisted upon accompanying her husband; this meant taking a covered carriage; inevitably it slowed them all down and the Governor had to suffer his wife's complaints on the long road north. He was, however, grateful to Appius for his appointment of the two companions had proved to be a life saver. They were both attentive and intelligent and Flavia kept them closely closeted, bemoaning her fate the whole way up the Via Nero. Aulus was more than disappointed that they were hidden from view and conversation, for both of them were young and very easy on the eye. Vibia in particular was vibrant and lively with a wonderful sense of humour. All of the troopers of the turma who escorted them were madly in love with her already; her reddish-blond hair and her flashing green eyes were a wicked combination.

"Well, Appius what do you think of this country?"

Appius, in truth was not impressed. His father had told him that it was a rich province but the only riches he had seen so far were rocks and trees. Admittedly the rocks were fine rocks and would make solid buildings but that was all. He decided to be diplomatic. "It has potential sir but there seem to be remarkably few settlements along the road." He gestured to the west where the land rose to the hills in the distance. "We have travelled almost eighty miles from the fort and yet we have only seen two forts with tiny vici. Where are the towns? Where are the villas?"

Aulus smiled triumphantly. "That will be my work Appius. I will transform this barbaric land into a civilised outpost of the Empire. It will be the talk of Rome. Those rocks you see will make buildings bigger and grander than anything in Camulodunum. We will send engineers into the mountains to find the iron, gold and copper which will make us rich."

Appius' attention was instant; gold and copper! Those were the treasures his father sought. "I will begin to make plans then sir, while we are at the fort to divide up the country and enable engineers to explore it."

Aulus Nepos appreciated the young aide. He worked tirelessly and seemed to anticipate his every move. "An excellent idea Appius." He turned to the escorting cavalry. "Decurion! How long until we reach the fort?"

The decurion sighed, how long did any journey take up here? Forever when you were asked the same question every ten miles! Could the man not read the mile markers? "Coriosopitum is just twenty miles ahead sir. If we push on we might reach it by dark." Both men looked at the slowly moving carriage.

"Send a rider to the fort to warn the Prefect that we will be arriving. Ask him to send a couple of turmae of his cavalry to escort us. Not that I doubt your ability decurion but after dark, this close to the forests and the frontier..."

Decurion Titus Graccus did not take offence. He actually did not give a shit if the Governor wanted a legion to escort him! The only thing he wanted was for the journey to end so that he could rid himself of his burden and enjoy the amphora of wine he had waiting for him.

At the back of the column Rufius, decurion of Marcus' Horse and one time Explorate also cursed the slowly moving column. He would have been at the fort already with his twenty recruits had the Governor not insisted upon them adding to their escort. He had had time to look the recruits over and he was impressed. They had none of the older ex-warriors who joined for the extra salary paid to horsemen; these were all young and keen, men who wanted to join the elite auxiliary ala they had become. The oldest of the recruits was Vibius Gemellus who looked to be in his early twenties but even he was bright-eyed and enthusiastic. Livius would be pleased. Metellus, his oldest friend would also be pleased for Rufius had called at their stud to collect some horses and Nanna had given him a letter and a cake for her husband. Rufius knew that Metellus would retire ere long and who could blame him? His farm was in the most beautiful part of the Dunum valley and Nanna was a wonderful wife. If Rufius had been married to her then he would have retired long ago.

"Sir?"

He looked around at the young Brigante warrior. "Yes er..."

"Aneurin sir. Will we be with these troopers, ahead, all of the time sir?"

"No Aneurin. They are the Sixth Legion and they do not operate as we do. We are the ones who patrol the frontier; they fight the battles and escort the generals. Why?"

"Just curious sir. I knew of Marcus' Horse from tales in the village but I had not heard of the troopers."

"Tell me Aneurin, why did you not take a Roman name. I only ask for I was not born Rufius, I took the name when I joined."

"Is it a problem, sir? They did ask me when I joined if I would change it but it was my father's name and I wished to do him honour."

"Not a problem at all. You will find that many of the troopers are Brigante and they will understand." He lowered his voice and gestured for the youth to ride next to him. "Some of the regular troops might give you a hard time. If they do, just ignore them. The ala is like a family."

"Thank you, sir. I will do that."

They reached the top of the ridge which overlooked the fort after it was dark. The four turmae met them a couple of miles from the valley. All of them were pleased to see the glowing welcoming lights of the fort which meant they had reached safety and hot food.

Aulus Nepos had demanded an escort of, not only the troopers of the Sixth Legion but also four turmae of Marcus' Horse; he took himself very seriously. Rufius took the recruits to the new fort whilst Marcus led the four turmae with the governor. Rufius had moaned to Marcus about the interminable journey and the decurion was just pleased that they did not have to lug the carriage around with them as Flavia felt the need of some time to recuperate with her companions.

"So tell me decurion what of the tribes hereabouts?"

Marcus knew what Livius had discovered but it was not his place to tell the Governor that. "It is strange sir. They just seem to object to the wall as an entity. It doesn't actually take any Selgovae or Votadini land. It is Brigante land. I think it goes back to the old religion; the religion of the Mother. They believe that you do not build anything permanent; you live in harmony with the land. They are a very religious people even though their gods are not ours."

Aulus' jaw dropped and Appius gave Marcus a questioning look, "Really! People still believe that."

"Look around you can you see any buildings? When you travelled north did you see any buildings or towns other than the Roman ones? Even if they do not believe in the religion the ideas are embedded deep in their hearts."

"So how do they feel about mining?"

Marcus shook his head. "They do not like it. The only mines I know are in those parts of Britannia which are peaceful. It is one reason why the Silures were destroyed as a people; they had gold in their land and we wanted it."

Aulus looked searchingly at Marcus. "You are half Brigante are you not?"

26

"Yes sir. My mother comes from the land near the Dunum and my father was an Atrebate who joined after the Boudiccan rebellion."

"I have also heard that you bear a special sword." He gestured at the gladius which hung from Marcus saddle. "That does not look particularly special; to me, it looks like a regular legion gladius."

Marcus laughed, as did the troopers behind. The Governor had a momentary look of anger until Marcus drew the sword from its scabbard on the opposite side of his body. "This is the Sword of Cartimandua. It was passed down through the royal line until it reached Cartimandua, the last Queen of the Brigantes and from there it came to my father and now me. I keep the gladius on my saddle should I need to fight with two weapons or in the press of a close battle where my other is too long to be of use."

Appius' eyes lit up. He could see the value of the sword in an instant. "That is magnificent and it looks ancient."

"Yes sir, it came from Gaul I believe but the metal comes from, I know not where for it is sharper and harder than any sword I have ever held."

There was disappointment on Appius'; face as the sword was replaced. The Governor examined the latest part of the wall with something like distaste upon his face. "So your people, the Brigante; they are at peace?"

"Generally, yes sir, but they have risen against Rome before and they may do again. It is why we have to be constantly vigilant."

Nepos reined in his horse. "Look at that wall, Appius, it would not stop a donkey. We must have the wall higher and we need more turrets and mile castles."

"The trouble is Governor that it is expensive in both materials and manpower to build. The Emperor was keen for it to be continuous and speed was of the essence."

"I do not dispute that decurion but once it is closed we will continue to improve it so that the barbarians here know who rules them! Rome."

Metellus was pleased to see Rufius return to the new fort. He had increasingly lost patience with the hundreds of mindless little problems which had arisen during the finishing off of the new fort. Now that the Prefect and the rest of the ala was in one place Metellus could get back to running the ala and not supervising a building. When Rufius gave him the letter and the cake his day was complete.

"I see you have recruits? We shall need them. Marcus suffered a few losses and eight men have retired."

"But not you eh, Metellus?"

"Not yet but soon Rufius. The fort has taken its toll. I can cope with the fighting and the patrols but not the lists and the ledgers. As for the new recruits, give the best three to Marcus. The Legate and Prefect Sallustius always seem to give him the most dangerous tasks and he is the best trainer of troopers we have." It had been on the tip of his tongue to say since Macro but it was not needed, Rufius knew what he meant.

"That will be Aneurin, Scanlan and Vibius Gemellus."

"Two recruits with Brigante names? That is unusual is it not? Most change their name when they are recruited."

"If you remember, Metellus, you were normally bullied into it until you changed. I think this bodes well for them that they stood up to the pressure. Besides they are Brigante and that will please Marcus. The other lad is a little older but he seems bright as a new pin and he is good with weapons. I saw him having a practice bout or two and he can handle himself."

"Good, for action is coming. The Selgovae and the Votadini are planning a joint attack. We don't know where but we know it will be soon."

"Any more good news! And the wall isn't even finished yet."

"I think that is why they are joining together to hit us before it is finished."

That evening the Camp Prefect decided to hold a small feast for his guests. It was not his first choice but the sniffy comments and dirty looks from the Lady Flavia ensured that he would have to do something. All of the senior officers were invited. The three women were highly flattered to have such attentive males. They had all put on a little extra make up and dressed just a little more provocatively. The Lady Flavia took the place of honour with Lucia and Vibia surrounded by the officers. Metellus was amused by the whole event and Livius found it irrelevant but the legionary tribunes and auxiliary officers fell over themselves to speak with the young ladies. Lucia found herself between a legionary tribune and a Tungrian Prefect; she fluttered her eyelids and laughed coquettishly at the jokes they made. Vibia, in contrast was coolness personified. Appius found himself more and more intrigued by the stunning green eyed beauty. She avoided the attentions of the younger officers and attempted to engage Livius in conversation.

"Didn't I hear somewhere that you are related to one of the last kings of this land Prefect Sallustius?"

Livius smiled at the memory. "Very distantly. My uncle, who was a former Governor, was descended from King Cunobelinus."

Lady Flavia stopped mid mouthful. "Royalty then?"

"Not anymore."

Appius watched the interplay with interest. The Prefect of Marcus' Horse showed politeness, nothing more and he wondered at Vibia's motives. He resolved to speak with her himself privately when he had the opportunity. She was intelligent and pretty; he felt certain that he could bend her to his will. She might prove an ally in the Governor's camp. He had noticed that Lady Flavia heeded the young girl's opinion. She was, of course, older than Lucia and her maturity showed. He noticed that Lucia flirted with officers who could not advance her; none of the officers was marrying material and would spend their lives on the frontier whereas Vibia was polite and nothing more He did not know about Livius' connections. He could not see how he could use the information yet but he stored it for future reference. The ala called Marcus' Horse was intriguing. Not only was it commanded by a royal, it also boasted a royal sword. If one added to that the fact that it was the most successful force on the frontier then Livius was a man to be cultivated.

When Livius excused himself Appius found himself next to Vibia. "You seem remarkably well informed about the men on the wall."

She shrugged and gave him a coy smile, "I lived alone in Eboracum for some time before gaining employment. I made a point of seeking information." Her looks became sad. "As an orphan I did not know what opportunities might arise and I was determined to make the most of them." She leaned in to speak more confidentially to him and he got a whiff of jasmine and rose, "to be truthful I was running out of funds when you found me. Eboracum is a cheaper place to live than Camulodunum but it still costs coin to eat. I am grateful to you."

Appius was suddenly aware that her voice had become lower and huskier and she was perilously close to him. He found himself becoming aroused. "I am pleased that I could be of some help to you and if you need me to do more then you just need to ask."

Her deep green eyes opened wide and her long lashes fluttered for just a moment. "Believe me, when I need your help I promise you that I will ask."

In the event, the Governor and Legate were wrong about the barbarian intentions. The plans were more subtle than the normal barbarian mass raid which ended in failure. This had been planned and thought through by leaders who had fought Rome before and lost. They would not lose again. Far to the south Briac and his warrior band were tracking the wagon loads of grain and cement as they left Cataractonium and headed the short way to Morbium. Although the land was flat between the two forts there were more than enough places for men to hide and swoop down on the slowly moving wagons. The half-century of Batavians who escorted the wagons hated the duty as did their commander; he always allocated his least dependable men for such a task. They escorted from Eboracum until Morbium and then the Prefect of Batavians changed for a better half-century. The journey north was dangerous country with more places for an ambush. Briac had watched the wagons on many occasions and knew the men and knew the route. He had over a hundred disenchanted Brigante with him as well as some who just wanted to kill and to fight. Briac didn't mind. This would be the nucleus of his army and with increasing success would come increasing numbers. Once the northern tribes flooded over the frontier they would have their insurrection.

When Briac had seen that there was none of the dreaded Marcus' Horse escorting the wagons, he knew that they could win. His men lay less than thirty paces from the roadside hidden by brown mottled cloaks. To the Roman escorts they looked like rocks but they were forty Brigante warriors, eager for blood. Briac and the remainder of the force were waiting on the ridge below the skyline. He had chosen an ambush site equidistant from the two forts and the only danger would be from a courier. He waited until the lead wagon was almost at the last of his men and then he and his Brigante screamed down the slope. Even without the men hiding close by he would have attained his ends for the soldiers in the half-century took too long to lock shields. Even as they began to move together the rocks moved and the forty warriors emerged with sharp daggers and swords, almost at their feet. The wicked blades found the spaces between their armour and their shields. There was neither cohesion nor order. The optio in charge tried to rally his men but Briac strode up to him with his two-handed axe and smashed it down onto the optio's shield. The arm shattered along with the shield and, as he cried out in pain, his life was mercifully ended by a hammer to the head.

The men with the wagons tried to escape but they were rundown and dragged from their seats and butchered like cattle. Taking the soldier's weapons, the Brigante began to plunder the dead bodies. Briac slapped, with the flat of a captured sword, the back of a man who tried to despoil a body. "We have no time for that! Get the wagons out of sight."

By the time the wagons were overdue and horsemen sent to find it, the grain and the cement were hidden in the hills far beyond any road. They had no use for the cement but it slowed down the wall building and they would be able to use the wheat and sell some of it. Their attack

30

had been totally unexpected and successful. Briac's war had begun. The Brigante were fighting back.

The Governor had completed his brief visit to the construction site of the new wall when the messenger from the south reached the frontier. He was busily engaged with Legate Demetrius discussing how to improve the quality of the wall and make it even more imposing when the clerk knocked on the Legate's door. "Messenger from Morbium sir."

"Tell him we will be out momentarily." Julius carried on talking to make his point to the opinionated Roman. "The trouble is Governor that making a better finish will only delay the time it takes to finish the wall. We need to use the two cohorts who are building the wall to conduct a punitive raid against the local tribes. They cannot do that if they are still building the wall."

"I realise, Julius, that you are a friend of the Emperor but you must see that I am only trying to make the best defence we can. Besides it will give us time to find the resources hidden beneath the hills to the west. I understand from my aide, Appius Serjanus, that they are extensive and might increase the coffers of the province."

Julius could see what a greedy pair they were and that they had no concept of military matters. He yearned for the days of Agricola and Paulinus. He would get nowhere with him. He smiled, obfuscation was the best option. Once the Governor was back in the south he would be able to complete the wall as he and Hadrian had planned. "Very well sir and now there is a messenger from the fort at Morbium. I suspect it may be important or they would not have bothered us." He went to the door, "Come in."

The messenger had ridden hard and the sweat could still be seen caked with the mud from the journey. "Sir, the Brigante have cut the road from Eboracum to Morbium. The grain and cement supplies have been stolen."

Julius gave a wry smile. "Well, it seems that we will be unable to actually finish the wall, let alone improve it Governor."

"You mean we are trapped here? That is appalling. My wife. The barbarians!!"

"Keep calm Governor. Morbium is many miles from here. We have two cohorts of legionaries and another two cohorts of auxiliaries to protect you. I will detail all but two turmae from the ala to deal with this problem."

"That is less than one thousand men. Will it be enough?"

"Trust me Governor it will be enough but the more worrying issue is that this confirms a rumour we heard that the three tribes had

31

combined. It means that the Selgovae and the Votadini will be on the rampage too. You and your wife had better make yourselves comfortable in Coriosopitum until we have sorted it out."

When the Governor told his wife she almost had a fit. "No! I am not staying here. It is barbaric. Eboracum was bad enough but this is little more than a hut. I want to return to Eboracum."

For once the Governor agreed with his wife. His conversations with the other officers had shown him that the most reliable auxiliary troops were Marcus' Horse. If they escorted them south then they would be safe. He told the Legate that he would be returning to Eboracum. Julius was relieved for himself but felt sorry for Livius who would have to travel at a snail's pace all the way back to Eboracum.

Chapter 4

"We will have to train the men on the road Marcus. Rufius only has four turmae and he will be hard pushed to watch the wall. He needs the best troopers he can get."

Marcus smiled, "We have done this before. I always say that the battlefield is a better classroom than the gyrus. Mistakes are more crucial there." Marcus had been the horse trainer when younger whilst his adopted brother, Macro, had been the weapons trainer. To Marcus, training was second nature.

"Metellus, you can lead the column with your four turmae. Marcus, you and your four turmae will form the rearguard and Gnaeus can escort the wagon." Both of the officers showed relief. Lucia had been flirting with every officer she could find; the two men were happily married and well past flirting. Gnaeus was young, he could endure it.

The weather was surprisingly clement as they headed south from Coriosopitum. Despite Lady Flavia's fears the two young women begged for the sides of the carriage to be opened and, when they were not attacked immediately, she too began to enjoy the pleasant pine scented breeze which wafted along the road. Lucia tried flirting with Appius but he and the Governor were busily engaged in a conversation about the possibility of opening a copper mine close to Glanibanta. One of the Brigante officers had told of deposits washed down to the lakes there in huge quantities. Both men saw the potential of copper in this part of the world; copper was almost as valuable as gold and silver. There was a port on the west coast and it could be quickly exported to the rest of the Empire. The young girl pouted at her rejection and turned her attention to Gnaeus. With his new officer's uniform he looked dashing and Lucia decided to try him.

"Are there barbarians over there?" She pointed to the east.

Gnaeus shook his head, "No my lady. We are south of the wall. We will be safe."

Vibia gave an innocent look. "But we were told that barbarians had stopped the wagons heading north. Is that not why you are travelling south?"

Gnaeus became flustered, partly because of the question but more because of the effect Vibia's voice had upon him. "They are Brigante, my lady, as I am. We are not barbarians. The ones who stopped the wagons are bandits, nothing more. We will stop their raids."

"Oh, I do feel safer now with such big brave men."

Both Gnaeus and Vibia ignored Lucia's empty words. "You are Brigante then? Have you seen this mighty sword about which I have heard so much?"

"Oh, it is a mighty sword. I have held it and it is a powerful weapon. To our people it is more than a sword, it is a symbol of our history and our heritage."

"I heard that it had driven all the enemies of Rome before it when used on the battlefield?"

"It has done that since the time of Ulpius Felix and Queen Cartimandua."

"Tell me, for I am intrigued, why does the Prefect not bear the sword if he is from the royal family?"

"It was passed down from Ulpius Felix to Marcus Maximunius who commanded this ala in times past, for he had been married to the Queen's sister. He gave it to Gaius Aurelius who was married to the last female relative of the Queen and he gave it to his son, the decurion."

"Women have been important in the sword's life then?"

Gnaeus had not thought of that before that moment. "I suppose you are right. Certainly, the Queen used the sword before she gave it to Ulpius Felix and I heard that she was a good swordswoman who fought against warriors."

"Do you think the decurion would let me hold it, the sword I mean?"

"I do not know but I could ask."

She leaned out of the carriage to touch his hand, much to the annoyance of both Lucia and Appius who had suddenly become aware of the flirting. "I would be so grateful if you could do that."

The journey to Eboracum was uneventful but tedious. The only ones who found the journey noteworthy were Lucia, Vibia, Appius and Gnaeus. Vibia enjoyed playing the two young men off each other and annoying Lucia. At the rear of the column, Marcus also enjoyed the opportunity to get to know his three new troopers. Aneurin and Vibius reminded him, very much of himself and Macro, his adopted brother. They got on well and they were both desperate to learn how to become good troopers. Their questions were intelligent and spoke highly of their determination to become good troopers. Vibius, in particular, seemed to be interested in all matters military but especially the history and traditions of Marcus' Horse. By the time they had reached Eboracum, he felt happier than he had in quite a while.

The ala was able to use one of the barracks as the Sixth was still building the wall which meant a comfortable bed and hot food. As they were in a safe place Livius allowed some of his officers to visit the vicus and the tavern, The Saddle. The original owner of the tavern had been a trooper from Pannonia who had lost his arm fighting Boudicca. It had become the unofficial meeting place of the ala for many years. His son now ran the place and always made the troopers welcome. The three officers settled into their usual corner with the amphora of wine. This was the only place in which they could relax apart from when they were in their own fort. They were safe and the landlord saw to it that no one bothered them.

"Those new lads look like they will work out Metellus."

"Makes a change from the ones we have been getting lately. Most of them just seem to want the extra pay but not the extra risk."

This was Gnaeus' first time with his superiors and he both looked and felt awkward. "Was I ever like that sir?"

"We are Marcus and Metellus not sir, Gnaeus. You are an officer. And no, you were not like that; you were born to be a trooper. Remember that and it will help you train your men up."

Metellus took a long swallow of the deep red liquid and sighed. A mischievous look appeared on his face. "I heard that someone was the sole attention and focus of a very pretty young lady today."

Gnaeus blushed and tried to look away. Marcus enjoyed his old chosen man's discomfort. "You are right Metellus. I was at the back but I could see the steam rising. I think something was going on."

"I was just being polite. She wanted to know about the ala." Gnaeus was desperate for the conversation to be changed but his fellow officers were enjoying themselves too much.

"Yes well so did Vibius and Aneurin but I wasn't riding close enough to count their teeth like you were with her."

"I'll go and get some more wine."

He rushed to the bar and the two older officers fell about laughing. "Oh that felt good!"

"Yes Rufius and I used to enjoy hazing you as well."

Gnaeus returned and quietly sat down. Metellus raised his beaker. "Here's to the ala."

"To the ala."

Metellus leaned forwards. "I probably shouldn't tell you this but when we interrogated those prisoners one of them said something strange. He said that we should watch out for knives in our back."

Marcus put his beaker down. "That is a strange thing to say. What do you think he meant?"

"None of us were certain but Livius and I thought it might mean we would not be safe in our own forts."

"But we know our people and…"

"Marcus you were an Explorate remember? We lied for a living. Is it unreasonable to expect that there may be barbarians out there who are willing to do the same? And remember Morwenna."

Gnaeus looked puzzled. Marcus said, in explanation, "Morwenna was the daughter of the witch Fainch. She was the mother of my stepbrother Macro but she pretended to be something she was not and Macro's father believed her."

"Not just Macro but all of us. Poor Decius believed her so much, he died for it."

"So it could be anyone?"

"Yes, except he was looking at the Prefect when he said it. I think there may be a traitor either in the ranks or in the fort." He looked at them both. "Keep this to yourselves but keep your eyes open too. If there are no problems then the Votadini was just trying to make us look over our shoulders." He swallowed off the last of the wine. "Anyway tomorrow we will hunt down these wagon thieves; we can worry about traitors when we get back to the fort."

Aula's two children met by the river quayside; it lay close to a large warehouse which hid them from the prying eyes of the curious. They had both covered their faces but there were few people there for the river was low and the tide was ebbing. "How goes it?"

"I have a good position and you?"

"I am well thought of. I have discovered where the ala is to be based but I have not had time to seek the gold."

"That will be difficult but we must be patient. The hard part was reaching here without being recognised and insinuating ourselves into the town. We have both succeeded and now we must watch for our opportunities." Giving each other the special handshake they had used since childhood, they parted.

Briac felt confident moving around the city of Eboracum. He had grown up there and played in the woods by the river. When his family had moved to the farm in the vale he had been a youth and still visited the shadier side of Eboracum; the taverns and whore houses in the vicus. In this way he had become familiar with both the criminal and the military world. He knew many of the soldiers from the garrison and, latterly, had shown them sympathy and remuneration when their salary had not stretched as far as they wished. His uncle had led an abortive rebellion some years ago and he had misjudged the soldiers. Briac would not make the same mistake and he had cultivated the friendship of the men his uncle had wanted to slaughter. His greatest achievement, however, was placing one of his men, successfully, in the thorn in the Brigante side, Marcus' Horse. There were problems with having a man on the inside of that force for they had tight security and it was sometimes difficult for Briac to meet with him but, as they were now stationed in the capital, it had become easier.

Briac knew that Dagger, that was the name they had chosen for their spy, would go to the inn called The Fosse. Few of the ala went there and Briac had been there for three nights just waiting for Dagger to meet. He had only been in the ala for a year or so and his intelligence had not yielded much but Briac and the other Brigante leaders knew that haste had been their undoing in the past. They needed patience. When his contact arrived, they ignored each other while they checked the customers for anyone who was paying undue attention to the two men. The Fosse was not noted for its gentility and most of the people inside looked like criminals of one type or another but once they were satisfied Dagger sat next to Briac in a particularly dark part of the dank and poorly lit tavern.

"Good to see you brother."

"And you. How goes life with the Romans?"

He ruefully rubbed his short hair. "I do not like the haircuts and I do not like the baths and they seem to live on bread and porridge but I am not with them to enjoy life am I?"

Briac patted his friend's arm. "No, but the work you do will free our people."

"I know when I feel like sticking my sword into the decurion's throat that thought restrains me."

"So what are their plans?"

"Two turmae have been left on the wall and the rest are to hunt you and your wagon thieves." He laughed. "As soon as we heard the news then I knew it was you."

"It is good to know that we have achieved our ends. But this is just the start. I will send word to our Selgovae and Votadini brothers of the weakness on the wall. They will pay. Where are you to patrol?"

"We have not been told yet. Some are to be sent to patrol the road and some to hunt you down."

"They will find that hard for we are well hidden."

"If I am on the road patrol then I will have my scutum on my back. If I am to search for you then I will carry it on my arm. If you have someone watching the gate then you can warn your people and ambush us."

Briac did not want to jeopardise his spy's position. "I do not want my men to hurt you. How will they know you?" He swept his arm up and down. "In your uniforms you all look to be the same."

"My horse has a white blaze on his head and only one white foot. He is the only one with such a blaze."

"Good. If you come too close to our camp we will ambush you. Where does the patrol go?"

"We have been designated to travel the road between here and Morbium. I think they will use two turmae from here to Cataractonium and two from there to Morbium. They intend to hold the grain wagons in the city until your threat is eliminated."

"So they still have wagons coming into the city?"

"Yes they have a century of guards waiting south of the fort at the river crossing to escort them the last ten miles."

"Good then we shall have more grain." He laughed. "Even now my uncle is taking the grain over to Deva to sell it to the legion there. As the price has risen it will cost them dear to buy back their own food."

"I will have to go back soon or they will begin to suspect my prolonged absence." He finished off his drink. "I will not be able to get a pass for another seven days and I may be on patrol."

"I will return in seven days for three days. You are doing a noble thing my brother."

"Until the Romans are driven from our land my father's death will not be avenged. I am resolute."

The Camp Prefect at Eboracum was worried. "The problem, Livius, is that I only have one cohort at my disposal here and using one of them to protect the grain convoy into the city stretches them a little too far." He held up his hand. "I know, it is the Legate's decision and I agree that we do need the grain, without it our men will starve but ...."

"I agree, Titus. How about this as a strategy? After I have looked for these bandits I will detach two turmae to head south and meet the convoy below the river."

"I will still be using one of my centuries though."

"It will be just this once. If our plans work then my horsemen can rotate."

Titus Plauca breathed a sigh of relief. "But will that not stretch your men?"

"The advantage my men have is that they can evade trouble by riding away. I am afraid the caligae of your men are not so swift."

As Livius left to give his orders he wondered about this sudden upsurge in Brigante activity. By the time he had reached his waiting men he had reached his decision. He smiled as he looked on the serried ranks of immaculately turned out troopers. They all looked ready for action. They had been trained well.

"Officer's call." His officers dismounted to join him. He kept his voice lowered when he spoke, not because he doubted any of his own men but there were non-military workers in the fort and, until they found the spy, or the possible spy, then they had to be discreet. "Metellus, take your turmae and patrol the road as we discussed. The first convoy will be leaving later today to head for Cataractonium. The men on the wall are on half rations and this precious cargo must be there within five days."

"Sir. What I think I will do is leave one turma just five miles from the fort and the other five miles from Cataractonium. It will save the horses and still give close protection to the wagons and their drivers."

"Good. "He turned to the other officers. "We will be heading west to try to find the Brigante. We will not return here for eight days at least so make sure you have enough rations for that period." His officers saluted and turned to leave. "Marcus, a moment, if you please."

"I have another task for you. Once we are out of sight of the fort take your turma and head for Decius' farm. We need a couple of Brigante scouts and I need intelligence about the mood of the Brigante. Your brother may well be able to help."

Marcus was dubious. "The problem is, sir, that they all know he is my brother and they know who my father was. I suspect that he would be the last person a rebel would approach."

"I know that but women talk and your mother and your wife may also have heard things. Remember you were an Explorate; it was the little things which gave us our information."

Marcus smiled, "You are right sir. It is just that those days seem such a long time ago. And do I then join you?"

"No, head south and pick up the grain convoy, escort it to Eboracum; it should be an easier initiation for your three new lads eh?"

"Sir."

The ala, all fourteen turmae, headed out of Eboracum heading west. Metellus waved his goodbyes and his turmae trotted up the road. Once they were out of sight and closer to the hills Marcus also waved his goodbyes. As he watched the lone turma depart the spy wrinkled his brow. This was not part of the Roman plan. What did it mean? He had been pleased that he was with the Decurion Princeps for that meant the heart of the ala could be pierced with a successful ambush but the departure of the sword also created problems for every Brigante yearned for the blade. He would have to hope that Briac had seen the sign and had an ambush prepared.

Marcus rode hard to reach the farm. It had been some time since he had visited and he wondered how much his son had grown. The farm was really a small fort for his father had created sound and effective defences to protect his family when he had been away and his brother, Decius, had continued with those improvements. The farm workers also served as an unofficial militia and guards. Thanks to the money his father and he had acquired and accrued they were a well off family and could afford to pay their men rather than having them as tenants or thralls. It bred loyalty and Marcus knew that they could fend off any bandit attack which dared to approach.

Decius had grown broader with a more pronounced paunch and Ailis, their mother, noticed the difference between her two boys for Marcus was like a lean and hungry wolf compared with his more comfortable brother. She had outlived all those she had loved, save her sons and, thanks to their wives and her grandchildren she was enjoying a new lease of life. She still worried over Marcus; any mother would and she was grateful to see him safe and sound when he visited.

"Sextus, let the men water their horses," he grinned, "and as I can smell bread baking, if you ask nicely at the kitchen door the cook may have something for the lads." One of the bonuses of serving with Marcus was the hospitality of his home.

Frann, his wife, ran to greet him. A freed slave from the land of the Tencteri she relished and appreciated every moment of her new life. She accepted her husband's absence but she was not lonely for Marcus' mother was as protective as a she-bear, as were the rest of the family. "Our son sleeps, I will wake him."

Kissing her gently he said, "No I cannot stay long and I know that his sleeping moments are valuable." His son, Macro, was just like his namesake, a bundle of energy when he was awake.

Decius and his wife joined them, his sister in law hugging him and kissing him, as she always did, on both cheeks twice. "Well brother what betokens this visit?" Decius loved his brother but he knew that bringing the turma meant trouble of some description.

Marcus sat at the family table with Frann on his knee. "We have heard rumours that the Brigante are becoming restive. Some bandits or rebels, we know not which, have captured supply convoys and the work on the wall is threatened. Have you heard aught?"

Decius shook his head. "You know that any rebel would stay away from me but I will go and ask the men. They have wider acquaintances."

40

"I am happy to hear rumours. Where is Drugi?"

"He is hunting in the western valley. Should I send for him?"

"No, I will visit with him after I have finished here."

"You are leaving today my son?"

"Yes, mother. The ala is to be based here until the threat is nullified. I meant to ask Decius if there were any of the men in the valley who would be suitable as scouts."

His mother gave a sad smile, "You miss Uncle Gaelwyn then?"

Marcus looked through the door to the place where they had buried the legendary scout. "Every day."

"I think there are a couple of boys towards Stanwyck. They like to work with Drugi and he has taken to them. If you see him then he may have more information for you."

By the time Decius returned, Macro had awoken and he and his father had enjoyed a playful tussle. Frann shook her head. "There will be no settling him now. He will be crying for his dada all the time."

Ailis smiled. "It is the same for all the boys in this family. One day we will have a girl and we will not know what to do."

"The men have heard rumours of people being terrorised along the valleys to the south. Wagon tracks were seen but no-one dared say anything. So your rumour may be true." The brothers looked at each other with unspoken words in their eyes. Decius would work on the security again and clear the trees back further. Rebels or bandits that close meant problems for the hardworking and loyal Brigante. In this area it paid to be careful.

"We have turmae on the road for a while so you can always send a messenger to Morbium." The proximity of the fort afforded the farm more protection than most. "We have to go now but I will visit again, alone next time." His last comment was for Frann.

Ailis nodded, "Good, it is time Macro had a sister. I am getting no younger and I would like a granddaughter before I meet your father again!"

Chapter 5

As they left the farm Aneurin ventured, "Sir!"

Sextus snapped, "Not when we are on patrol son. Save your questions for the halts." He shook his head and said, to no-one in particular, "I have never known such recruits for fucking questions."

Marcus did not turn around but smiled. Aneurin reminded him of himself riding with Rufius and Metellus all those long years ago. "Just one question Aneurin."

"Why doesn't the ala patrol this part all the time?"

"That is a good question Aneurin and the answer is a simple one. We are the only cavalry this side of the divide and the barbarians in the north fear us. Once we have quashed this latest threat we will return home." He saw Aneurin's face drop. "Where is your home?"

He pointed to the east. "Over there by the hills, close to the old hill fort."

"I know it. We may return but not for a while and now no more talk we have to find a giant who is invisible."

Sextus saw the question rising into every face and he growled, "Not one fucking word!"

They reached the valley and Marcus held up his hand. They just waited. There was total silence but all of the troopers, not just the new ones stared at each other. Eventually, Scanlan held up his hand and said, hesitantly, "You said a giant sir?"

Marcus laughed, "Just wait and see Scanlan. We have time to wait so do not worry. Out next journey is an easy one down the road towards the south."

The troopers stared at the water. Suddenly a figure stood next to Sextus, who drew his sword and said, "Stand to!"

Marcus shouted, "Stand down! It is Drugi." He smiled at the genial giant who stood taller than a horse's head. "You have not lost your touch old friend."

Drugi snorted, "Around these I could have worn full armour, banged a drum and they still would not have seen me." He smiled at Marcus. "How long since you saw me?"

"Had I had my bow, enough time to put three arrows into you when you moved behind the elm tree!"

"Hah! This land is making me soft."

"What have you heard, Drugi the king of all trackers?"

He pointed to the west. "There are men with wagons in the high valley, to the south"

"Brigante?" The old scout nodded and Marcus turned to one of his more experienced troopers. "Livius, ride and find the Prefect. Tell him Drugi says they are in the high valley. Stay with him." Livius kicked his horse and trotted off. "Drugi, we need scouts."

His face fell. "You want Drugi to leave the farm and follow the wolf?" He pointed at the wolf standard carried by the signifier.

"No Drugi. Your work is here, training my son and protecting my family." Drugi's face split into a huge smile. "No, we need you to find us a couple of boys or young warriors who can scout." He held up his hand. "They will not be as good as you but we need someone who can follow a trail."

He looked away to the west, as though he had not heard the decurion's words. Then he turned. "I have two trackers in mind. I will bring them to your brother's farm in a few days."

Marcus leaned down to clasp the former slave's arm. "Thank you, old friend. I can always rely on you."

"Without you and the hawk I would not have a life. My life is yours and it is now full." In the blink of an eye he was gone.

Sextus looked around in amazement. "How in the Allfather's name does he do that, sir?"

"Practice, Sextus. He was born to it."

When Livius received the news from Marcus' trooper he held a meeting with his officers. "If they are in the high valleys then we will have no cover and they will see us before we can see them. We only have three turmae which handicaps us a little. Gnaeus you know this land as well as I do. Take your turma on a long loop to the south and approach the valley from the southern side. They use heavy wagons which means they could not get to the head of the valleys and I suspect that they will be where the wagon trail ends. Lucius, you are new to the region so you will be the bait." The young decurion grinned; he liked living life on the edge. "You will ride up the wagon trail. Follow the ruts. It has been raining so even Julius Longinus could follow them. I will approach from the north. Remember that we want the wagons secured but, even more importantly we want these bandits caught. Do not risk your men. If you can get prisoners then all well and good but I would rather have a turma whole than a prisoner caught."

"Sir."

The spy stared with eyes filled with hate at the back of the Prefect of Marcus' Horse. Briac had hoped to ambush the horsemen but now it looked like his fellow warriors would be ambushed themselves. Now it was up to him to try to thwart the grey haired officer.

Briac and his men had seen the spy's signal and had trailed him. Briac was disturbed when one turma headed north, especially as it was led by the one with the sword. He had been tempted to have him followed but he had decided that the three turmae merited his attention. Now as the three turmae split up he was in a dilemma; whom should he follow? The fact that his spy was in the leader's turma determined him. They would ambush that turma; without their leader they would flee. His men easily followed the horsemen for there was little cover on the fells. An occasional copse made them briefly disappear but they soon returned in sight. He kept his men between the turma and his precious wagons. The grain had long disappeared south but the cement he held close to the end of the wagon trail, guarded by his men. His people had no use for it but the fact that the Romans wanted it made it precious.

Suddenly the horsemen turned south and headed directly for Briac and his band. Had they been spotted? His men quickly found cover where they could and Briac peered from the rocks to the east of the turma. The Allfather and the gods of his people were with him for the turma would pass beneath them. "When they are close enough we will attack them!" He outnumbered them by over two to one and he had the advantage that they could not attack him, the Brigante had the high rocky ground.

The Prefect's horse's ears suddenly pricked and the experienced officer knew that there was something amiss. The wind was from the east and his horse had detected an unusual smell. "Stand to!"

The fact that the attack came from the left, added to Livius' warning command meant that the turma had more protection than they might have had. Their shields came around to protect them and the arrows and spears found few vulnerable targets. One horse went down in a tumble of legs and the trooper rolled down the hillside. He was in danger only for a heartbeat as two of his comrades shielded him with their mounts whilst a third picked him up. Livius could see that they had no chance of defeating the Brigante while they were on their rocky perch and he cursed the lack of scouts. Scouts would have seen the enemy trail. There was but one thing to do; ride to the other turmae where they would have a chance of defeating them. "Let's ride!" Kicking hard into his horse's flanks the turma sped away from the missiles still being hurled in their direction.

Briac cursed. Their very safety meant that they could not easily get to the horsemen who galloped off and it was then that the Brigante leader realised that their course would take them to the wagons. He hoped that the thirty men he had left guarding them would be sufficient.

44

Gnaeus and Lucius arrived at the wagons at the same time. Although the Brigante sentries had spotted them, their hastily improvised defences were not enough to stop the javelins and swords of the sixty troopers who fell upon them from two directions. They fought bravely enough but when Aed, their leader fell the others fled. They had enough wit left to climb the crags and the horsemen had to halt. "Secure the wagons! Appius, Publius, take four troopers and form a screen four hundred paces from the wagons." Gnaeus dismounted and inspected the wagons. They still contained their cargo, the white dust rising in the air as he lifted the covers. "Lucius, see if they have left the horses somewhere."

Gnaeus was not optimistic but at least they had achieved half of their aims. He scanned the skyline for the Prefect. As he turned away he sensed a movement and looked back as the Fifth Turma, with their Prefect at their head, tumbled over the ridge line. Gnaeus was experienced enough to know that his commander was in trouble. "Stand to! Javelins!"

A quickly formed line protected the wagons as the Prefect brought his turma through the gaps left by their comrades. The Brigante appeared on the skyline and halted. Briac looked down at the ninety Romans. He could not defeat them. This round had gone to the Romans but there would be others. His men melted away like morning mist.

"Should we follow sir?"

Livius looked ruefully at the four wagons. "I am afraid not Gnaeus. They will have gone in many directions and the rocks up there prevent us following. No, we have achieved what we set out to do, we have recaptured the wagons. Well half of them at least. We will take them back to Eboracum."

"How sir? They have taken the horses."

Livius gave the newly promoted officer a long hard look. "It may have escaped your attention but we are riding horses."

Gnaeus was horrified. "You mean use our horses to pull the wagons?"

"Got it in one. Two horses to a wagon, pick the biggest ones." He looked at Gnaeus mount. "Yours will do Gnaeus!"

Gnaeus bit back his retort and took his saddle off. "What are you grinning at Decimus? Yours is a big bugger too. Take off your saddle and join me eh?"

Marcus halted his turma close to the road. He looked to the east and saw that they were close to the place where the Prefect's brother had escaped Britannia. "We will halt here lads."

45

Scanlan asked, "What are we waiting for sir?"

Sextus growled and Marcus smiled as he held up his hand. "We are waiting for the next wagons and we will escort them into the fort but, as you are so interested in what we are doing then take Vibius a mile down the road to wait for them. The rest of us will water our horses at the river; it is only eight hundred paces east of us."

Sextus laughed, "That'll teach you not to be a nosey bugger! Shall we feed the horses as well sir?"

"Might as well Sextus. I have no idea how long we will have to wait. Let the lads eat too."

"They ate at the farm sir. You are spoiling them."

"When I was with the Ninth legion they taught you to eat as often as you can, when you can. You never know when you might not have the opportunity." The brief time he and his stepbrother had spent with the Ninth had been during his formative years and the lessons and traits he had learned, ran deep.

Vibius didn't mind the excursion. He wanted to see as much of the country as he could but he found it amusing that Scanlan took it to be a punishment. He was sure that Aneurin, the other Brigante would not have done so.

"All I wanted to know was how long we would be there?"

"Why?" Scanlan's broad face looked puzzled. "I mean what difference does it make?"

"I dunno. I thought we would be fighting more than we have been." The young Brigante seemed to notice Vibius for the first time. "I meant to ask you, why did you wait so long to join up? No disrespect Vibius but you are as old as some of the troopers who have been in for five years."

Vibius' face clouded over. "Let's just say things didn't work out the way I intended when I was younger and leave it at that. "He glanced back up the road and then to the river, not far east of them. "This must be a couple of miles from the turma, let's wait here." There was a small hill fifty paces west of the road and Vibius led Scanlan towards it. "We will see further from up there and yet be close enough to the road." Scanlan suddenly realised that he would not have thought of that but it was a good idea. He would stick close to Vibius; he was bright and the decurion liked him. Thinking wasn't what Scanlan did best; he was a fighter. After they had fed their horses, they took it in turns to sit atop their mounts to watch for the grain wagons which would trundle slowly from the south.

The warband sent by Briac to capture the latest convoy was smaller than the ones on the first raid. Briac had needed his men for the ambush of the Prefect but Tadgh, their leader was happy enough. He had forty men and the Romans would not expect them to strike so far south of the city. Their leader was both wise and wily and he would outwit the Romans. They saw the wagons approach and noted that they were unguarded. This would be even easier than the first raid. His men had covered themselves with brown and green blankets and were invisible to the bored wagon drivers. They knew that north of Eboracum there were raids but here they were safe. Tadgh raised his arm to signal the attack.

Scanlan was watching to the south and he suddenly saw a strange movement; the white arm, rising from the ground looked out of place. "Vibius. I can see the wagons but…"

Vibius sprang on to the back of his horse. He took in the situation in an instant. "Quick, ride back to the decurion. The wagons are under attack. I will try to…."

Scanlan never heard what Vibius would do for he was riding as quickly as he could for the turma. Vibius checked his shield and hefted his javelin. As he kicked his horse on he wondered just what he would do. He counted that they were at least thirty or forty warriors that he could see. As he rode to meet them, a vague plan began to formulate in his mind. They would not know that the turma was a mile or two behind. He began to look behind him and to shout as he neared them. "On! Turma Two! Charge!"

Tadgh looked in horror as the lone Roman horseman hurtled towards him. The first wagon drivers were dead and his men were busily dispatching the others. Had he had horses he would have charged the maniac coming towards them but they were afoot. "Get those wagons off the road and up the hills. You eight, form a shield wall."

His eight warriors locked their round shields and stood steadfastly in the middle of the Roman Road. Vibius had gone beyond the point of no return. He hurled his javelin and had the satisfaction of seeing it plunge into the surprised head of a Brigante bandit who had failed to use the full cover of his shield. Emboldened by his success he threw a second which merely struck wood. He tugged fiercely back on the reins and his horse stopped but ten paces from the Brigante. The warriors could see that he was alone and they roared towards him intent upon killing this bold and foolish warrior. As he wheeled quickly back along the road he saw, to his great relief, the wolf standard and the turma galloping towards him. He could see the Sword of Cartimandua held aloft by the decurion and he felt real pride in the men with whom he served. He slowed up his mount and, as the turma galloped by him he heard Sextus say grudgingly, "Lucky little bastard!"

Marcus led his line of troopers directly at the would-be robbers. Unarmoured as they were they stood little chance against the accurately thrown javelins. By the time Vibius had turned his horse around to rejoin his comrades it was all over and the last few Brigante had been captured. Sextus grinned at Marcus and pointed at the prisoners. "A little profit for us then eh sir?"

Prisoners meant slaves and the money would be shared out amongst the turma. Marcus nodded and then gestured towards Vibius. "That was bravely done Sextus."

"He was lucky sir." Then he added grudgingly, "I was impressed with his accuracy though. If the others are as good then we might have a good turma again."

The dead carters were placed in the cement wagon while the dead Brigante were stripped of weapons and left as a reminder to others of the perils of stealing from Rome. The century awaiting the wagons a few miles from Eboracum were delighted that it was escorted by the ala. Marcus disappointed the centurion by telling him that they would have to escort the wagons in without the aid of the ala. Sextus asked, "Are we not going into Eboracum then sir?"

"No Sextus, the Prefect is still out there bandit hunting and I do not want to waste a turma of cavalry doing what the caligae can do equally well. But you can take the prisoners in to the slave market. Take Scanlan with you and then meet me at my brother's farm."

Sextus went off happily. He would manage to get a beaker of ale at least at The Saddle. "Come on gormless. Let's see how fast these bandits can run." Giving one rope to Scanlan and taking the other, the gruff chosen man began to trot towards the distant fortress.

Marcus rode over to Vibius who was still flushed with both his success and the excitement of the skirmish. "You did well Vibius but remember there are thirty other troopers to aid you. It was a little reckless. We were coming to your aid."

"I know sir, sorry but it just seemed the right thing to do."

"Do not get me wrong Vibius it is what I would have done when I was your age but when you get a little older you realise the dangers in being isolated amongst enemies."

"The men say that you were an Explorate when you were younger. You hid amongst the enemy." It was a statement which required both an explanation and an answer.

"True Vibius but that was different. We were hidden in plain sight. We dressed as the people dressed." He gestured at their uniform. "We did not look as different as you do. Tell me Vibius, you are a well-trained youth, why did you wait so long to join?"

"What you really mean, sir is where did I learn to throw so well?"

Marcus could see that talking to Vibius was different from talking to the other recruits. He had a maturity about him which was lacking in the other youths. "Not just the weapon work but the riding as well. You look to have had some military training and I can hear from your voice that you have been well educated."

"My family had money and I was given every opportunity to better myself but my parents and the rest of my family were taken by the plague which visited us and I found that my father's business dealings were not as sound as they might have been. I was left with a small amount of money." He shrugged. "Had I been a citizen then I might have contemplated joining the legionary cavalry but as I was not I chose Marcus' Horse."

"You had heard of us, in the south?"

"Your fame is known throughout the land and besides my family was of the same tribe as the Prefect and it seemed fitting somehow that I should be a warrior with the nearest thing to a chief that I could."

Before Marcus could reply, his horse's ears pricked. He held up his hand, "Stand to!"

A trooper from the Fourth Turma appeared from the nearby copse. "Sir."

"I take it your turma is close by Septimus?"

"Sir! The Prefect has managed to recover the wagons and we are taking them to Eboracum." He pointed behind him where the line of wagons could be seen.

"Good. Carry on with your scouting duties. Turma, ho!"

The column of riders quickly closed up with the rest of the ala. When Marcus had reported their success he said to Livius. "With your permission sir I will head for my brother's farm. Drugi promised me a couple of trackers."

"Good. I will keep your turma with me and we will meet you in Eboracum when you have secured your men." He smiled at his young decurion. "It will give you the opportunity to spend a night with your wife. I am aware that you have not had leave for quite a while."

"She understands sir. And my mother knows how it works."

Chapter 6

Marcus could see that his brother had heeded his warning about the Brigante and his workers were deepening the ditch which surrounded the huts. The men waved at Marcus as he rode through the thick oaken gate. Ailis watched her youngest son as he dismounted; he was the image of his father. Decius was more like his mother in the face but his body was far bigger than his little brother. It was strange that the brothers could be so different and yet, inside, they were still the same. They had never fallen out and there were no sibling jealousies. She and Gaius had been lucky, she knew that. "Frann, your husband is here."

Frann raced out with Macro, asleep, in her arms. "Will he be staying the night do you think?"

"He is alone and I would think so. Here give me the boy and I will prepare your room." As she took him she said, "You need to make the most of all of these moments for who knows when they may come again."

When Macro had been put down in his grandmother's room and the family were seated around the table, Ailis felt content for the first time in a long time. She had been lucky to have lived so long and she cherished every moment that her sons were with her.

Decius leaned back and wiped his mouth with the back of his hand. "I do not know what we would have done had you not brought Drugi back with you. He is invaluable around the farm and he refuses to take anything from us."

Marcus reached over and took Frann's hand. "Had you seen his life before you would know that the freedom he has is payment enough."

"Is the threat from the bandits over then, brother?" Decius was a typical farmer and worried about the weather, the animals and bandits. If one threat could be eliminated, he could spend all his time worrying about the other two.

"Not yet. We have had a little success but we have not found their leaders yet. When Drugi brings me the trackers we may be able to find their lair but the land of the Brigante stretches from sea to sea."

Marcus awoke with Frann in his arms. The touch of her was soft and welcoming; the bed was warm and soft. This was as close to heaven as Marcus ever came. She looked up at him and snuggled in a little closer. "We have been lucky husband."

"I know and I treasure each moment. The next time I am home I expect that Macro will be running around like a mad thing!"

"He does that now!" she laughed. "Your mother has given us this quiet time and she will be ready for a rest herself when you have gone back to the turma."

When they emerged into the main room Drugi was waiting for them, the remains of the meal he had eaten scattered on the table top. "I thought you were going to spend all day in your little nest." The smile on his face belied the words he spoke.

"If you had such a bird in your nest old friend then you might not leave so readily. I take it you have found my trackers?"

"Aye, they are outside."

"Why did you not bring them in?" scolded Frann.

Drugi spread his arms wide with an outraged look on his face. "They did not wish to do so! Come we will meet them."

When Marcus went outside he saw a youth of about fifteen summers and a dog. The youth had the tanned look, much as Drugi did, of someone who spends their days outdoors. His hair was long but clean and he had not yet begun to shave. Although he was thin Marcus could see that it was a leanness that implied fitness and not a sign of malnutrition. The dog was one of the common sheepdogs Marcus had seen on the fell sides. It was brown with sharply pricked ears; one long white sock and three short ones. At the very tip of its tail was a white spot. Its eyes watched Marcus carefully as he approached them. The decurion peered around for the second scout. "I thought you said two scouts?"

"Can you not count Marcus? There are two."

"But one is a dog!"

Drugi laughed, "And a better tracker you have yet to meet. This, my rude young Roman friend, is Felix." The youth stood and gave a nod of his head. "And this is Wolf!"

Marcus smiled apologetically. "I am sorry for my rudeness, Felix," he looked at the dog, and Drugi. "Forgive me. I can see from Drugi's face that there is a story here. Pray continue old friend."

Felix's face opened into a huge smile and Wolf wagged his tail. "Drugi is right, decurion; Wolf is the best scout you will ever meet."

"Well then. On with the story, Drugi."

"Felix can tell the tale as well as any." Drugi gestured for the boy to sit.

The boy sat on the chair Ailis used to watch the farm workers. "I lived with my family near the high falls and we had sheep." He pointed to Wolf. "His mother was the best sheep dog we had. When I was but five summers old the Selgovae came raiding. They stole the flock,

51

killed Wolf's mother and slaughtered my family." Marcus glanced over to Drugi, a question on his face.

"He will tell you decurion; learn patience."

"I was playing with Wolf by the falls and when I returned, I found my family dead. I buried them and Wolf and I tried to follow the Selgovae but the snows came and we had to return to our burnt-out home. The Roman soldiers found us seven days later. They had killed the raiders and they were heading back to the fort. They gave me the name Felix."

"Lucky eh?"

Felix nodded. "They took me to their fort and I lived there for a while with Wolf. They were kind to me and we learned to help them. They had found some of the flock and we looked after them. The Gauls liked the meat. When the fort was abandoned and they were sent to the wall Wolf and I stayed around the fort for we were used to it and that is where I met Drugi."

Drugi nodded and continued stroking Wolf's head. "I came across them when I was hunting and they found me." He nodded as Marcus' face showed the surprise that anyone had sneaked up on the master tracker. "I showed him how to hunt. Sometimes he stays with me and sometimes I visit his home but he needs a purpose in his life."

Felix stood. "I want to pay back the Selgovae for their murder and I owe Rome much for I would have died were it not for their kindness. I would serve you." He looked over at Drugi. "I am Brigante and my father told me of the sword you carry. Drugi also told me of it. I would follow the sword."

Marcus walked over to the youth and clasped his arm. "Then I welcome you to Marcus' Horse and you shall be my scout. Do you ride?"

For the first time, Felix looked uncomfortable. He shook his head. "I know not how."

"Then I shall teach you as we ride to the fort. Do you have any belongings?"

He looked over to Drugi who said, "Just his weapons. Does he need more?" The boy held up his bow and quiver.

"He will need a leather jerkin for our enemies do not discriminate between those with and without armour."

"I have one in my hut. By the time you are ready to leave I will return."

First, we will get you a short sword and dagger. Marcus led him to the barn and, after moving a calf out of the way, cleared some straw from the floor. A small trapdoor was revealed and when it was opened

52

Felix could see that it was filled with weapons and mail shirts. The decurion took out a short sword and a dagger. He saw the question on the boy's face. "We have collected these over the years so that when my brother and his men fight they are prepared. We will replace those weapons the next time we fight. And now to your horse."

Marcus took Felix to the stable. The dog did not need an instruction, he just followed the youth. In the stables Marcus went to the most gentle of the horses who were there. Marcus was the ala horse master and, like his namesake, Marcus Maximunius, he knew horses the way a shepherd knows his sheep. "This is Blackie. He is descended from a fine line of horses and he will carry you safely. Speak with him and breathe into his nose while I get a saddle for you."

Wolf had his head cocked to one side, watching Felix as he stroked Blackie and spoke with him. Marcus could see, immediately, that Felix was one of those special people who could relate to all animals. He was another Drugi. "Here, I will show you how to put the saddle on. You can ride without one, but it is more comfortable with one." Felix was also a bright Brigante and the expression on his face showed Marcus that he was eager to learn.

Marcus led the horse out by his reins. He looped the rains over the placid horse's mane. "Now, mounting a horse is only hard the first time. Once you know it won't move, and this one won't, trust me, then you will gain confidence." The decurion put his hands together. "Put your foot in there, grab a handful of mane and pull yourself up." Marcus almost laughed aloud when he saw the look of fear on Felix's face and then he remembered when he had been taught, many years ago. Perhaps he had been as afraid then too. Felix was quite light and Marcus easily boosted him up so that he did not need to pull hard on the mane. Once he was seated he looked less afraid. Wolf still looked dubiously at the huge black horse and the boy who had raised him. "Now take the reins and kick with your heels. Make this sound." Marcus clicked his tongue three times in quick succession. As soon as Felix obeyed him the horse set off quite calmly.

As soon as the horse moved Wolf began to bark. Felix looked at the dog and pointing with his left hand said, in Brigante, "Stop!" The dog stopped barking but still watched carefully.

"Now just ride around the outside of the building and become familiar with him and I will get my horse."

Frann and Ailis had come from the kitchen when Wolf had barked. Drugi strode into the yard with the leather jerkin. "You ride well Felix. Talk to him as you do with Wolf and he will become your friend too."

53

When they disappeared around the back of the farm Ailis asked Drugi, "Is he alone in the world then?"

"He is and he lived with just his pup for seven days, just him and the dog with the snows around. I do not know what would have happened if the Gauls had not found him. The Allfather watches over him I think."

"Well someone does." She put her hand on the huge man's arm, "and I think that you watch over him too Drugi."

"I will never have a son but Felix is the son I would wish to have had."

Felix appeared around the corner of the building with a huge grin on his face and Wolf trotting quietly behind him. While Drugi gave the jerkin to Felix, Marcus gave his mother a hug, his wife and son a kiss. He watched Felix don the jerkin which would give him some protection in combat and then clasped Drugi's arm. "Stay close to the farm old friend until we have rid the land of these bandits. I have a feeling that they mean ill to folks like us."

Drugi gave a slight bow, "I will my friend." He nodded to Felix. "As I know you will care for the boy."

Marcus nodded and sprang easily on to the back of his horse. He put his arms out and Frann handed him Macro. He held tightly to his son and they trotted around the yard; Macro giggling and squealing with delight. When he gave him back to Frann the child let out a wail. "Thank you, husband! He cries and you go."

Marcus shrugged apologetically. "Send to Nanna and ask her if she has a small pony. It is time my son learned to ride!"

As they rode down the road towards Eboracum Felix asked, "How could you ride without using your hands? Why did you not fall off?"

"You use your knees to guide it and you become one with the horse. You will learn and when you scout you will not use your horse but it is easier for you to ride when we are on patrol for we cover great distances." He looked down at Felix. "The weapons I gave you will need to be kept sharp and you must use them to protect yourself."

"I want to hurt the Selgovae who killed my family."

"Felix, when we join the ala you will have to obey orders. You must know this and promise that you will do so or you can return to Drugi now. We fight all Rome's enemies, not just yours."

"I am sorry decurion. I will obey orders. I promise." The intense look on the boy's face told Marcus that he spoke the truth.

It was dusk by the time they entered the fort. Marcus did not know who was more surprised, the sentries who stared at the wild boy and his dog, or Felix who had never seen a building made of stone before. Marcus nodded to the optio. "This is Felix, my new scout."

The optio grinned; he had known the ala for years. "So they have replaced old Gaelwyn at last."

"I do not think we can ever replace Uncle Gaelwyn. Ride on Felix."

As they approached the barracks Marcus saw Felix's eyes drawn to the standard which stood outside the Principia. He pointed at it, "Decurion what is that?"

Marcus smiled, he had anticipated this moment all the way from the farm. "That Felix is the standard of the ala, it is the Wolf. Your dog is coming home."

Felix nodded. "Now I know that this was meant to be."

Appius Serjanus read the reports again. According to the engineers who had surveyed the land on the west coast, there were huge copper deposits as well as granite and slate. There was also the hint of gold. He had been a perfect aide to the Governor and dealt with the tiresome paperwork. It had only cost him a few late nights to copy down the report but he had scaled back the potential. When he showed it to the Governor he would volunteer to oversee the development of the mines. He would ensure that the miners and the officer who extracted the ore would report directly to him. His father had been right; this was a rich land with potential for someone with a shrewd brain and the courage to take action. All he now needed was to engage men whom he could trust. Despite all of his plans and strategies the young patrician still could not get the lovely Vibia from his mind and his thoughts. Every time he saw her around the Governor's residence, which was frequently, he found himself intoxicated by her perfume and drawn to her fluttering green eyes. He knew that she was toying with him but he could not help himself. He was just grateful that his rival, the young decurion was kept busy, out on patrol with the over-worked ala.

The object of his desire was fully aware of Appius' feelings for her. She had been taught well and knew how to captivate and entice a man. One of her servants had been an adherent of the Mother cult and Vibia had been a devoted learner. She understood about the use of herbs and potions to enhance one's beauty. She had enjoyed the knowledge that she could concoct a potion to make a man become infatuated with her. So far she had not needed it but she knew it was there when she wanted it. Even more than the knowledge of potions she had voraciously absorbed every fact she could about poisons. As with the love potions she had not needed them yet, but should anyone cross her then they would see the other side to Vibia. Appius suited her plans; she intended to be rich and she had seen in Appius Serjanus a likeminded soul.

Randal and the Selgovae warriors he led had watched the wall with increasing interest for the past week. Gone were the cavalry patrols which kept them penned and pinned inside their settlements. The narrower the gap became between the forts the more confident they became and there were now eight warbands of Selgovae and Votadini within a thousand paces of the wall. They had watched the infrequent cavalry patrols and counted the troopers. No more than thirty ever patrolled at one time and Randal had learned the value of caltrops. They had begun to manufacture crude ones; not of the same standard as those of the Romans but effective nonetheless. They were not afraid of thirty horsemen. They had also noted that it was not the legionaries who patrolled the length of the new wall for they continued to build, it was the warriors with mail, the warriors with the oval shields and the warriors Briac had told them they could defeat. Their scouts who had crept close to the wall told them of the grumblings from the auxiliaries. Briac's plan had begun to work and the supplies had been interrupted. They were hungry and unhappy. He knew that they had planned to wait until the wall was finished and the legionaries left but Randal saw an opportunity and he would take it.

The ditch on the frontier side of the wall had been deeply dug but, so far, it was free from either traps or lillia. The wall had yet to be faced and the stones afforded some grip to men determined to climb. Not all the mile castles had been built and Randal chose places with a large gap between them. He had his largest warband, two hundred warriors strong, waiting for the moon to dip behind the clouds. The previous two nights had been bright but the rain during the day had left clouds in the sky and it was a perfect opportunity for the Selgovae to inflict damage upon the wall and the men who manned it. The ten agile warriors, with ropes wrapped around their half naked bodies, slipped across the ditch and began to climb the stones. Although they were well finished there were holds between them which gave these warriors purchase. Once they reached the ramparts the warrior at each end of the line slipped away to deal with the sentry who watched there while the other eight threw their ropes over the side of the wall, tying them around the ramparts themselves. The two sentries died noiselessly as their throats were cut.

Once they were all safely inside the defences Randal led them towards the gate. Here he knew would be a half-century of auxiliaries. They had counted the eight who would be upon the walls and spotted

56

the stairs leading to the barracks housing the others. The optio who was on duty stared northwards across the rolling hills of the frontier. This was the real frontier. It seemed a lifetime away from his home by the sea in Northern Gaul. He had yet to see a Selgovae or Votadini but he had heard of them and their blue painted bodies. Someone had told him that it was not paint but they scarred their own bodies. He shuddered at the thought. The slight movement from his left was his only warning of something untoward. Randal's war hammer smashed through his helmet and split his skull in a single blow. The sound of his body crashing to the floor alerted the others but only one brave Gaul managed to shout a half warning before he too was despatched with the others. The centurion was an old frontier hand and the sound awoke him. "To arms! We are under attack!" One of the auxiliaries began to turn over. "Get up you dozy bastard. Those are barbarians!"

The centurion just grabbed his gladius and a spare scutum. Barefooted he ran up the stairs. Behind him he heard the sound of the door to the barracks being wrenched open as his gladius slipped up into the belly of the Selgovae racing down to kill even more of the Romans. Stepping over the body he punched his shield into the face of the next warrior and the Selgovae fell screaming to the barrack's floor. Once he emerged at the top of the tower the centurion could see that it was hopeless but he would not die without a fight. "On me!"

Four auxiliaries ran up the stairs to join him. "Sir, the men are being slaughtered!"

"You three form a shield wall, Titus, light the signal." Every tower had a signal which was there to warn of an attack. As Titus began to chip sparks off the flint the centurion and the other three began to hack their way through the Selgovae. There were only four of them and they had no armour but with swords and shields, added to their experience they began to force the Selgovae back. Suddenly the sky was illuminated as the flames took hold and the beacon flamed. "Titus, get your arse here!"

The five of them turned to face the barbarians who streamed up the stairs to get at them. The five Gauls fought well but once the Selgovae found the javelins it was all over as they stabbed under the shields into the unprotected bodies of the auxiliaries. Even though he was bleeding heavily from spear thrusts to his thighs the grizzled centurion continued to fight. As the life blood seeped from him his defence became weaker until Randal ended it by smashing his war hammer into his skull and the last defender died.

Randal was disappointed to have lost so many men. "Put their heads on spears. Burn it! Burn it to the ground!"

57

Briac waited in the shadows in the tavern at the vicus. He was not in a good humour. This was the third day he had waited for his spy and so far he had not shown. The two disasters caused by the ala had meant that they needed another plan. The patrols along the road had made the area much more secure for the Romans and more hazardous for the Brigante. When his spy entered, he ignored him while they both checked the room for any sign of someone showing undue interest. Briac had three of his men outside and they were ready to intervene should it become necessary.

"What went wrong?" Briac was blunt.

"The Prefect went wrong. He makes sudden decisions and doesn't tell, even his officers, what he intends."

"We lost men and we lost the wagons. I begin to wonder what the point of is having a dagger in the heart of the Roman cavalry if we cannot use it!"

The spy threw an angry glance in Briac's direction, but he knew that his leader was correct. "I can tell you now that the ala will be patrolling the northern road and the southern road and three turmae will be hunting you. And," he added ominously, "they have a new tracker; a Brigante who is half man and half dog."

Briac waved away the last comment. "The tracker is nothing. It is the Prefect who is the problem. He must die."

"That is easier said than done. What would you suggest? A knife in the night?"

Briac had not got as far as the details but the spy's idea seemed reasonable. "How close are you to the Prefect?"

As close as any in the turma but not close enough to be able to stick him like a pig."

"Who stands in your way?"

"Gaius, the chosen man. The signifier is another." The spy thought he knew what Briac intended. "It would be difficult for me to eliminate those two and not arouse suspicion."

Briac's clever mind was already ahead of his spy. "I know that. Leave it to me to get rid of those two. You must be ready to step into the breach and gain his confidence so that when you are the one closest to him then you can strike. This may not be as swift as we would like but if he is eliminated then Marcus' Horse will lose its power."

Aula's children were also meeting this time at the Temple of Augustus. Towards evening it was not as busy as during the day and they looked like two penitents, cloaked and hooded against the night chill. "Have you had the chance to find the gold yet?"

"No, but I know the place for it is close to the road. And you? How close are you to the Prefect?"

"Not close yet but I have a plan to make him come closer to me. Remember that mother said that we should be patient. We are young and the important thing is to succeed. It matters not when." A smile played upon the lips. "Besides I am enjoying this life and this deception, are you not?"

The smile which came back was identical. "Of course I am. They are fools and we are leading them by the nose!"

Chapter 7

The Legate, Julius Demetrius, came himself with the news of the raid and the destruction of the gate to the Praetorium at Eboracum. When Livius received his summons he left immediately and found the Governor, Julius and Appius studying the map of the Stanegate and the wall. "Ah good, Livius, you know the area as well as any. Julius has brought grave news. The Selgovae scaled the walls and slaughtered a half-century of men, destroying a gatehouse in the process. It has not only set our building programme back but caused a dip in morale. Following on from the shorter rations the auxiliaries are not happy about their losses and we do not want a repetition of the Batavian revolt of a few years ago do we?"

"They chose their target well. The section they attacked had not had the mile castles added and the sentries were isolated."

"How did they scale the walls?"

"They just climbed as a spider does. Appius here has a solution to that, however. Tell them Appius."

The preening aide puffed himself up so much that Livius though he might explode. "If we were to make the faces smooth with concrete then they could not climb."

"If the ditch had been finished and lined with traps and lillia then we might have had warning." Julius Demetrius was beginning to become a little annoyed with the aide and his ideas.

"Yes, Julius but there is little point in going over what we did not do. What do you think of Appius' suggestion?"

"It will work but it is expensive and it means sending for more wagons with the materials to make the cement. This will also tie up the ala. I am sure that, had we had the ala on patrol then this would have been less likely to happen."

"There you go again Julius. Stop worrying about what we didn't do and concentrate on what we can do. I do not care about the expense. The wall must be built to give us security. As we both know the Emperor needs the wall to hold back the barbarians and also to provide a base when we invade again."

Livius could see that Julius and the Governor were on a collision course. "Perhaps we could send another four turmae north to boost Rufius. I am sure that the other twelve turmae can patrol the road."

Appius looked at the Governor who nodded. "Eleven turma for I need one turma to travel to the land of the lakes and escort Appius while he sets up a mining operation."

Julius looked to the heavens in exasperation. "The frontier threatens to boil over and you want to waste a valuable resource escorting one man! Where are the priorities?"

"You forget yourself, Legate. It is my decision and besides which it will pay for the new materials we need to face the wall and to build new forts."

"New forts?" Julius and the Emperor had spent long hours meticulously planning the wall and the forts were already there to the south of the wall.

"Yes. I plan to build forts here and here on the wall and then some north of the wall, here and here."

"Think of the manpower you would need, not only to build them but to protect them!"

"It will make the frontier secure. I have made my decision. Now Prefect who will be escorting Appius to the west?"

Livius hated to detach one turma and he was loath to use Marcus or Metellus. "Titus, for he came from the region and he knows the area as well as any. He will make the expedition as short as it needs to be and return to the real work of the turma." Appius shot a look of pure hate at the Prefect who assiduously ignored him. "I will send Marcus north with Gnaeus, Lucius, and Septimus. Metellus can be based at Morbium and patrol the road to Eboracum and I will remain here in Eboracum to try to catch the rebels."

Nepos looked up in surprise. "Rebels? I thought they were bandits?"

"From their weapons and their tactics they are rebels. Bandits would not have wasted time taking the concrete. No, they want to disrupt the wall building and the intelligence we had from the prisoners is bearing fruit. There is a conspiracy amongst the tribes, Governor and that bodes ill for us all."

Far to the north along the wall, Rufius was acutely aware of the threat and the anger from the tribes. He had long grown from the keen young Explorate into a sound leader of men. He took pride in the fact that Livius had left him with just two turmae to patrol a frontier riddled with enemies. It did not make the task any easier, however, for every time he sent Decius off with his turma he worried about the young decurion. He knew that Decius was a good officer but he had learned much from watching men like Cassius and Livius. The frontier was an unforgiving classroom.

The Gallic Prefect had been angry about the loss of his half-century. There was no blame attached to Rufius but Prefect Ambrinus knew that his men were spread out too thinly. "Rufius what can your men do?"

61

"I think that the fort is too far to the east to be much good; especially as the building work is so far to the west now. I will leave the fort to the Sixth. They can continue to improve the wall here and I will build a camp between the Stanegate and the wall. How is that? We can then patrol directly north of the wall and give some protection to the vulnerable parts."

"I appreciate it. We didn't realise what a good job you lads did until the Governor sent them south."

"We will leave today and I will take my men up the old road and head for the gap on their side of the frontier. It may help us to surprise them."

Julius Longinus sniffed disapprovingly when Rufius told him of his decision. "Leaving me here with a bunch of legionaries! The sooner the Prefect returns the better." He pulled out a piece of parchment. "Here this may help. It is a map with distances showing the forts and the walls. It may be of some service. Make sure you bring it back!"

For all his bluster the old man was very fond of the men in the ala. He had been with them so long that they were like family to him. "Don't worry. We will be back."

The gate to the northern road was at the far end of the bridge. Rufius remembered the fierce fighting which had taken place when they first erected the fort. Now it was peaceful but he knew that it was an illusion. They were being watched. As they waved to the sentries at the far side of the bridge Rufius turned to Decimus, his chosen man. "Take young Julius and ride west. There is a trail which cuts through the forest. Let us see if we can flush any of the Votadini scouts out."

Grinning Decimus snapped a, "Be delighted to sir!" and galloped off with Julius in tow.

The old road north had been built by the Ninth during the heady days of Agricola and his successful drive north. To the ala it was a valuable lifeline for it enabled them to travel north rapidly and with little chance of ambush. "Decius you bring up the rear and watch for any sign of our barbaric friends. They are up to no good and it is time we taught them a lesson."

The down side of travelling along the road was that there was neither sign nor tracks to follow but Rufius only intended to travel far enough north to spook the scouts he knew would be watching them.

As soon as he felt they had travelled far enough he shouted, "Turmae, left wheel." The whole column turned into a sixty-man, two deep line, and thirty men wide. Keeping a good distance between the troopers meant that they could cover a large area. Their tactic soon reaped results as Rufius saw the warriors trying to out run the horses.

62

The younger troopers became excited and he could see them kicking their horses on. "On me! Keep the same pace." Rufius wanted the fleeing warriors exhausted and he knew that he had two men just waiting to head them off. There was no hurry; the cavalry mounts could keep this pace up all day. He had time to count them. There were twelve of them and most looked to be the younger warriors; they would have stamina and would run further and longer than older warriors. Equally they would be easier to break when it came to questioning. "Drive them to the middle!"

Just like hunters driving game their quarry began to draw together. The frantic looks over their shoulders told Rufius that they were becoming increasingly concerned with the proximity of the horses. The Votadini were not men of the horse, they were the foot warriors and horses frightened them. Rufius tried to imagine what they would be seeing as the sixty horses thundered after them.

When the first one stumbled Rufius yelled, "Secure him!" He heard, rather than saw the two troopers stop and wrestle the scout into submission. Two more fell this way until Decius and Julius loomed ahead of the fleeing men; they saw not two warriors but more of the hated horse warriors who would kill them. Four of them tried to attack the two troopers but Decius casually slew them with his long spatha and Julius made his first kill. The others were too exhausted to fight and they prostrated themselves on the ground. "Bind them!"

As his men secured the prisoners Rufius signalled Decimus and Decius to join him. "Did you see any others Decimus?"

"No sir, these were the only ones. When we heard your hooves, we knew they were heading our way."

"Good. We will continue east and scout the wall gap. These prisoners can be interrogated later."

The eight prisoners were tethered to a trooper each and led through the woods. They were in no condition to struggle and Rufius kept up a steady pace to discourage any attempt at escape.

At the gap in the wall the third century of the Sixth Legion was toiling away in armour. The latest attacks had meant that they could not strip off and work as they would have preferred. Their piles of weapons were gathered in tent party groups and the centurion, Gaius Colonus felt the hairs constantly prickling on the back of his neck. The brazen attack on the Gauls had shaken even the most experienced veteran and they worked with one eye on the forest. The ditch they were digging would, eventually, form the northern boundary of the Roman Empire but at the moment it seemed a little isolated to the centurion. The sooner they had finished the building and could get back to real soldiering, the better. He rubbed his neck. It was becoming uncomfortable to have to keep looking over one's shoulder to watch the forest. He turned to look again and this time saw a flash of white flesh which should not have been there. "Stand to! On me!" Grabbing his helmet, he looked for the signifier as the legionaries quickly donned their weapons. They had not seen the danger but the fact that Gaius Colonus had warned them was enough for them.

The Votadini raced from the tree line, their cover blown. Unhampered by armour and any kind of order, they raced across the open ground to hurl themselves at the legionaries who were desperately trying to form a defensive line.

"Lock your shields!" Colonus cursed the fact that they would not have time to get their javelins and would have to defend themselves with gladii only. This would be a bloody business! The first Votadini threw himself at the rapidly forming shield wall and died at the hands of the centurion who chopped down at the unprotected neck, severing the head. His momentum, however, caused him to knock over the legionary who had no one behind him to brace. The next Votadini exploited the gap. The centurion and the optio were on opposite sides of the barbarians and they both urged their men to close the gap. The warriors were desperately throwing their own warriors into the shrinking gap and both sides were taking casualties. Colonus could see that they were well outnumbered and the Votadini could afford a battle of attrition. At least they would know they had been in a fight. "Come on ladies! These are fucking half dressed barbarians! Kill the bastards!"

Rufius heard the clash of metal and knew that meant trouble for someone and in this part of the world that someone would be Roman. He shouted to the men holding the prisoners. "You men wait here. The rest of you, javelins, and ride like the wind is behind you!" The line spread out trying to make up the distance to the rear of the warband. Rufius gripped his knees and hurtled his javelin, watching with satisfaction as it thudded through the back of the surprised warrior. He drew his spatha and, as the Votadini warrior turned to face him, cleaved his skull in two. Around him his men were carving a path of death through the barbarians who were caught between two camps, defeating the vaunted legionaries and defending themselves from the unknown horsemen behind. They failed and the warband broke and scattered.

"Form a perimeter!" Rufius knew that they could return and he saw that the century had suffered many casualties.

The centurion mopped the blood from his scalp wound. "Nicely done, decurion. You timed that well!"

"The Allfather smiled on you today. We had prisoners and were heading for the gap."

The centurion held out a gnarled and muscular arm. "Whatever brought you here you have my thanks for I thought I had fought my last."

It had been a close run skirmish and thirty of the century lay dead whilst another twenty had suffered wounds of one type or another. "I think, centurion that we can end the work for today and we will escort you back to the fort."

"Aye and a beaker of something when we get back eh?"

"Decimus, fetch the prisoners."

As the line of prisoners was brought from the forest one of the younger troopers, Publius approached Rufius. "Sir, can I have a word please?"

"Yes, Publius what is it?"

"Sir, I can speak a little Votadini and when we were waiting in the woods I heard the prisoners talking to each other. Some of the other troopers wanted to stop them but I didn't see the harm, they are little more than lads." Rufius suppressed the smile at the young trooper's words. "Anyway, one of them is the son of a chief, Iucher."

"Which one?"

Publius pointed to a tall red-haired youth who had a number of amulets around his upper arms. "Him sir. I think this was a part of an initiation ceremony you know, watch the Romans and report back."

"Well done Publius. You take charge of the prisoners and let me know if they say anything else."

Julius Demetrius was tired of the journeys to Eboracum and back. He longed for the simpler days when he had been a Prefect of cavalry and had little else to worry about than a barbarian ambush. He saw Rufius leading his patrol back into the fort with his string of prisoners. At last they would have increased ala support now that the Governor had released more turmae.

The Legate slumped into the seat in the Principia. Julius Longinus looked up from his work. "Hard journey sir?"

"At my age every journey is hard. Is it my imagination or is it very quiet around the fort these days?"

"I will be glad to see the Prefect and the men back sir. I hate to say it but I do miss them."

"I know what you mean. They annoy the life out of you when they are there but when they are not…" The sound of a challenge and then hooves clattering into the fort alerted them to the arrival of horsemen and they both left the office.

Rufius' face told the two men that he had something important to say. "Legate. I am glad you are here. We have captured a war chief's son."

"Which one?"

"Iucher."

The clerk looked in his lists and said, "His name was mentioned by those other prisoners. He is one of the important warriors."

"Well done Rufius. Now, the question is how to use him to the best effect?" He offered Rufius a beaker of wine and continued, "You never met Julius Agricola did you?" Rufius shook his head. "He was a brilliant general and a cunning leader. He often avoided battles by holding hostage the families of his enemies. Queen Cartimandua did the same. Bring me one of the other prisoners and someone who can speak their language."

Rufius returned with a surly youth and Publius who seemed proud of his achievement. "This is Publius; he is the trooper who discovered the boy's identity."

"Well done, Publius. Tell this one that we are going to let him go." Publius looked surprised but Julius continued, "Just tell him son."

Publius did so and the boy's surly expression changed to one of suspicion. The boy said something in his own language and Publius said, "He asked why sir."

"Tell him I want him to take a message to Iucher." Even before the word was translated the boy's eyes flashed back at the Legate. "Well that confirms Iucher's identity anyway."

Publius translated and there was no change in the barbarian's face. He still looked suspicious.

"Tell Iucher that unless the attacks cease then I will execute the other boys, one by one. I will crucify them."

Publius showed surprise but he translated the words. The Votadini lurched forward; fortunately, his hands were still tethered behind his back. He yelled something and Publius grinned as he said, "He doesn't like you sir! I won't translate what he wants to do with you but it isn't pleasant."

Julius laughed wryly. "Many barbarians have promised me such pain in the past." He turned to Rufius. "Have Decius take him north of the wall and let him go."

When Rufius returned he asked, "A bit of a risk sir. What makes you think he won't try to rescue the others?"

"Oh he might but if we can't stop one youth from breaching our security then it is time to go home eh Rufius? We will know soon enough if we have succeeded. According to Julius here they are attacking somewhere along the wall every day. If we go two days without an attack then it means our threat is working and we will then have to worry about the father trying to rescue him. And hopefully, the other turmae will be here soon and we might actually be able to do our job."

Marcus and the four turmae arrived shortly before dark. They had been slowed by the wagons they had escorted. Now that the Governor wanted the wall facing they had had to ensure that there were enough materials to do the job. Rufius looked at Felix and the dog. "New recruit Marcus?"

"A couple of scouts Drugi found for me. This is Felix and the other is Wolf. This is Decurion Rufius." Felix bowed formally while Wolf eyed the officer suspiciously. "Go with the other men Felix and they will show you where the stables are and your barracks." Felix clicked his horse after the other troopers while Wolf sniffed everything his nose could reach. "How are things?"

"Interesting. We have a chief's son as a hostage and the Legate is threatening to kill him if the tribes don't behave. We will find out how successful a ploy it is in the next two days."

Iucher took the news remarkably calmly. The surly boy had told of the attack and their capture and Iucher had blamed himself for allowing his son to join such a reckless adventure. Torin was his only child, for the boy's mother had died in childbirth and Iucher was loath to throw away his son's life. Besides which they had lost more men in the last few days and he wanted his warband to build up their numbers and then they could have a night time attack. The first one had been so successful that it was worth repeating but this time it would be near the horse fort where his son was being held. "I will travel south of the wall and visit our Brigante brothers. It is time they delivered what they had promised."

Chapter 8

Briac was shocked to find Iucher and ten unhappy Votadini warriors waiting for him in his camp. Not only were they unexpected, but they had also managed to evade his sentries and the Brigante chief felt foolish. "Chief Iucher, I was not expecting you."

"No? Perhaps that is because you have not delivered on your promises. The Romans on the wall are still well supplied and they still attack. My son is now a hostage Briac. What will you do about that?"

"I am sorry Iucher but the horse warriors have prevented us from stopping the wagons. We intend to kill their leader."

"Well, do it quickly. And what of my son?"

Briac chewed his lip. Suddenly an idea came to him. "We could gain a hostage of our own."

Iucher was intrigued. "It would have to be the son of one of their chiefs."

"They have them not but there is a wife and she would make a valuable hostage."

"How will you get her?"

"I told you, I have a spy in the fort. I will go with some of my men and we will bring the hostages to you and you can take them back to exchange for your son."

Iucher could see no flaw in the plan and, north of the wall his men were still gathering for an attack on the horse fort. If this kidnap failed he would do it his way and sever his ties with the false Brigante. When the Romans fell he would deal with his faithless allies himself. "Very well. I will return to my people but our alliance depends upon the success of this operation Briac. Make sure that you succeed."

The spy was less than happy when he met with Briac and the other Brigante warriors. "You want me to kill the Prefect and kidnap the Governor's wife? You do not expect much from me Briac."

"Instead of a knife in the night we will use poison and all I need from you is to let the five of us in. We will do the rest. Your identity will still be safe."

The spy relaxed a little, "You have poison?"

Briac handed over a small earthenware jug. "Pour this in the food he is to eat and he will die. We will strike tonight. Draw me a plan of the Governor's quarters and where the guards are."

As he did so the spy explained. "You will need to don Roman clothes for no-one will question you once you are inside. I know how to get you inside too. Bring a deer and tell the sentries that you come from the farm of Decius Aurelius, his brother serves in the ala and they are well known. They will allow you in. Bring it here," he marked a place on the drawing, "to the kitchen and I will await you there."

Livius preferred being on the road with his troopers for being stationed at the fortress meant he was at the beck and call of the Governor. He now knew why Julius had left as quickly as he had for the frontier. He had spent the whole afternoon poring over maps with Appius and the Governor so that the aide could find the putative copper mines as quickly as possible. The only advantage of being in the fort was the comfort of the dining arrangements. He and his officers were able to eat hot cooked food in comfort. Metellus and the others had finished their escort duties. Marcus' journey north had meant that they, too, could spend a comfortable night in barracks and, perhaps, a night in the vicus.

"Have you managed to see Nanna yet Metellus?"

Metellus was too honest to lie and he and Livius shared a long history of working together. Despite the difference in their ranks they were friends; a friendship forged in Aquitania when hunting Livius' traitorous brother. "Yes, we always manage to call in, however briefly on our journeys north."

"I envy you at times Metellus but then I think that I am glad that there is no one to worry over me. Ours is a perilous profession and few reach their pension."

Julius, the decurion of the tenth Turma shook his head. "Your problem, sir, is that there are over five hundred people who worry over you."

"Kind of you to say so Julius but some commanders would feel that that showed a weakness of leadership."

"No Livius; it shows you care for the men and they respect that."

Their conversation was interrupted by the bowl of stew which was carried in by two of the fortress cooks. "Venison stew sir. Courtesy of the decurion's brother, Decius!"

"Excellent! It is an advantage having the farm so close. One gets tired of the constant porridge and bread. And I am starving."

The other officers had all ladled the stew on to their plates. Julius could not resist a mouthful. Livius stood and help up his beaker. "To Marcus' Horse!"

The officers all stood and roared "Marcus' Horse!"

"And now the stew…"

Before Metellus could even sit Julius had fallen over and was clutching his throat. A white, green froth erupted from his lips. "Poison!

Don't touch the stew! Send for the capsarius. Metellus get the charcoal!"

Metellus was already going to the cold brazier to get a piece of charcoal. Livius sniffed the water jug and tested a drop on his finger. "Tastes fine." Metellus used the pommel of his dagger to grind up the charcoal and mix it with the water. Julius' eyes were already rolling back in his head as Livius forced the black liquid into his throat. "Hold his nose!" While Metellus held the decurion's nose Livius poured the whole of the concoction into Julius' mouth. Once it was in, he held his mouth closed.

The capsarius raced in. He took one look at Livius and said, "Charcoal?" Livius nodded. "Well done sir. Best remedy for poison. I assume it was poison?"

"Yes looks like the stew."

Just then Julius started to retch and vomit. The green and black liquid smelled foul but the capsarius looked pleased. "Good lad, get it up it'll do you good." The capsarius took a water skin from his bag of equipment. Let's try some pure water." He cradled Julius' head in his arms much as a mother would do with a baby. "Keep drinking son. The more you drink the better chance you have of living."

"Metellus. Take some men and get down to the kitchen see if you can find out how the food was poisoned. I'd better see the Governor."

The Governor, his wife, his aide and his wife's companions were just sitting down to eat when Flavia Nepos noticed that she did not have her fruit knife. It was an ornately made piece of cutlery but particularly special to Flavia because the Emperor Trajan's mother had given it to her and she always said that the fruit tasted better cut by the Empress' knife. Lucia began eating and avoided eye contact; Vibia sighed, "I will get it, domina."

She walked down the long corridor to the rooms the Governor used. She was already tired of working for the annoyingly fussy woman who bored her to death with every utterance. If only Appius had more money then she would marry him and enjoy a much more luxurious life, the life she had been born to. She was, therefore, somewhat distracted when she opened the door and was suddenly grabbed by the four huge and foul smelling Brigante. Her eyes opened wide as she recognised one of the troopers from the ala. "You!" A fierce warrior clamped his hand across her mouth, his other gripping her tightly across the chest, pinning her arms at her side.

The spy cursed, "Shit! This is not the wife of the Governor. This is one of her servants!"

Just then Livius and the other officers clattered down the corridor outside. "She will have to do! Just get us out of here and then see if the poison has worked. Adair, smack her one." The warrior holding her dropped her and, before she could shout, hit her hard on the chin with his enormous fist. She passed out and Adair slung her over his shoulder. The spy led the way as they made their way to the northern gate. Already word had got out about the attempt on the Prefect's life and the guards at the gate were alert and watching the buildings keenly.

Briac halted them in the shadow of the barrack building. "We need a diversion." Taking out his sword he stabbed the spy in the leg, just below the knee and avoiding an artery. "Crawl out there and shout for help." He turned to his other men. "Put the girl down and when they come to help him kill them." He was already working out how far they could get. Their horses were tied up in the vicus with three more of their men.

The spy rolled out from the barrack building and, with blood smeared on his hands from his leg wound shouted, "Help! There are Brigante."

The four sentries were so shocked and surprised that they forgot their training and all four of them raced over to help their wounded comrade. As the spy thrust his pugeo into the throat of the first man, the others were butchered where they stood. "Grab the girl." Ignoring the spy who was busy replacing his bloody dagger with a clean one from one of the sentries, Briac led his men out of the fort and into the vicus. The shouts and the commotion had drawn other guards who raced to find the wounded trooper and the dead sentries. The spy lay in a pool of blood, it was not his but it served its purpose. "Brigante! They have one of the Domina's companions." He then pretended to pass out.

As he lay there he heard the optio say, "Brave bugger. Capsarius!"

By the time the gate was again manned, Briac and his men had fled with their victim. They had the hostage they needed. Their next task was no less daunting; to get their victim north of the frontier which meant passing through the Roman forts and patrols. Briac was determined to show the Votadini and Selgovae that the Brigante were still a powerful tribe.

Governor Aulus Nepos was still trying to calm his hysterical wife and Lucia by the time Livius reached him. "Where have you been, Prefect? My wife was nearly kidnapped and they have taken Vibia. What were you and your men doing?" Livius could see that Appius was also unhappy and scowled at him. He felt the unfairness of it. He and the ala were not the garrison of the fortress. The legionaries of the Sixth

Legion were responsible for that while his ala were merely guests. He did not think that arguing that would do him any good.

"I am afraid it is more serious than that Governor."

"More serious than trying to kidnap the wife of an Imperial Governor?"

"Someone managed to poison the stew my officers and I were going to eat. So you see in the scheme of things kidnap is slightly less serious than murdering all of us."

Flavia stopped crying. "You mean we could have been poisoned too?"

"If they could get at our food then yours would have been doctored just as easily. We have questioned the cooks. The food they used was not poisoned but the men who brought it were not from the farm they said. Brigante rebels managed to breach our security." He said '*our*', but he meant the Sixth's. It was not in Livius' nature to blame a fellow officer. "However the most serious element is that no Brigante went near to the food. Someone from inside the fort is a traitor."

After Livius had finished speaking there was a stunned silence. "Were the two events linked do you think, Prefect?"

Livius noticed the slightly more placatory note. "It would make sense. If there were rebels inside the fortress then they would have the opportunity to kidnap one of your party. The question is why? It is not their usual tactic. If you kidnap someone then you want something in return. And I am at a loss to see what."

Appius stood and went to the desk in the corner. "I think I can help there. We received a letter from the fort on the wall, your fort, Prefect. It came from the Legate. Apparently, your men have captured the son of a war chief and he is being held hostage for their future good behaviour. My guess would be that they will want an exchange."

Livius sighed more with exasperation than anything else. Had he been informed of the letter then he would have been able to do something about it. The Governor looked shocked. "I will have a word with the Camp Prefect about the security. From now on we will allow no Brigante near the fort. But what about food? Are the cooks to be trusted?"

"That is simple enough, Governor, just have the cooks taste the food in your presence and then you will know."

Appius stood up, suddenly angry, "What about Vibia? How does this help here? What do you intend to do about her?"

"You forget yourself Appius!"

"I will send Titus and his turma with the news. Rufius and Marcus are both excellent officers they will find her."

72

"How!" The contempt in Appius' voice made the Prefect want to punch him.

"Well apart from the fact that they are both Explorates, Marcus is a Brigante and they both know the area very well, the fact that I say they can do the job should be enough for you." Livius' voice also had an edge to it.

Governor Nepos waved his arms in attempt to calm things down. "I think that is an excellent suggestion, Prefect and I think the sooner you and your men can catch these Brigante killers then the sooner you can get back to the wall and rid us of Rome's enemies."

"I am going too!"

"No I forbid it Appius. We need you here."

Both Flavia and Lucia looked equally shocked but Appius was adamant. "My task was to find the copper mines. With the turma in the north then I have nought to do. When we have recovered Vibia then I can go with the turma to the west. Is that not true, Prefect?"

Suddenly Livius was an ally. How he hated politics, politicians and political appointees. "Yes, it is possible. But believe me, if my men cannot rescue her then no-one can."

"Nevertheless, I will be going north and that is an end to the argument!"

Titus and his turma rode hard for the north. They needed not Appius' constant orders and demands for speed for they were going to join the rest of the ala and that was all they wanted. Titus had taken spare horses and they made the journey in one day, although the horses were ready to drop by the time they arrived. Appius had complained when Titus had insisted upon telling the commanders at the forts on the roads to watch out for Brigante heading north. The patrician fop who complained did not know, as Titus did, that the forts were the best defence they had against barbarian enemies. They could shut the stable door and make it even harder for the Brigante to get to the wall unseen. When they reached the fort, although they did not know it, Briac was still south of the Dunum. The ala had an edge.

Rufius took charge of all six turmae when Marcus arrived. He was pleased that they had a new scout; even though both he and Marcus were excellent trackers they missed having one of Gaelwyn's ability. It looked like Felix fitted the bill perfectly. "Marcus, take your turma and Felix out. Just let him get the feel of the land. This is new country and we both know how different it is to the land near to the Dunum."

So, even while Titus and Appius were racing towards the frontier Marcus and his turma were north of the wall. "I will leave the horse in the stable sir for I need to feel the land."

Marcus had never seen the two of them working before and they were a remarkable pair. Wolf ranged from side to side and would suddenly disappear. Felix never seemed to worry or mind that his dog was no longer close by. For his part, Felix constantly touched, smelled and tasted everything he could see. It was he who made the first discovery. He held up his hand and gave a whistle. Wolf appeared, apparently from nowhere and Felix pointed to the ground. "Seven days ago, perhaps longer, seven warriors crossed here heading south. The warriors went in single file. They returned north two days ago."

Sextus was as impressed as Marcus. "What do you make of it sir?"

"Interesting. It meant they went further south than the fort, the question is why and where were they going?" He suddenly slapped his head. "What a fool I am Sextus. Felix is a Brigante we need to let him see and smell Votadini and Selgovae. There are Votadini prisoners at the fort. It could be these warriors were sent to scout out the fort." He looked up at the sun. "We might as well head back to the fort and report to the decurion."

The fort was a hive of activity when Marcus and his men rode in. He saw Titus and recognised the unpleasantly arrogant Governor's aide as soon as he dismounted

The Legate waved him over. "Sextus, see to the men and Felix. It looks like something big has happened."

Julius Longinus gave Marcus a rare smile as he came in. The old man was fond of all the original decurion but Marcus held a special place in the old man's thoughts. The Legate waved them to their seats. "Titus has just briefed me." Marcus could see that the aide was red faced and obviously unhappy that Titus was afforded more respect and credibility than he was. "It seems the Brigante have kidnapped the companion of the Governor's wife. We think, or at least Livius does, that they were going for Domina Nepos."

Rufius interjected, almost absent mindedly, "Well then that will be what happened." He held up a hand. "Sorry for the interruption Legate."

"You are right and I agree with you Rufius. I also agree that this is likely to be in retaliation for our hostages and it may well result in an exchange. Now, thanks to Titus, the frontier should be shut up tightly and they may not even reach this point but let us work on the assumption that they will reach us and they will make a demand."

"Then you will exchange her!"

All of the officers stared at Appius in amazement. Julius Demetrius · just said quietly, "I understand why you are upset but you have neither status nor rank here. I am allowing you to stay here out of courtesy but I would appreciate it if you would keep your mouth shut." Titus hid a smile. This made up for the diatribe he had suffered on the long road north. "Now to get back to the matter in hand; we have time to find their camp and to try to ambush them as they travel north."

"Sir?"

"Yes, Marcus?"

"We found tracks which led south and then returned north. They seem to tally with the time the hostages were captured and the lady kidnapped. It means that we have a place to start to look."

"Excellent! Take your turma out in the morning with Titus and see what you can discover. Rufius, you can take the other turmae south and try to intercept them. It is a long shot as they will try to avoid the roads but I trust your Explorate training to give you the edge. And you," he looked at the aide with a cold hard look, "can wait here and try not to get in the way!"

Chapter 9

Vibia awoke as they approached the Dunum. Briac had contemplated waking her before but, as she was quiet, he had allowed the sleeping dog to lie. The kidnapped girl was tied over the back of a horse and Vibia felt slightly nauseous as a result of the motion. As she came to and felt the bruise on her jaw the kidnap came flooding back to her. She reflected that had Lucia been asked to go then the situation would now be totally different. Pragmatic as ever she would find a way out or her dilemma; she had been taught well. Vibia was not afraid. Had her captors wished harm to come to her they would have done so already. "What do you want of me?"

Only Briac understood her and he held up his hand. "Halt! He went to her. "I will untie you and seat you on the horse but if you try to escape my men will catch you and they will hurt you. Do you understand what I mean?"

Vibia looked at the men and shuddered, she knew exactly what they meant. Their leering faces left her in no doubt that she would suffer pain as well as the unwelcome attentions of her Brigante captors. She would have to go along with them until she could escape. She had no doubt that she could escape them for they were mere barbarians. It would be a case of being patient. "I will do as you wish but as it is going to become cold I would appreciate something warm about my shoulders or did you kidnap me merely to have me freeze to death?"

Briac did not like Romans and he did not like being told what to do by a woman. Here a Roman woman was ordering him around and he did not like it. He would, however, have to accede to her demands. There would be little point in kidnapping and risking his spy merely to have her die on the road. He reluctantly gave her a cloak, ironically stolen from a dead Roman. "Here, but two men are behind you at all times. Remember that."

Vibia feigned difficulty in sitting correctly on the horse when in fact she had been taught to ride from an early age. She could even ride bareback but now was not the time for escape. She needed to know where she was. She had no idea which direction they were travelling in and she had only a vague idea of the geography of the region. She knew they were Brigante but she also knew that the land of the Brigante stretched from coast to coast. She had heard that they sometimes sold people to Hibernian slavers although it seemed a little farfetched that she would be taken. She also knew that the Via Nero went north and south of Eboracum and, from the direction the shadows were falling the sun was in the east. That was as far as her knowledge went. She wondered, as they headed north, if they had mistaken her for the Governor's wife. Then she remembered the Roman trooper she had recognised. He had known who she was. It was planned to take her; the question was why?

They reached the Dunum which was forty paces wide and flowing deceptively slowly. Briac halted them and tied two halters to the woman's horse. The water was not shallow enough for them to walk but the horses were able to swim. Briac had taken the journey many times and he knew the best angle to enter and leave the water. He was not afraid. He led the party across the water, ensuring the party stayed close together. Vibia herself was a little wary about the dark sinister water and she hoped that the horse knew what it was doing. Although the water was deep it was not flowing very quickly and she breathed a sigh of relief when she felt the horse's hooves bite into the river bed as they approached what she assumed was the northern bank. Once they reached the other side one of the warriors loosened his halter and took up a position behind her. It did not go unnoticed by Vibia; she was being closely guarded. She noticed the direction of the river's flow and deduced that they must be travelling north which meant that they were heading for the wall. That gave her some comfort for she knew that the wall was garrisoned and that the horsemen she had met were in that region. The hope grew in her but she knew she would have to watch for an opportunity to escape. She would only have one chance; she knew that and failure would result in pain at best and death at worst.

Marcus looked at the churned-up ground. Wolf had taken a good sniff at the Votadini who appeared to be more than a little wary of the snarling dog. Marcus had wondered about that for the dog had shown no aggression towards any of the ala but he did not know if Wolf had been given a sign by Felix. Felix too had sniffed at them and felt their clothes. When one of them began to raise his arm, Wolf snarled and Marcus smacked him in the face. The combination cowed the others. Felix had nodded happily when they left. "I will know them," was his confident statement.

Now, as they rode north Marcus reflected that he would have had no chance of discerning evidence from the churned up mud but Felix and Wolf happily trotted on ahead of the turma. As they went deeper into the forest Wolf and Felix separated; Marcus kept following the human tracker. A whistle occasionally brought the dog back. The decurion wondered how the dog would communicate what it had found for it did not bark.

77

Eventually, Felix came back. "Sir, wait here and I will return."

In a heartbeat he was gone and Titus rode up to join his colleague. "How does he disappear so quickly and quietly, sir?"

"He isn't riding a horse but even so he is impressive." He turned to the two turmae. "Get your weapons ready in case we need them in a hurry."

The forest seemed unnaturally quiet and Marcus began to imagine he was seeing Votadini all around him. Suddenly Felix appeared next to him. "If you dismount sir I will take you to their camp."

Marcus dismounted and put his helmet and shield on the pommel of his saddle. "Titus, Sextus keep watch until I return. Put out a perimeter guard."

"Are you sure about this sir?"

Marcus grinned, he was an Explorate again. "You are getting more like an old woman every day Sextus. Of course, I will be fine." He set off after the swiftly moving and silent pair of trackers. He felt as though he was a bull charging through the forest for he was aware of the noise he was making but Felix did not seem to mind. There was a smell of wood smoke and noises ahead, the vague murmurings of people, the sound of metal on metal, an occasional laugh and shout; the Votadini! The Brigante boy held up his hand and dropped to all fours' Marcus did the same emulating Felix's action. It seemed like years since he had done this. He crawled slowly across the forest floor, watching where he placed his hands and feet before he trusted them to the ground. He saw Wolf's ears drop and the dog lay close to the ground. There looked to be a slight ridge ahead and Marcus, like Felix, lay on the ground and slid slowly, like a serpent to where the dog waited. Felix's left hand came out and stopped him from moving further forward. The scout's right hand scooped some mud and smeared it across Marcus' face and then his own. He nodded and began to raise his head. When Marcus did the same he saw that they were about fifty paces above a clearing. In the clearing there were at least three hundred warriors. Some were sharpening weapons some were practising with their weapons and others were seated around open fires talking. Even as they watched another party, forty strong strode into the camp to be greeted warmly by the ones already there. This was a large warband. This one was close enough to attack the men building the wall and expect to succeed. He had seen enough and he slid slowly backwards. When he reached the place he had started he stood up. They began to make their way back to the rest of his men. Both humans kept silent and Marcus noticed that Wolf trailed them by a hundred paces and would occasionally loop back on himself.

78

When they reached the troopers Sextus laughed, "Fall in the mud then sir?"

Marcus realised he still had a mud covered face. He went to his horse and poured some of the water from his skin to clean his face. He mounted his horse, "There are three hundred Votadini at least over there. I think they are planning something. Let's get back to the fort."

As they rode back the three new recruits trotted alongside each other. "Did you hear the decurion Aneurin? There are three hundred Votadini! It looks like we will be getting some action at last then."

"I don't know, Scanlan, three hundred and more I heard. There are only five hundred in the whole ala and almost half are still stationed near Eboracum."

"I'm not worried. We have the sword with us you know. I heard that the sword had oath brothers who all swore an oath to defend the sword and that it has never suffered defeat."

"Really? That sounds a little too primitive for Romans. What do you think Vibius?"

"What?"

"I was just saying that swearing an oath on a sword seems a bit primitive for Romans. They are more civilised than that."

Vibius shook himself from his reverie, "Roman legates still make sacrifices before battles so I suppose swearing an oath on a sword is no different. It depends upon how you feel about the sword doesn't it?"

They rode in silence through the forest. "You have been quiet lately Vibius. Is there a problem?" Aneurin felt quite close to the older trooper since their encounter with the bandits and was somewhat in awe of the older and obviously brave trooper.

He laughed easily, "No Aneurin, it's just that we left the fortress so quickly I am not sure if I brought everything."

Suddenly Sextus' gruff voice growled behind them. "Well if you have forgotten any equipment then you will be on a charge Trooper Gemellus!"

"No Chosen Man, not equipment, just some personal belongings."

Sextus shrugged, "Well that's alright then. A word of advice troopers, if you can't carry it on yourself or your horse then don't bother with it. We may not get back to Eboracum at all and even if we do there are some thieving bastards stationed there."

Vibius looked round in horror. "What? Never? But I thought we moved up and down the road all the time."

"Aye lad but we can't guarantee it. We could be based at Morbium, Cataractonium, and Derventio... I have been in all of them. We are cavalry and they like to move us around and deal with problems

79

quickly." He softened his voice a little, "No son, this is where we are based so whatever you left in the fortress you better hope the Decurion Princeps picks it up for you."

In a distracted voice, Vibius looked to the south as though he could see the fortress and his barracks. "Thanks, Chosen Man. I will take your advice."

"So you see Legate the warband could be up to a five hundred strong or even more."

"And until we recapture the hostage we will not know when and where they will attack." He stared at the map and the freshly marked site of the camp.

"I saw nothing either, Marcus. But I doubt if they could have beaten you north which means they are still on their way and if they are going to get across the wall they will have to get by us."

Far to the west a second huge warband was gathering. Randal was not worried about the Votadini hostages. He would still carry out his part of the pact. He and his war chiefs saw a great opportunity. The vexillations from the Twentieth and the Second were already shifting men towards the gap. The Tungrian auxiliaries had built a new camp to help cover the possible invasion when the Votadini spilt over. Randal had not yet attacked the wall. It was part of his cunning that he had not done so. He was trying to lull the soldiers on the western side of the wall that the Selgovae were docile and accepting the monstrosity of the wall without even a whimper. He had a thousand warriors gathered and he had chosen his point of attack carefully.

To the west of the high rocks and the deep water the Romans had built a turf, not a stone wall. It was close to the sea and not as well guarded as the centre and the east. He would take his men over along a two mile stretch of the wall and then use the very artery the Romans had built to service the road, the Stanegate, to attack them in their rear. Briac had been correct in one matter; the Romans were most vulnerable in their camps, where they thought they were safe. The Selgovae might have difficulty with a stone wall but wood was different, it burned!

The turf wall had been completed early in the wall building programme. The vexillation of legionaries who had constructed it had moved eastwards. The wall was not as high as the one Iucher had attacked but it was wider. There were more mile castles but they were all made of wood and not stone. The only stone they used was in the foundations. The Tungrian auxiliaries enjoyed a quiet life in the west. They enjoyed a healthy diet of fish from the river and the sea. The original member of the cohort had been from the low lands of the Rhenus and even the new recruits had carried on the watery tradition. The Prefect, Gaius Culpinus had heard of the problems in the east and thanked all the gods he could that his posting was a quiet one. He had five more years to go before retirement and he had a small place in Gaul already picked out where he would grow grapes and make wine.

It was his custom, just after the last watch went on duty to take a walk down the wall with Centurion Garbo, the first spear of the cohort. It enabled them to plan the next day's work programme while reflecting on the cohort and its morale. They had both served in Britannia for twenty years and knew what it took out of a soldier. They had served together for many years and had an easy and comfortable relationship which made for an efficient cohort. "I think we should deepen these ditches. The Gauls in the east were slaughtered because they weren't deep enough to stop the barbarian bastards getting over them."

"I'll put the third century on it tomorrow. It is about time they pulled their weight. I think we will pour some water on them and make them slippery." He pointed at the river. "That is one thing we have plenty of."

Prefect Culpinus looked towards the western end of the wall. "Where is the light?" He pointed away. Isn't that where the eighth century is on duty?" The lights were used to mark the mile castles and to help the guards see further along the ramparts.

"If those dozy bastards have been using the oil for cooking instead of the torches I'll have then digging shitters for the next ten years!"

They both began to speed up as they headed towards the darkened area of wall. Every sentry saluted as the two men passed by, absentmindedly returning the salute. Suddenly the sentry who was about to salute was pitched off the wall by an arrow. Both officers knew what it meant. The Centurion roared, "Stand to! We are under attack."

The Prefect drew his sword and turned, "I'll get back to the gate."

"I'll take charge here sir!" The look they exchanged was one of goodbye for they could see a horde of barbarians racing down the wide wall sending the sentries to their deaths. They had breached the wall and, once its integrity was gone, it was no longer a barrier. The first tent party had joined the centurion. "Right lads, shield wall here until the rest can join us." The centurion joined six of them in a defensive line with the other two soldiers behind. The Selgovae were without armour but they were all armed with a shield as well as either an axe or a sword. They had learned from the Romans that a shield could make all the difference in combat but they did not have the training which still gave the Tungrians the slightest of edges.

"Steady! Throw!" The six pila all struck home, those that missed the barbarians still found a shield and rendered them useless. Garbo did not have a shield, he did not need one. Using his vine staff, he stabbed one barbarian in the stomach while whipping the staff across the eyes of a second. A spear from the two-man reserve finished off the blinded man and then all nine of them were in a hand to hand melee. The sheer weight of numbers forced the Romans back but their training took over and they all punched with their shields whilst stabbing with their swords. As more auxiliaries arrived the line was stabilised. Centurion Garbo cursed and swore at the Selgovae whilst exhorting his men to stand firm. Suddenly there were no more barbarians before them. Instead there was a mound of bodies. He turned to look at the men behind him. "We did it lads! Well done!" He turned to find just four men. Before him lay fifteen dead auxiliaries, testament to their bravery. "Well at least we put paid to their attack."

A wounded optio who was leaning against the ramparts tried to stand while a capsarius dressed his wound. "No, Centurion. The main warband are there!" He pointed to the Stanegate and Garbo could see the warband streaming down the road; peering to the east he could see even more of them.

"Get the torches all lit. I want a full report on casualties. I will be with the Prefect." As he hurried towards the gatehouse, he saw the carnage on the wall. This was not a small attack; this was a full scale invasion. When he reached the gate, he could see that it was wide open and the bodies around it showed the fight that the century there had put up.

One of the other centurions, a bandage around his head approached him. "Sorry First Spear, the Prefect didn't make it. He's there."

Centurion Garbo went over to one of his oldest friends; someone who had been in the cohort almost as long as he had. He had fought well but the bodies around him showed that he had had too many enemies. To no-one in particular he said, "Well your last plot of land won't be in Gaul, Gaius, it will be here in this godforsaken shithole."

The warband ran all night and halted close to the small camp housing some of the men of the Twentieth Valeria Victrix. The four centuries were building a fort which would be on the wall itself. They had only arrived there the previous day having received the instructions by messenger from Governor Aulus Nepos. The Selgovae rested in the dips and hollows close to the fort. Randal was happy to let his men rest for they had done well and killed more Romans already than he had hoped. This, however, would be the greatest success if he could destroy the legionaries. He would have achieved far more than Iucher!

The centurion in charge of the vexillation gathered his officers around him. "We will be here for some time and it gets fucking cold so Marius you keep a half century here and start to make some proper barracks I would like to be dry for at least part of the night."

Marius sighed in exasperation. "And where will I get the wood?"

The senior centurion, Claudius Culpinus, shook his head and pointed at the forest to the south. "The two things they have plenty of here are trees and rain. Just cut down some trees. It doesn't have to be the Temple of Claudius, just a roof and walls to keep us dry and warm!" Turning to the rest he roared, "Get your tools and quick march; let's get this fucking wall built and then we can go home to Deva!"

The three and a half centuries started to tramp out of the camp singing a particularly dirty marching song.

When Randal saw them, he waited until they were three hundred paces from the camp and then raised his sword. Five hundred Selgovae were suddenly unleashed upon the unsuspecting Romans. As soon as he saw them the senior centurion knew that they had moments to react or they would be dead. "Testudo!" Even as he did so he hoped that Marius would have seen the attack. If the camp could be held then they might just make it. The legionaries quickly formed the four-wide testudo as the Selgovae battered in smashing their war hammers and axes at the scuta of the legionaries. Some of those who had fought against the Ninth remembered the vulnerability of the legs and thrust spears below the shields' lower edges to try to hamstring the soldiers of Rome. The soldiers who had their legs gashed gritted their teeth and pushed on knowing that to fall out would mean death. Inside the fort the centurion, Marius, had sent ten men to guard the gate while the rest went to the ramparts with a supply of javelins. The Selgovae who came too close were plucked from their feet and killed but still the warband roamed around the edge of the testudo like a pack of wild dogs with a lone bull at their mercy.

Inevitably, with the distance they had to cover there was a break in the integrity of the testudo and it came in the middle. Three huge Selgovae warriors battered two scuta in the middle of the armoured beast. Although a pilum stabbed out to gut one of them, the damage was done and the laminated scuta cracked open. The other warriors saw flesh and threw everything at the gap. Once the legionary fell the whole column was disrupted. Lucius Garbo, the senior centurion realised the danger. "Century testudo!" Immediately four testudo were formed but the one with the gap in it was surrounded by the Selgovae intent upon slaughter. While three testudo made their way slowly towards the safety

83

of the camp the last one was whittled down by warriors who battered and hacked at the doomed men.

The first testudo reached the safety of the camp and the centurion shouted, "Shield wall!" The legionaries changed into a two-deep line with a bristle of pila peering from behind their shields. The second century made the gates and filled the ramparts. Soon the Selgovae found themselves under attack from the men on the walls and the men at the gates. By the time Lucius and the last century reached safety the destroyed testudo lay three hundred paces from safety a mass of bloodied and wrecked bodies.

"Get that bloody gate closed and light the signal fire! Marius, give me a head count." Even as he asked the question, he knew that it would be a grim total. They had done well to reach the safety of the camp but it had cost them men, men who could not be replaced, and the Selgovae were now surrounding the camp. Even as he wondered how they would extricate themselves he saw two hundred of them heading towards the construction site, it did not take much imagination to realise that they were going to cause mischief. "Two steps forwards and one step back!"

On the Via Nero, close to Eboracum Livius was trying to stretch his depleted and limited forces. The wagons and carts were still streaming north in increasing numbers and that meant that Metellus and the turmae were doing double duty. Metellus came to see him; his Decurion Princeps was looking exhausted and haggard. "We can't keep going like this. The horses are suffering. We can order the men to keep on but the horses will just drop if we don't rotate them."

Livius sympathised. "The trouble is the cement. We have the local stone but the wall cannot be built without the cement and that has to come from the south."

The decurion princeps was nothing if not a thinker and he had been running the problem through his head. He suddenly saw the solution. Metellus suddenly grinned. "Ships sir! That's what we need."

"What do you mean ships?"

"The wall is north of the Tinea sir. Why not send the cement by ship. A couple of boatloads equate to twenty or so wagon trains and it means we could be based on the wall. From the reports we have been getting it is becoming a little lively up there."

"Of course. It would be even easier if we had a better port there. I will see the Governor."

Surprisingly the Governor was all in favour of the idea. If it meant the Brigante would not be raiding the road then he and his family would be safer and if the supplies could be sent in greater quantities then so much the better. "An excellent idea Prefect. I will send for the Navarchus and see what he can do."

"Then I will leave the Decurion Princeps here with four turmae and take the rest of the men to the wall. It will increase our search capacity for the girl."

"Yes, my wife and Lucia are still highly upset. I want her back sooner rather than later."

"Perhaps it is good news that we have not had a ransom demand yet."

Far to the north a dirty and dishevelled Vibia was becoming desperate enough to try to escape. The problem was that she was tethered to a guard at all times. She had tried to demand a little privacy for her toilet but her guards merely laughed and she had had to suffer the indignity of them watching her. They had crossed another couple of rivers and she had seen Briac, for she now knew his name, becoming more anxious as they negotiated the obvious signs of Rome. She sensed that they were near to the frontier and had long ceased to use the roads. This made an escape even more unlikely for she was completely lost in the forest and would probably die of starvation even if she did manage to escape.

Briac was grateful to see the Stanegate up ahead. He knew that, during the day, it would be impassable due to the heavy military traffic but night was another matter. He knew that he had to head towards the gap in the wall. Although regularly patrolled by many Roman units, he might be able to sneak through during the hours of darkness and he hoped that Iucher had men watching for this was his usual route to the barbarians in the north. He watched the cavalry patrols return at dusk along the road and then saw the sun set slowly in the west. He led the small group off. If his hostage shouted or screamed he did not know what he would do; he couldn't kill her, that would ruin her as a hostage and he contemplated gagging her. That too, was not really an option; he did not want her choking to death. He would have to rely on the fact that she was afraid. As he glanced at her he had to admit that she had held up remarkably well and still did not seem intimidated.

Crossing the Stanegate was heart stopping. The cobbled surface meant that the horses made a noise which seemed to echo along the frontier. He halted them on the far side and listened for the tell tale sound of soldiers rushing to find them. Thankfully there were none. He knew where the gap had been but he assumed that work had been done since his last visit and he headed further west. He saw increasing signs of Roman activity; there were more trees cut down and more trodden down and churned up patches of mud. He held his hand up to signal silence. To the east he could see the shadow of the wall and he headed his group further to the west. The horses were well chosen and they carefully picked their way up the rocky ridge. One dislodged stone could bring the guards Briac knew were nearby. Suddenly he heard a noise, as did his men. Their swords slid from their scabbards. A grinning face appeared next to Briac. It was a Votadini warrior, "Took your time didn't you?"

Vibia's heart sank as they were surrounded by the small warband. Her escape plan would have to wait. She was north of the frontier and Roman help.

The news filtered down the frontier that the Selgovae had launched their attacks in the west. Julius was beside himself. Although the Votadini still appeared to be holding back, the reports from Marcus showed that they were still a dangerous threat. That meant he could not despatch troops to aid the beleaguered soldiers in the west. The senior centurions had been told to deal with the problem as best they could. Of course, it meant that all construction had slowed down dramatically. Ironically having the supplies did not help them so long as the threat in the north remained. He summoned Rufius. "Any sign of that girl?"

"Not on the road sir."

"They must have reached here by now."

"The trouble is they could have come up through the forests we wouldn't know where to look."

"I am not blaming you Rufius but we must know if she is up here. Where would they cross the frontier?"

"It would have to be through the gap. If they came up at night they might get through."

Julius Demetrius had been a determined Prefect when he had led the ala and he showed those qualities of leadership now. "Right, send Marcus to the gap, and see if his tracker can pick up their trail. Leave one turma here and you take the rest to the west and try to dislodge the Selgovae from the road. If they cut the Stanegate then we are in trouble. I will send a messenger to request the rest of the ala to join us."

"But the convoys!"

"We have supplies but there is little point if we can't use the damned things." His tone softened. "Just be away for one night Rufius. Perhaps the presence of Marcus' Horse, might just dissuade them."

"Sir. Well at least Marcus will be happy. Another adventure for him eh?"

Chapter 10

Not only Marcus, but all of his troopers were happy to be on their particular patrol. There was a great deal of interest in the young Roman captive and the troopers all felt offended that someone had been kidnapped from their fortress, and that someone was a pretty Roman virgin. It was almost as though it was a matter of honour to rescue her. The three new recruits, in particular, wanted to be the ones to rescue her and as they prepared their mounts assaulted Marcus and Sextus with questions.

"Are we going to follow them into Votadini territory then sir?"

"That all depends, Vibius, on what we actually find. If we don't find tracks or evidence, then the answer is no."

"Could we not wait and ambush them when they travel north sir."

"Well, Aneurin, that might prove problematic for the young lady."

"Sir?"

"Arrows, spears and swords can go awry in an ambush and we wouldn't want her hurt would we?"

"Aneurin you are an idiot!" Vibius seemed particularly annoyed with his young comrade.

"If you lads just do your duty and let the decurion and myself plan strategy we will all get along much better." Sextus was not one for discussions and debate. He liked orders and discipline. The decurion might be young but he was the best officer Sextus had served alongside; the decision making, when it was needed, would be flawless.

Marcus drew Felix to one side. "We are seeking the Roman woman Felix. Is that a problem? She will be amongst Brigante."

He grinned. Marcus had seen him grow daily in confidence as he had been praised by all. He seemed to revel in the task. "No sir. It should be easier. Wolf knows the smell of my people and even you should be able to smell a woman. There are not many up here, certainly not many who smell as sweet as a Roman."

Sextus growled at the insult but Marcus held up his hand. "No Sextus, the scout is quite correct. There was a time I would have used my sense of smell but you become lazy and let others do it. Thank you, Felix. I will remember your words." He turned to the assembled turma. "We are looking for the lost Roman hostage and we will be travelling through Votadini country. There is a large warband ahead of us. I want you to watch where we go and, if we are ambushed or attacked, then you will know the way back to the fort."

They looked shocked that their decurion would even think that they would desert their officer. Cassius, who had only been with the turma for a couple of years, suddenly blurted, "We would die defending you sir! And the standard."

The standard bearer, Julius, shook his head and mumbled, "Well that makes me feel much safer."

Marcus raised his voice, "No you will not. This is a rescue mission. If it goes wrong then you must get back to the Legate with the information so that next time it will succeed. Understand me?"

"Sir, yes sir!" chorused the turma.

"Good. Cassius take the pack horse which I had prepared and the spare mount."

With the barbarians on the rampage at the western end of the Stanegate, Marcus led the turma over the bridge to follow the outer edge of the wall. They rode just three hundred paces from the wall and Marcus was pleased and reassured at the waved greetings from the sentries, most of whom were doubtless glad that they did not have to venture in the land of the Votadini. The area which had been under construction was now the scene of much activity as the Sixth Legion assembled to make that vulnerable point more secure.

"You see Sextus, had we started there," he pointed at the gap' "then Felix would have had a hard job to sort the tracks out. If they did cross anywhere close by then we should find them easier here where there is not as much activity from our men. Right Felix, off you go."

The two scouts ranged ahead. Marcus kept the turma in defensive formation while the two of them searched the area immediately before them. They found nothing and Felix turned to beckon them on. They continued westward keeping one eye on the barbarian north and one to the south where they knew the Selgovae were raiding. They would be in the middle of any sudden attack. Even Sextus felt a little vulnerable. "I feel like a worm on a hook you know sir. And there are hundreds of hungry fish out here!"

Suddenly they saw Felix halt and search the ground. He waved Wolf away and the dog raced northwards. Marcus was amazed how low it kept to the ground. Unless you knew what you were looking for it would just be wind blowing over the tufty grass; at times just the white tip of his tail could be seen. The scout beckoned them forwards and waited for them.

"I have found where they crossed. There were six horses." He held up some dung. "Not Roman, they are grass-fed but not Votadini ponies. These are Brigante horses. They had the woman with them." He looked up at Marcus. "Can you not smell her?"

88

Marcus dismounted and walked to where Felix was stood. He sniffed. At first he could detect nothing and Felix said, "Close your eyes sir and picture her."

Marcus did and, remarkably, a perfume came up and that was mixed with a human smell but not that of a man. He smiled to himself. It had been years since he had used his skills but he was pleased that they were still there. He opened his eyes. "Well done, Felix." He looked north. "Is Wolf looking for them?"

Felix nodded. "He will find the trail and then return here." He shrugged. "He likes to run."

The dog soon returned and lay down next to Felix. He fished something from his pouch to reward him. He took out his bow and strung it. When Marcus threw him a questioning look he said, "They were here last night. They will be close."

Marcus turned to the turma. "We have the trail of the hostage. Be on the alert and keep your weapons at the ready. Anyone we meet from now on will, most likely, want to kill us."

Sextus added, under his breath, "Or at the very least take your bollocks for a necklace!" Scanlan laughed. "Now, you are safe lad. You have to have them for them to find!"

The trail led up and over bumps, hollows and rocky outcrops. Marcus felt naked and longed for some cover. They had to keep to the trail which led inexorably northeast. He soon realised that they were heading for the Votadini camp which Felix had found on their last patrol. The Brigante must have had the same thought for he looked at Marcus and pointed to the distant forest. The decurion turned to Sextus. "It looks like they have taken her to the Votadini camp. You and Julius ride at the rear. If anything happens up here and we get ambushed, you ride back and tell the Legate. You know where the camp is too and you can bring the others." Sextus opened his mouth to say something. "Sextus! Just do it."

"Sir!"

Vibius and Aneurin took the place of the two sesquiplicarii. Both of them grinned at each other. They were riding behind the decurion; it was a place of honour and they would not let down the decurion with the sword. As soon as they reached the forest edge and sheltered within its eaves Marcus halted them. "I want two lines fifteen men wide. Keep at least eight paces from the next man. Sextus you and Julius ride behind the second line." He beckoned Felix over. "Are they still heading for the camp?"

"Like an arrow sir."

"It is in that direction isn't it?" He pointed northeast. Felix nodded. "We can use the moss to guide us. You and Wolf get to the camp and see if she is there. We will follow." Felix threw him a dubious look. "I was doing this when I was your age, Felix. Go!"

The two disappeared quickly and Marcus led the men forwards, slowly and carefully to avoid making too much noise. He thought it unlikely, but there may have been scouts and sentries in the forest. Suddenly Wolf raced up to the turma when they were still well over a mile away from the camp. Felix appeared close behind him. "The girl is there. The Votadini have many more warriors who have arrived in their camp since our last visit."

"How many? "

More men than I saw at Eboracum."

Marcus had never thought that he could attack the camp but the numbers mentioned meant that it would be difficult to get in and out. "Where is she kept?"

"I saw her close to the fire. She was tied to a post and there were two men guarding her."

Marcus dismounted and cleared some of the leaves and debris from the ground. He gave him a stick. "Show me."

Felix drew in the soil and Sextus came to look over his shoulder. "That looks impossible."

"Yes, Sextus but we have to try." He turned to look at the men he had brought. "What I need is a couple of the lads who don't look Roman." He looked up at Sextus who looked every uncia a legionary, "which rules you and Julius out. That suits me. I am going to get close and I want you to wait here with the turma. You need to make some traps and deadfalls. When we leave it will be in a hurry. You need to leave a safe route for us. Mark the trees." Sextus threw him a puzzled look. "An old Explorate trick. You cut a piece of bark from pairs of trees. We ride between them and we are safe. When we reach you then you and the troopers throw your javelins at those following us." The standard-bearer and chosen man exchanged a befuddled look. "If we do get the girl out then we will need Nemesis to be on our side anyway."

"Who are you going to take then?"

Marcus looked at the troopers he had. "Felix obviously, Cassius," he grinned, "he looks like a barbarian. Scanlan and Aneurin."

"The new recruits? You are joking!"

"No Sextus, think about it. They are Brigante. We can walk around the camp speaking Brigante. We know there are some Brigante there don't we? And they are both young. They look like young warriors.

90

They don't look like Romans. My mind is made up. Gather the men around."

When they were all gathered Sextus and Julius rode towards the camp to act as sentries. "The hostage is in the enemy camp. I am going with the two scouts." They all smiled, Wolf was now seen as every bit a member of the turma as any trooper, "Cassius, Aneurin and Scanlan will accompany me." He heard the gasp and saw the reactions. "They are Brigante and we are not going in uniform." He nodded to Cassius. "Bring your pack horse, Cassius. You three get your uniforms off." He started to take off his mail shirt and caligae.

Vibius noticed, for the first time, that the decurion was not wearing the sword of Cartimandua. It told him much about the decurion. He had planned this out whilst still at the fort. "Sir, why can't I accompany you?" He wanted to be the one to rescue the Roman hostage but the others who hadn't been chosen cast him looks of pure disgust. He sounded like a whining, petulant child.

Marcus took out the clothes from the pack horse and handed them around. He said, softly, to Vibius. "You are not Brigante and you do not look as young as these three. We will be playing Brigante rebels and you, well, you look too Roman besides you do not speak Brigante. Do not worry, Vibius, your time will come and you will be needed when we escape for then, every barbarian north of the frontier will be after us." He looked at the men he would take with him. He remembered Felix's trick and, smearing mud on his hands he daubed the faces of the three troopers and himself. "Can't have us looking too clean. Now the rest of you; Sextus will have you making deadfalls and traps. Watch over our uniforms. When we leave it will be in a hurry." He gestured at the three troopers now dressed in barbarian attire. "You three. We will follow Felix to the edge of the camp and tie our horses there. Cassius, get the spare horse. The hostage will need that. When it is dark we will enter the camp. From now on we only speak Brigante. I can manage a few words in Votadini so if we are stopped let me do the talking. We are trying to avoid attention. The girl is tied to a post in the centre of the camp. Cassius and I will take one of the guards, Aneurin and Scanlan the other. Felix will release the girl and then we will walk out." He threw a dirty cloak to Felix. "You cover her with this." He looked at them again. "Keep your hoods up but walk as though you belong there. With luck they will see what they want to see; warriors such as they. May the Allfather be with us."

They led their horses through the thick forest to avoid detection. Wolf patrolled in front; sometime they could only see his one long white sock as he sinuously moved through the pine carpet. Felix led them to a rock formation hidden in a stand of trees. They tied the horses to the stump of a lightning struck pine. Dusk had descended and they followed the young Brigante scout as he led them down the path towards the encampment. A bubbling stream disguised any noise they might make but Marcus was acutely aware that it would disguise the Votadini noise too. When they reached the bluffs above the stream they watched. They were two hundred paces from the camp but the gloom and the trees hid them.

The camp was busy and Marcus became alarmed when a party of men gathered near their tethered horses. He could see, even from that distance that at least one of the men who mounted was a chief from his torc. Aneurin tugged at Marcus' arm. The decurion turned and Aneurin said, into his ear, "The one near the chief. I know him; he is Briac the Brigante and those four with him are Brigante also."

Marcus nodded to show he had understood. Had they been spotted? He watched as the twenty men left the camp. They waited and watched. Marcus slid his sword out of its scabbard and then replaced it. It was a nervous action for he knew not if they were coming for them. It was only when the men in the camp began to relax and to begin to drink and chat close to the fires that Marcus knew that the party of horsemen would not be back soon. He had no idea where the chief and Briac had gone but he would use it to his advantage. They saw men and boys coming to the stream to draw water. He also saw a number of warriors, obviously the worse for wear for drink, coming to relieve themselves.

Gradually a plan formed in his mind. It took him back to his Explorate days when he had travelled behind enemy lines with Cassius, Metellus and Rufius. They had taught him to think on his feet and improvise. He did so now. He turned to his men. "We are going into the camp. Follow me and do as I do." The four young men were extremely excited and nervous. They were going into the bear's den; willingly!

As they made their way down the slope Marcus was amazed at the lack of security from the Votadini. Apart from the two guards they had seen by the hostage, there did not appear to be any sentries, or indeed anyone who looked alert. It seemed they were relaxed. Perhaps the lack of their leaders made them feel as though they were off the leash. Three warriors wandered back from the stream, having relieved themselves downstream from the point they collected their water. They were a little the worse for wear, staggering a little, and they stared at Marcus and his party. Wolf started to growl but Felix gave him a signal and he dropped to all fours, his eyes darting from the barbarians and back to Felix.

The tallest man, who had many arm rings and scars, spat some phlegm at a tree as he idly scratched his groin. "Who the fuck are you sorry bunch?"

He had spoken in Votadini and only Marcus had understood him. "I am glad that we have found you. We seek Briac for we are his warriors and we bring important news."

The warriors visibly relaxed. "Well you missed him and he won't be back until tomorrow evening. Come, join our camp. I am Belenus, war chief of the Votadini." The way he puffed himself up made Marcus think that he was not as important as he obviously thought himself, "Chief Iucher has left me in charge while he goes to the Roman fort to demand the return of his son." He slapped his arm around Marcus' shoulders. "Your people did well to steal the hostage. Perhaps you are not the women we thought you were!" He laughed and Marcus gave a weak smile. It was fortunate the others had not understood his words. He looked at the po-faced companions of Marcus. "What is up with them? Didn't they understand my little joke?"

"I am sorry, I am the only one who speaks your language."

"Well none of us understand your language so we will have to use signs and gestures eh? Come we will sup."

As they walked in they were seen as non-threatening because of the presence of the war chief. Marcus could not remember if Vibia had seen him. He would have to hope not or pray that she was quick witted.

"And who are you Brigante?"

"I am Gaelwyn," Marcus had learned when he had spied and lied before, to keep the story simple and memorable and his uncle's name came easily to the tongue.

"I have heard that name before. I wonder where?" They had reached the fire with the post. "Here, clear some space for some of the Briac's Brigante brethren." Some Votadini cleared a space on a log and they sat down.

The movement made Vibia look up and her eyes widened as she recognised Marcus. He gave a slight shake of the head and she closed her eyes and gave an imperceptible nod. Marcus thanked the Allfather that she was a good actress. A jug of beer stood on the table. There were some empty beakers there and Belenus waved an imperious hand. "Help yourselves."

Marcus turned to his men. "We are welcomed and the chief," he nodded meaningfully at the war chief, "bids us drink. He is sorry that they do not speak Brigante but has told me that Briac is returning tomorrow. Take beer but pretend to drink and pretend to get drunk. That way we can fall asleep here. The girl's guards look to be alert; we must be careful."

They all filled a beaker with the frothy beer and sat down. They were silent and Marcus could see the question on the chief's lips. "Talk, tell jokes, act as though you are happy to be here. You all look like you are about to wet yourselves."

Aneurin gave a weak smile. "Sorry, sir. We aren't used to this."

"I know but just pretend and we will get out of this." He turned to Belenus. "We have stopped the wagons of the Romans in the south."

"Aye, and we have bloodied them here too. The Selgovae have destroyed a camp and part of the wall and with your spy in the Roman camp we will soon drive them from our land."

Marcus froze. A spy! It confirmed what the prisoners had said and that he was a Brigante. "Yes, he gives us good information."

Belenus took another swallow of the beer. "Aye. It is a pity he is not in one of the legions but still the horse warriors are a fierce force and it is good to know what they do."

This was even worse. The spy was one of their own. He suddenly looked at the three men he had with him. They were all Brigante; could one of them be the spy? Then he dismissed the idea, they did not volunteer for this, they were chosen and a spy would have revealed himself to the Votadini straight away. Still, it paid to be patient and he would wait until he had returned to the fort to tell someone. He knew whom he could trust but it shocked him to his core to think that there could be someone who was an enemy.

They talked and joked for a while; Marcus made sure it was inconsequential but he also learned that the tribes were planning a big offensive and it would be timed to coincide with a Brigante uprising led by Briac. It was obvious to Marcus that Briac was the key and, having seen him, he would do all in his power to capture him. He also discovered that they had been stockpiling weapons for some time and were prepared for a bigger war than hitherto.

When he could, he caught the eye of each of his men and nodded. They returned the nod and, one by one they fell asleep. Even Wolf feigned sleep; Marcus did not know how Felix told him to do so but he did. After Marcus, who had pretended to drink copious amounts of beer, fell over and feigned sleep, the Votadini left them by the fire and returned to their tents. Marcus had deliberately fallen so that he lay on his arms and could watch the two guards. The guards had been changed once and Marcus had to wait until everyone was asleep and the guards relaxed. He whispered to Felix, who was the nearest one to him. "Go and take a pee and when you return, sleep a little closer to the pole."

Felix rose and Marcus watched, through half lidded eyes, as the guard gave him a cursory look. Wolf followed obediently and when they returned, the two of them curled up in a ball about five paces from the pole. The guards did not seem to mind. Vibia, too, was watching with interest what was happening. When she had seen Marcus and recognised him her heart had soared but she still could not see a way out of her dilemma. When the boy with the dog came a little closer she began to gain hope.

Marcus stretched and sat up. He held his hands to the dying embers of the fire. A subtle glance told him that the sentries were ignoring him. He leaned forwards and murmured, "Cassius and Aneurin go and have a pee. When you come back, go behind the guards, one each and have your knife ready." Marcus was proud of the way the two troopers slowly stood, unsteadily and, holding on to each other, as though still drunk, they staggered away.

"Scanlan, get ready; when I tell you, get to the guard on the right and put your hand across his mouth." A slight nod, as though from a sleeping man, told the decurion that he knew what to do. He saw Felix wink, his knife already in his hand. Marcus stood and warmed his backside against the fire and then began to walk slowly towards the guards, a smile on his face. Behind them he saw his two men approach. Marcus' movements made the two guards suspicious and they pointed their swords towards him. He feigned surprise and held his open hands out. He watched their eyes relax and he grinned as he said, quietly in Brigante, "Now!"

The two troopers behind moved so quickly it was though a snake had struck. Marcus walked quickly to the guard nearest to him and holding one hand with his right hand put his left hand over the man's mouth. The sticky hot blood from his throat spurted all over him. Even as the man was dying Felix was slicing through Vibia's bonds and the second guard was joining his fellow in the hereafter.

"Can you walk?"

"Of course and tha…"

"No time for that. Felix, take Wolf and check the way to the horses. You three watch the girl and I will bring up the rear."

Vibia didn't know what to make of it as the five men took her swiftly from the encampment. She kept glancing over her shoulder at Marcus who was fifty paces behind, sword drawn watching for enemies. They climbed through the forest and they all became aware that it was not as dark as it had been. Dawn was breaking. At the rear Marcus knew that men's bladders would begin to work and when they saw the girl gone, the pursuit would be on. Even as he scanned the land

95

below him he knew that they had been more than lucky to have achieved what they had done. Everything now depended upon Sextus and his traps and deadfalls.

By the time Marcus reached the horses, they were all mounted save Felix. "Felix, get behind the girl we have no time for you to run." The scout looked as though he was going to argue but two things happened, firstly Marcus snapped, "Get on the horse," and there was a roar from the camp as the Votadini discovered that their prisoner had been spirited away.

Cassius summed it up well, "Well there it is lads! We are in the shit now! Felix, get on the fucking horse now!"

Felix clambered up and they fled. Felix shouted, "Wolf! Go!" The dog raced off.

Marcus shouted, "Watch for the marked trees. Ride between them!"

Behind them the camp was in an uproar as Belenus roared around berating everyone in sight. One of the warriors spotted the trail and the warband hurtled up the path after the Brigante. They grabbed whatever weapons they had. They did not have many horses, they did not need them but Belenus grabbed one as did the other leaders. The war chief cursed his luck and the spies who had fooled him. He would be the laughing stock of the tribe unless he could recapture the precious hostage. He kicked viciously into the flanks of the horse as it struggled up the hill with his weight. One of his scouts was waiting at the top. "They had horses waiting. They are heading for the wall!" He pointed south at the trail which led to the frontier.

"After them. They must die!"

Sextus heard the hooves, muffled by the pine carpet, of Marcus and the others. He was in no doubt who it was but he had to be certain. "Stand to!" He hoped that the trail had been clearly marked or this would be a disaster. The deadfalls and traps would, he knew, slow them up but the trail had to be accurate. To his relief he saw Wolf racing towards him followed by the girl and Felix. He had never been so glad to see a dog before. "Sir! Here!"

The girl, it had to be admitted, was a good rider and she deftly steered her horse towards the waiting turma. The five horses reined in. Marcus voice barked. "Get your helmets on and shields we may need them. Sextus, they are behind us. Give them one volley of javelins and follow us."

Sextus grinned like a child at Saturnalia. "Good to see you, sir. Don't you worry, they won't get by us! Get your javelins and mark your targets!"

Belenus was fortunate, or perhaps just lucky, that he managed to follow the safe trail. As he heard the screams and shouts of his men to the left and the right he realised that his enemies had laid traps. "Follow me! Stay in the trail!" His men began to move towards the central line which appeared to be safer. In the forest men lay with legs broken, arms and torsos pierced by stakes.

Sextus and the twenty odd men held their shields before them and their arms braced with their javelins. They were beyond the traps and spread out in a wide semicircular line. "Wait for my command!" Dawn was now breaking to the trooper's right as they saw the warband hurtling towards them. Sextus waited until the enemy were less than forty paces away and then roared, "Loose!"

Belenus and his horse took three javelins and he was dead even before both his and his horse's necks were broken by the bole of the tree into which they crashed. The other riders were also plucked from their mounts. "Retreat!" Sextus had taken out the only riders; the rest were on foot and now, after the traps, cautious.

Marcus knew that they had a long ride ahead of them and the barbarians could move as swiftly through the forests as horses. He kept up a steady, ground eating pace. He never once turned around; he trusted Sextus and knew that he would follow. He kept his eye on Felix and Vibia in front of him. He needed no scout on point for Wolf ranged ahead and he would alert them to a barbarian quickly. Dawn broke slowly to his left but it made him feel better. He could see the wall now, albeit in the distance and it shone like a beacon in the new day. He hoped that the Selgovae had not overrun the defences for if they had then the Votadini behind him would rip through the frontier like a knife through butter. He now had even more reason to get back as swiftly as he could.

Chapter 11

Iucher, Briac and the other warriors reined in at the bridge of Cilurnum. The Tinea rushed below, the recent rains in the hills having sent it surging towards the sea. Its white flecked waves perilously close to the bottom of the stone bridge. The sentries at the gate were not worried for there were few riders before them. The barbarians just sat there impassively viewing the wall. One of the auxiliaries turned to the optio. "What do we do then sir?"

The optio stroked his face. He felt the stubble; it meant that his relief would be here soon. He would let him have the problem of sending for the Legate. "Nothing son. They aren't going anywhere. We'll let the next shift worry about what they want. I can't be bothered trying to talk to some hairy arsed barbarian at this time of the morning."

The sentry pointed to Iucher. "That one there has one of them torcs on that means he is a chief. Shouldn't we send for the Legate?"

"If you think I am going to risk waking the Legate just because a bunch of barbarians with fancy jewellery come calling then you are out of your mind."

Iucher turned to Briac. "Why do they not speak with us?"

Briac shrugged, "Their chiefs are in the fort, across the river. The men guarding it are not important."

One of the Votadini fingered his bow. "I could hit them easily from here."

Iucher restrained the eager warrior. "We will wait until we get our boys back." He turned to the Brigante. "Briac ask to speak with their chief."

Briac rode a few paces closer to the gate and looked up at the eight men on the gate. His Latin was imperfect but was understandable. "We would speak with the general. We have a Roman hostage."

"Shit!" The optio could not ignore the barbarians now. The whole fort knew that an important relative of the Governor had been kidnapped. He turned to the grinning auxiliary next to him, "All right smart arse. Go to the Principia and tell them that we have a delegation of barbarians with news of the hostage." As the auxiliary descended the stairs and ran back across the bridge the optio shouted down. "I have sent for him."

A heavy atmosphere hung over the gate as the two groups stared at each other. It was the first time either had seen their enemies when they were not intent on death. They were able to look and examine them. To the auxiliaries, the barbarians seemed fierce but vulnerable. The

98

ordinary soldiers identified the lack of armour and the many weak spots their blades would find. The barbarians wondered at the soldier's courage, or lack of it, that they needed to hide behind stone walls and wear such awkward armour. To the Votadini it just proved that the Roman soldier was an enemy who could be defeated easily once he was prised from his wall.

Julius Demetrius eventually arrived having put on his full armour. He had paused to tell the duty centurion what he intended and what he wanted him to do. When he reached the bridge gate he shouted to the optio. "Open the gate I will go and speak with them."

"Sir? Isn't that dangerous? They might take you as hostage too."

Julius gave a wry smile. "Son, I have been fighting these barbarians since you were sucking your mother's tit. They have come to talk but if it makes you feel any happier then aim your bolt throwers at them eh?"

"Open the gate." As the men opened the gate and the tent party aimed the bolt thrower the optio said, "He's a game 'un. I'll give him that. Mad as a fish but game."

Julius strode across the bridge and Iucher said, grudgingly, "This is a warrior."

Julius saluted, "Hail, Iucher and you," he looked at the Brigante, "are you the Brigante who took the girl?"

Briac nodded. "I am he, old one. My name is Briac. We have the hostage. We took her from the fort in the south."

Julius nodded, "And?"

Briac looked confused. "And we want to exchange her for the prisoners you took." He pointed at Iucher. "The chief's son and the other ones."

"Those prisoners are surety against your good behaviour. Taking a hostage from the Governor's residence is not classed as good behaviour by the Emperor. I am afraid that one of the hostages will have to die." He held up his hand. His guards appeared at the top of the gate holding one of the hostages. The centurion put a noose around the youth's neck. "Unless the hostage is returned to this fort by sunset I will execute one prisoner each morning, beginning with this one."

Iucher laughed, "You would not do this."

In answer Julius dropped his arm and the youth was thrown from the gate. The crack of his neck was so loud it sounded loudly even above the torrent of water rushing beneath. The barbarians all grabbed their weapons. "Before you compound your error look at the wall behind me." The small party looked up to see twenty archers and two bolt throwers all aiming their weapons at them.

Iucher angrily thrust his sword back into its scabbard. "This is not over Roman and I will eat your heart while you watch for this treacherous act. This I swear!"

As they galloped back towards their forest camp, Iucher knew that he would never see his son alive again. The Romans were ruthless. But he would bring the girl back to this very spot and have his men rape her where the Romans could watch and then he would have her dismembered. He would show them that he was a true leader who paid back acts in kind. This day marked the beginning of the end for Rome.

When he reached the gate Julius glanced up at the body dangling from the gate. The centurion asked, "Should I cut him down sir?"

"No, leave his body there as a reminder to the Votadini that our word is law."

As the Legate entered the gate the centurion turned to the optio, "Well lads it will get a little smelly here before too long."

The optio pointed to the birds already gathering at the forest edge. "I wouldn't worry too much sir. The birds around here will soon get rid of him, they are hungry buggers and they don't care who gives them the food!"

Rufius and his turmae had spent the night camped close to the Sixth Legion's camp. The Selgovae were somewhere ahead and it had not seemed prudent to Rufius to go wandering in after dark. He and First Spear discussed their options. "Have we any idea how many Selgovae there are?"

"No decurion. We know, from the survivor of the Gallic cohort who made it here, that they have over run the wall and surrounded the vexillation. To hear the survivors talk the army is the size of Boudicca's but I suspect they are exaggerating."

Both men knew that the ones who were stouter and had stood would have given a more accurate description and the fact that they had escaped spoke of their terror and fear which inevitably meant every barbarian became ten. "Even so my hundred and fifty men will be outnumbered. "

"All me and my lads need you to do is find the buggers, stop them escaping and we will do the rest."

"Oh we can find them. We will leave now and head west. I will send a messenger back when we have them. How many are you bringing?"

"We have four centuries of Gauls here. I will leave them to guard the camp." He sniffed in a derisory fashion showing his opinion of the

Gauls. "They would be about as much use as a one-legged man in an arse-kicking contest."

"You don't rate them then?"

"Your lads are all right. They have proved it over again but my men still hold out. These ran. Get my point? Anyway, I will bring the First Cohort, eight hundred men. If they can't deal with them then we might as well pack up and go home."

Rufius shook his head. He had yet to meet anyone from a legion who did not think he could defeat the barbarians single-handed. "We'll be off then."

Rufius sent out his best scouts to range ahead while the turmae, all five of them, rode in a column of four. He wanted to be able to deploy into line as soon as possible. His direction was obvious for there was a pall of smoke to the north-west. The Selgovae were still burning the wooden gates and destroying the recently constructed parts of the wall. The first scout returned.

"Sir. The camp is surrounded and they are attacking its walls." He pointed behind him. "About a mile up the Stanegate sir."

"Right Gaius, get to the Sixth and tell First Spear. We will try to discourage them." As his scout rode off Rufius turned to the turmae. "Get your javelins ready we are going to charge the Selgovae as soon as we see them. Attack by turma. Charge, throw the javelin and then wheel behind the next turma." Marcus Aurelius had devised the tactic as a variation on the Cantabrian circle. It kept a constant rain of missiles and the troopers did not tire as much.

Rufius led the way, his grey eating up the road as he rode along at a steady lope. He could hear the noise of the battle and see the smoke rising from the places where the Selgovae had started fires. They had arrived none too soon. "Third Turma, deploy into line." Rufius had one of the two buccinas in the ala and he turned to the signifier who carried the instrument. "Sound the charge. We might as well let them know we are coming. It will give hope to the poor buggers in the camp."

As the strident notes echoed across the Stanegate the thirty two men galloped forwards in a single line. Had they not sounded the charge then they might have caught the Selgovae at the rear with their backs to them but Rufius wanted the pressure relieved if he could. A line of Selgovae turned to face them and they began loosing arrows. A charging line of men and horses is a hard target to hit and every trooper knew how to use his shield to best effect. Most arrows flew harmlessly overhead and those that struck hit the large scuta each man carried. When they were forty paces away Rufius roared, "Loose!" Even as they threw their javelins he shouted, "Wheel left!" Every trooper executed a smart turn

101

as the next turma charged in and repeated the manoeuvre. As Rufius rode back he saw that the arrows were more accurate and some of his troopers and horses lay on the field.

"Reform!" His turma formed a line again and each man took out his next javelin. The brief respite had rested the horses but Rufius knew that this charge would be slower and they would be more likely to take casualties. "Charge!"

Galloping forwards he was pleased to see the field littered with barbarian bodies and noted with grim satisfaction that the walls were no longer being assaulted as the Selgovae turned their whole force against the horse warriors. This time the Selgovae had improvised a shield wall from behind which their archers and slingers could hurl missiles at the charging horsemen. Many of the troopers' javelins smacked into the Selgovae shields while the troopers themselves began to take casualties. Rufius could see that he had done all he could. "Sound recall!"

The other turmae were not in range and they pulled back to their start point. The Selgovae began to bang their shields in exultation. They had defeated, or so they thought, the vaunted Marcus' Horse. "Roll call!"

The horses were ready for the rest and the capsarii began to treat the wounds sustained by the survivors of the charge. All of the troopers kept their attention firmly focussed on the barbarians for they were known to be fleet of foot and could cover the ground to them very quickly. The single-minded Selgovae, however, resumed their assault on the camp.

The decurion from the Tenth Turma, Septimus, reported. "Sir the vexillation has lost ten troopers and we have eight wounded. None of them serious."

"Good. Septimus, take your turma beyond the Stanegate and warn of any barbarians joining the fray from the forest." Rufius could still see the smoke from the north which meant there were still warbands on the loose. The last thing First Spear would need would be to be attacked from his flank while relieving the siege.

The messenger galloped up. "The First Cohort is half a mile away sir."

"Good." He turned to the remaining four turmae. "Form a single line."

One of the younger recruits said, in a worried voice, "We going to charge again sir?"

Rufius smiled while his chosen man glowered at the unfortunate recruit. "No son, not yet but I want them to think we are and I want to hide the legion from them until the last possible moment."

The trooper grinned, "That's all right then!"

Chosen Man roared, "And it will be all right for you son when you are cleaning the shit out of the stables for a nundinal!"

The Selgovae still kept a wary watch on the horsemen but they could see that the Romans were not a threat so long as they kept a wall of shields before them. Their axes began to tear chunks out of the wooden walls which topped the mound of earth that marked the camp boundary. The centurion within had had his hopes raised when he had heard the buccina and seen the charge and the respite had enabled him to reorganise his defences and have his wounded seen to. Now, as he heard the axes biting into the wood he wondered how long they would last.

First Spear appeared behind Rufius. He nodded at the line. "Good idea." Stepping next to the decurion he surveyed the scene. "It looks like we got here in time. If you stop them escaping we will take it from here."

"Will do!"

Behind them the centurions were arranging the centuries in blocks so that there appeared to be six arrow heads peering from the line. Rufius had seen the tactic before and it worked very effectively, giving the attack of a point and the security of a shield wall. "Marcus' Horse, wheel right. Column of twos."

As the horsemen moved off the watching Selgovae wondered why they were leaving. When they saw the eight hundred legionaries advancing quickly towards them they knew the reason. In the camp the centurion knew they would survive; it was the First Cohort. They were the finest soldiers in the legion and they were coming directly for the Selgovae with revenge imprinted on their faces. The warband chief could see that the threat from the legion was more dangerous than that of the horse soldiers but they had seen off one attack; this second would not be a problem. Taking his war axe in his hand he roared his warriors forward, exhorting them to charge the advancing Roman line.

First Spear almost licked his lips in anticipation. If they wanted to die quickly then so be it. "Pila! Loose!" Four hundred spears flew through the air and stopped the Selgovae charge in an instant. The heavy spears either struck the few shields rendering them useless or punched the warrior backwards, immobilising them if it did not kill them. Over three hundred warriors were taken out of action in an instant. The First Cohort gave them no chance to recover and they marched quickly into the attack. The second volley of pila flew beyond the ragged and disorganised front line to decimate the ranks behind while the gladii of the legionaries began to hack and slash at the

103

unprotected bodies of the wild Selgovae. The war chief fell in the first attack and the warriors began to lose heart. They had started their attack so well and the Romans had fled the field but now they had nowhere to run.

Septimus' messenger found Rufius. "Sir the decurion says there is a warband coming from the forest. There look to be over four hundred of them."

"Tell him to delay them and we are coming." He turned to the trooper behind him. "Ride to the First Spear, tell him there is another warband coming from the forest. We will try to slow them down a little."

"Turmae. Form two lines." The remaining troopers formed two lines behind Rufius. "Forwards!"

It was but a few paces beyond the Stanegate when they saw Septimus' turma retreating and then charging to throw their javelins. Rufius knew that it was effective but exhausting. He turned to the signifier. "Sound recall!"

As soon as the turma heard it they galloped quickly back to the rest of the ala. "Charge!" The warband was hot on the trail of the turma and charging blindly. Rufius' men left gaps for the survivors of Septimus' turma to pass through and then they struck the warband. There was no volley of javelins; they all threw at the nearest target and then they drew their long cavalry swords. The warband had run from their attack on the wall and were not a cohesive unit but they outnumbered the auxiliaries by five to one and Rufius knew that they could not fight them for long. He slashed and stabbed on either side of the grey's head. His mount helped by trampling and kicking all who came within range of its deadly hooves. A spear was thrown at him and his instincts took over as he raised his shield and it glanced off. He stabbed down at the two men trying to strike his horse. It was time for a withdrawal. "Sound the retreat!"

The retreat began but ended halfway through for the decurion when the signifier was stabbed in the leg. Rufius wheeled around and grabbed the loose reins to lead the signifier's horse from the battle. The men who still lived galloped back towards the legion. To his relief Rufius saw that the legion had despatched one warband and were marching resolutely towards the forest. Glancing around him he saw many empty saddles. It had been costly but it had saved the First Cohort of the Sixth from an even greater disaster.

The warband which emerged from the forest had its number suddenly swollen by the warriors who had avoided the blades and shields of the Sixth. They poured back from whence they came. Had the cavalry not charged four times they could have pursued and destroyed them but Rufius knew it was too big a risk. "Septimus keep your eye on them but don't pursue."

The big decurion grinned, "I am afraid that none of us could sir. The lads are just about out on their feet and," he ruffled his horse's head, "as for these poor boys, I reckon they need a feed."

"That seems reasonable." To the rest, he shouted. "Get the grain bags out; they deserve it. Decurions go around and check the wounded, see to the dead." The officers dismounted to begin the grim task of finding who had died and who was merely wounded.

Leaving his chosen man in charge Rufius rode over to the legionaries who were busily dispatching the wounded Selgovae while the capsarii were busy with the Roman wounded. Quintus Licinius Brocchus strode over and clasped Rufius' arm. He gestured at the dead troopers. "Thank you decurion. I know that without your sacrifice we might have lost more men than we did." He looked over to the camp, still burning and looking as though it was ready to collapse of its own accord. "Shall we go and see what we fought for?"

"Aye." Dismounting he followed First Spear across the battlefield.

Centurion Culpinus was lying on the floor with his leg supported by two legionaries while a capsarius tried to sew together the flap of skin which had been torn open. "Sorry I can't stand sir. This dickhead reckons I need to lie like this to stop losing my blood."

The two legionaries were grinning while the capsarius carried on sewing. "You'll be glad when I save your leg. Or should I carry on doing what the barbarian was doing and chop your leg off?"

"You try that sunshine and you'll get a gladius enema."

First Spear bent towards the wounded man, "Well I am glad to see that you haven't changed much Claudius. Still the same sour centurion with the silver tongue." He leaned over to clasp his comrade's arm. "Well done. Sorry, we couldn't get here sooner."

"Not your fault sir. We need signal towers or something like that. They came out of nowhere."

"You were the lucky ones, centurion. They overran the Gauls in the west."

The capsarius put the leg down. "Now, no walking on it for at least three days. If you pop those stitches, I really will cut off your leg." The fussy orderly marched off to deal with another wounded warrior.

When he had gone, and the three officers were alone, he said, "He's better than a Greek doctor that one. "He seemed to notice Rufius for the first time. "Are you the lad who brought the cavalry?"

Quintus laughed. "He is the officer commanding the cavalry, yes Claudius."

He held out his arm. "Then thank you, son. You just about saved what is left of my command. You gave us time to reorganise."

"My pleasure centurion. How many men did you lose?"

He looked grimly around the field. "We have less than one hundred effectives left out of four centuries. I reckon there are thirty who are wounded and will fight again but at least twenty of the lads are crippled." He looked up at Quintus. "Bit of a cock-up sir eh?"

"As you say. Bit of a cock-up."

The three of them looked around the carnage and devastation in silence until Rufius said. "And the good news is more of the ala is returning north."

Quintus looked at the piles of bodies being reverently placed by the troopers and said, "Well I think you may need some recruits as well decurion."

Chapter 12

Their pursuers were relentless. None of them wished to risk the ire of Iucher. They had been left to guard the hostage, the price of his son's freedom and they had lost her. Honour demanded that they get her back or die trying. At the rear of the turma Sextus could hear them closing on them. The horses could go little faster than a running man in this thick forest and the only advantage the horsemen had was that they would not be as tired as their enemies when it came to a fight and the Roman warrior knew that it would come to down to a fight. If only they had something they could deploy to slow them down.

Sextus almost slapped his own head at his stupidity. He turned to the trooper next to him. "Take out your caltrops." To the two in front he said, "You two, take out your caltrops and then throw them on either side of you." He reached down to his saddlebags and took his handful out. To the trooper next to him he said, "Throw them behind you." The four of them dispersed their small number of caltrops; they were wicked pieces of metal which always had a spike upwards no matter how they landed. Sextus was counting on the fact that their pursuers might either be barefoot or only have fur shoes. Either way it would hurt.

Suddenly, from behind there came a scream, followed by another and then a string of what sounded like Votadini obscenities. "That'll teach you, fucking barbarians, if you had proper shoes you might have caught us." He risked a look behind and saw that the barbarians had dropped back as they negotiated what they thought was another trap-laden area. It gave them time to increase their lead.

Marcus saw the edge of the forest looming up when the light in the dim murk began to brighten. They had almost made it. He could see, four miles away the magnificent stone monument that was the wall. He could not see a gate but it didn't matter, the wall meant safety. He halted the turma. The horses needed a breather. Sextus rode next to him. "We slowed them up with caltrops sir."

"Excellent idea." He turned to the rest of the troopers, "All of you sow your caltrops in a line behind us." His men cheerfully emptied their bags of the handfuls of caltrops that they all carried. "How far Sextus?"

"There they are!" The first Votadini could be seen as a white face a hundred paces back.

"Right! Let's go. We should be able to outdistance them on this open stretch." He led them at a brisk pace and then, to his horror, saw the band of riders who had left the camp the previous night. It was the chief returning from the fort. The Romans were seen at the same time and, with the girl at the front it was obvious what had occurred. The Selgovae and Brigante riders kicked hard towards the turma. Marcus knew that he could not risk the girl being caught and the rest of the tribe were hot on his heels. "Head west, try to out run them. Sextus lead them off and stay with the girl."

The men needed no urging but the horse carrying Felix and the girl was struggling with the double weight. Felix was aware of the dilemma and, saying, "Sorry," slipped from the horse. He ran alongside it with Wolf ahead of them.

"What are you doing Felix?"

"I will keep up." He grinned. "I have had a rest now."

The girl's horse picked up the pace and they began to stretch away from the running barbarians but those on horses closed with them. Marcus knew he would have to delay them. "The last ten troopers on me!"

He slowed his horse down and began to angle away from Sextus and the others. "Javelins!" He turned to see who had followed him and that they had done as he asked. To his surprise three of them were his new recruits. Their faces did not look worried but excited. "Stay close to me you three. These warriors are the best the Selgovae have and these are neither half-asleep nor drunk! We throw one javelin and then we run. Clear!"

They all chorused, cheerfully, "Sir, yes sir."

Iucher had seen the girl and was incandescent with rage, if they returned to the fort with her then his son would die and this would have all been a waste. He urged his horse on. If he could cut them off from their escape then his men could close with them and he could recapture the girl and show the Romans true torture. When the ten men rode towards him he almost laughed. Some of them, he could see, were no more than boys. He was a warrior who had fought many times and never lost. These Romans would die at his hand.

Marcus watched the angle at which the enemy approached. "Go for the horses!" Part of Marcus was thinking of slowing down the enemy but another part remembered that they were largely recruits - a horse was a bigger target. "Loose!" His men threw their javelins and two horses pitched to the ground throwing their riders. One struck a warrior and hurled him to the ground. Two others struck men but they still rode towards them. "Wheel right!"

Anxious to get away the eleven troopers dragged their weary horses around. One of the troopers, Publius, was unfortunate; his horse found a hare hole and he was thrown to the ground, landing less than thirty paces from the warriors, eager for blood. Iucher, Briac and the remaining riders homed in on the dazed man as he struggled to his feet, still dazed and winded from the fall. Before they could reach him, and Marcus react, Vibius and Scanlan had turned their mounts around and as Vibius slashed his sword to half sever the Votadini warrior's face, Scanlan grabbed Publius and hauled him across the neck of his horse. Marcus managed to halt his horse and hurl his javelin to strike Iucher's horse in the chest. "Ride! Ride like you have never ridden before!"

When Iucher fell to the ground, the heart went out of the rest as they raced to help up their leader. He cursed and struck them as they helped him to his feet. "Catch them! You imbeciles! Catch them! They take with them the life of my son!"

By the time Marcus caught up with his men they were within bowshot of the wall and the sentries were looking down on the scene with a mixture of curious and concerned expressions. Sextus held the reins of Vibia's horse and he led her towards the gate which they could see. Felix was already there with Wolf, having taken a short cut across the rocky outcrop which meant a detour for the horses. The optio on the gate recognised the standard and the uniforms and ordered the gate opened. Here was a story to alleviate the boredom of sentry duty on the wall; where had the horse warriors found such a beautiful girl out here in the middle of nowhere? It just didn't seem fair, they were paid more money, they could ride and not walk and now they were finding women in the middle of the barbarian's forest.

They had reached a gate some fifteen miles from Cilurnum. Marcus briefly told the Gallic centurion at the gate what had occurred. "There is a huge warband in the forest to the north and their war chief was one of those on horses. They may be just pissed off enough to attack. I should watch out."

The Gaul nodded. "I wouldn't worry too much decurion, your lads and the Sixth knocked the Selgovae about a bit. We have a little more support."

"Good!"

"Too right. It means we can do a bit of proper soldier work and not spend all our time shitting concrete."

"Turma wheel left!" As they rode along Marcus shouted to Scanlan and Vibius. Scanlan was still riding double with Publius. "That was very brave of you lads." They both blushed and grinned at what they took to be a compliment. "And also stupid. If you ever do that again I will have you on a charge." The joy dropped from their faces in an instant. "I am only letting you off because you are recruits." They looked at each other in confusion. "What are my standing orders Publius?"

"If a man is dismounted the rest leave him." He smiled at the two recruits. "I am grateful you came back for me but I didn't expect it. I would have slowed down the enemy and you would all have escaped."

Vibius asked, "Truly?"

"Truly."

Leaving the recruits to ponder his words he rode forwards to Sextus and Vibia. "Take the rear Sextus. It is time I spoke with our guest."

Vibia Dives turned to him and gave him a smile which melted his heart. Her green eyes glowed like those of a contented cat. Marcus forced himself to think of his wife at home and resist the stirring in his loins. "I want to thank you for coming for me decurion."

"I was just following orders."

She pouted, "You mean had you had a choice you would have left me there?"

Marcus blushed, "No, er, what I mean is you don't need to thank me for doing my duty. None of us wish to see Roman women as prisoners."

"Ah!"

"My mother was held captive for many years by the Caledonii until my father rescued her so I understand what you must have been going through."

"Sorry for what I said. What I really meant was thank you for risking so much. You may have been under orders but I do not think those orders included sneaking into the enemy camp and spiriting me away. That was not only brave but showed great resourcefulness. And with such young boys too."

"They were chosen because they could pass for barbarians. Any of the men could have done as they did."

"Even so I am grateful and I will endeavour to show my gratitude when I can." Her eyes fluttered and she leaned over to place a hand on his.

Marcus smiled and withdrew his hand; there was something about this beautiful young woman that was dangerous. He had been amazed at how calm she had been and how well she had reacted to the ordeal. There was more to her than met the eye. "No need to, miss. It is all in a day's work here, at the sharp end of the frontier." He would be glad to reach the fort and hand his charge over to the Legate. He could deal with her then.

"There is one thing, decurion, one of the men who helped them to abduct me was one of your troopers."

Marcus looked behind him at the turma, "One of my lads?"

"No, not these but a trooper dressed as your men in Eboracum. I recognised him."

That gave Marcus pause for thought. It confirmed what Belenus had said and was even more specific, it was the unthinkable, and the traitor was one of their own.

The first thing Marcus noticed as he led his weary turma towards the southern gate, was the number of birds across the river. As he saluted to the sentry on duty he asked, "Where did all the birds come from?"

The sentry grinned. "The general, he hung one of the hostages when the barbarians came calling this morning. You could hear his neck snap all over the fort. The birds are enjoying a very pleasant meal." The sentry had obviously had a perverse pleasure in the prisoner's pain and death. He also had money in the century sweep to see how long the body would last before it became nothing but bones. He was still in with a chance!

Marcus suddenly realised that was another reason why the barbarians had been so keen to apprehend them. They had seen the ruthless side of Rome. If you broke the law then you would be punished but Marcus wondered if that might be the spark which engulfed the frontier in flame. Legate Julius Demetrius reached the gate as they entered. "Well done Marcus." He embraced his young decurion. "Any casualties?"

"No, but it was a close-run thing. I'll tell you later. I have to see to the men. Here is the hostage Vibia, Legate. Safe and sound."

Marcus helped her from the horse and the Legate summoned the four female slaves who stood nearby. "Take this young lady to my quarters and see to her needs." He looked at her in a fatherly way. "Whatever you need, my dear, just ask. There is a bath house and the slaves have clean clothes for you."

"Thank you, Legate, and I would like to commend the decurion. He and his men put themselves in harm's way to rescue me and I do appreciate it."

"As we all do. Will you join the officers and me for our evening meal? I know that Appius will be desperate to see you."

"Appius? Is he here?"

"Yes, he will be sorry he missed you. He took the opportunity of hunting this morning. He said he hated having nothing to do while you were in the clutches of the barbarians. I think he is quite fond of you my dear."

"So it would appear. I will join you and thank you."

The troopers were in high spirits as they rubbed down their horses. They had survived a dangerous mission and their only casualty was one horse. They stood to attention when Marcus walked in. "At ease. Well done. We will not be riding tomorrow. Use the time to check your mounts and equipment for defects. I suspect that the Votadini will return sooner rather than later so make the most of the space. The rest of the ala and the new recruits are arriving soon. We'll be cosier than fleas on a barbarian!"

Marcus would have loved to take a bath himself but he suspected that Vibia would be there and he did not want to have another run in with the green-eyed beauty. Instead, he went to the Principia. Julius Longinus looked up at him with the hint of a smile on his face. "Returned safely eh decurion? I look forward to hearing your report. The Legate is in the inner officer if you would like to follow me."

The clerk was used by the Legate to write up the reports first hand rather than a second-hand account from the Legate himself. That way they could compare versions and end up with a truer picture. The clerk was the most trustworthy man in the whole fort.

"We found their camp easily enough and saw their leaders leave. I assume they came here?"

"Yes, Iucher and a Brigante called Briac. I deduced that he is the man behind the problems we are having in the south."

"Yes we entered the camp as his men when we saw them leave and they told us much. Briac is the man behind the raids but even worse, he has brokered an alliance of the three tribes. They are working in concert."

"That is bad news."

"Yes, it is Legate but not the worst news." The two men both raised their eyebrows at once. What could be worse than that news? "There is a Brigante spy in the ala! One of our men is working against us. The girl confirmed what the war chief said. It is one of Marcus' Horse who aids the enemy. She said he was not one of my turma." He saw the quizzical look on the Legate's face, "I asked."

The two older men looked at each other, "Which might explain Legate, how the Brigante entered Eboracum and managed to poison the officer's food."

"Yes and with the whole ala being gathered here soon we will have almost six hundred suspects!"

Julius Demetrius sank a little lower in his chair as he realised the magnitude of the problem. The clerk stood and, putting his hands behind him, began to pace the office floor. "Not so, Legate. There are some men we can eliminate."

"Such as?"

"Anyone who was with the ala more than two years ago. I mean we could say one year but let us set a realistic time frame. We can also deduce that he will probably be a Brigante."

"How do you work that out?"

"The two years?" They both nodded, "I cannot see them having a spy and waiting two years. The Brigante are not that patient and the Brigante? Well if Briac is the man behind it then it would make sense for him to use someone from his tribe."

"That is still a lot of men."

"True but nearer fifty or sixty I would say. The recruits might be favourite but for the fact that he knew his way around Eboracum. That would suggest an experienced man."

Julius Demetrius banged the desk. "The information stays in this room. When Rufius, Livius and Metellus arrive we will tell them and then we will try to catch our spy. Well done you two. And now, Marcus, you had better get changed for the evening meal eh? You are a little aromatic, shall we say?"

"I would have said smelly, Legate, but I will bathe as you suggest."

When Appius returned to the fort and found that Vibia had been rescued he was beside himself with a mixture of joy and anger. He had wanted to be the hero who rescued the love of his life but at least his rival, Gnaeus was still in Eboracum and he would be able to woo her at the meal. His wit and his charm would show her what buffoons these country officers were. He went directly to his room to choose the toga with the narrow purple stripe. Although not yet a narrow stripe tribune, he knew it was merely a matter of time.

The meal, which the cooks had prepared, was brought in. The cook was an old servant of the Legate's but, with the news that there was a spy in the fort meant that he asked for the cook to taste and then serve the food. Titus Carbinus was not offended, especially as the Legate had briefed him on what he would ask of him. He would happily taste his food for any. The Gaul gave an imperious sniff as he left the dining room. Julius had done this deliberately so that when the whole ala was based in the fort he could repeat it and no-one would think anything untoward. Fortunately, no-one seemed to notice. Vibia had used her time well and her hair cascaded from a carefully crafted design which the slaves had helped her to create. She had applied the blue makeup to her eyes and the red cochineal to her lips to enhance their natural beauty. Perfume had been a problem until one of the resourceful slaves had found some rosemary, lavender and roses. When they were combined in the correct proportions with just a hint of olive oil they were applied to Vibia's wrist and neck. As she entered the room, later than anyone else, she knew she would have an immediate and lasting effect on the men in the room. All the younger officers and Appius visibly drooled as she sinuously glided in. Marcus and Julius exchanged a look. Julius could now see the change marriage had wrought on Marcus. A flirtation did not appeal to him and he could watch the male displays with detachment as the beautiful Vibia fluttered her eyes at all the young men who drank in every gesture and flick of a red painted finger. Marcus and the Legate had more things on their mind than a siren luring young bloods on to the rocks of lust. They spent the evening talking of the serious implications of the news they had garnered.

Livius and Metellus were glad to be heading back to Cilurnum. At the fort by the river there were no distractions and, thankfully, there was no poisoned food. They could, in a strange sort of way, relax more. Even though they were close to the frontier and to danger they knew who their enemies were and that was not always true in Eboracum. Livius, in particular, had tired of the Governor and his constant whining about gold, copper and money. It seemed that all he cared about was acquiring and spending money. The men on the frontier, the soldiers who fought to keep the province safe, did not appear to figure in his calculations. They were an incidental while to Livius they were the cement which held the province together.

"I am sorry that you could only have one night in your home Metellus."

"It matters not sir. Two years from now I shall have every night at home and a healthy income from selling horses to the ala."

Livius gestured back at the herd which followed them. "You have not done so badly this time old friend."

"True and poor Marcus will have the difficult job of training up these new horsemen who follow us."

"I am just pleased that the Governor authorised the payment to enlarge the ala. I had thought he would spend all the money on making a pretty wall."

Metellus shook his head in disbelief, "What difference does it make if the wall is faced or not?"

"To the barbarians? None. To someone who wishes his name to be remembered a thousand years from now as the man who built Nepos Wall? Everything!"

As they rode through the gate to the fort they saw Rufius and the remnants of his turmae riding along the Stanegate. It was a harsh lesson and a warning for all. Livius and his men had suffered few casualties

114

but here, on the wall, it was a dangerous place and a short life span for the auxiliaries of Marcus' Horse.

"Hail Rufius. I can see from your empty saddles that many men have gone to meet the Allfather and our comrades."

"Aye Prefect. It was a hard-fought battle but we succeeded in our mission and the Sixth was saved; not to mention this bloody wall."

Metellus gestured behind him. "Well, we have many recruits to fill the empty saddles and horses too."

"Which is all well and good Metellus but can you give me the experience of the brave men who died? Can you give me the spirit that my turmae had?" There was a silence and Metellus leaned over to touch the arm of Rufius. "Sorry old friend. I yearn for the days when the three of us could roam at will knowing that the only men we could hurt were ourselves."

Livius shook his head sadly, "And now we have the responsibility of command. Another reason why I never envy Julius nor aspire to be another Agricola. This ala is all that I desire."

Chapter 13

"We have no time for niceties. Let your chosen men see to the troopers, we five need a conference with Julius. I think his maps and his information may be of help." Livius detected a nervous tone in Julius' words. He wondered what it portended.

Once in the office, Julius Longinus had spread his neatly drawn map on the table. Eboracum, Morbium and the wall were marked clearly. The Legate made to speak and Marcus held up his hand saying, apologies sir." He put his head out of the door. "Lucius. I want no one closer to this office than twenty paces. And that means anyone. Understand me?"

"Yes sir."

Metellus cocked a curious eye at Marcus but Julius smiled grimly and said, "Young Marcus does right and I should have thought of it myself. We have a traitor in the ranks."

"Impossible!"

"Hear Marcus out, Livius, and then make your judgement."

Marcus then told of the rescue of the girl and his conversation with Belenus. "So you see, if we add that to the attempt on the officer's lives then it makes sense. And when we add to that their early success with the wagons until we began to behave in an unpredictable manner then it becomes more obvious. It is just that none of us can believe it."

Livius paled. This was his ala. He trusted every trooper he had under his command. "Do we mistrust everyone?"

Julius coughed, "Our clerk and part time intelligence officer has done some work on this. Carry on Master Longinus."

Julius nodded and, like a schoolmaster, took his pointer. He had the lists of the ala pinned to a wall and there were men marked with red. "We deduced that the spy had to have been in the ala for less than two years. We also worked out that it was likely that they would be Brigante. The men in red are all in that category. Rufius, Livius and Metellus all spoke at once.

"That one is impossible!"

"Gaius saved my life."

"He would die for the ala!"

Julius tapped his pointer against the desk. "This may all be true. There is but one spy so your comments may well be true, however, until we can prove their innocence then all of these fifty men are suspect."

Mollified the three officers leaned back. "But what can we do?"

"If you notice they are spread around the turmae. I suggested to the Legate that we move them all into your turma, Prefect. Use the excuse of new recruits and new officers being needed." The Legate nodded his approval for the clerk's words. "That way we contain the threat. We watch and we, perhaps, set a trap."

"What kind of trap?"

Julius put his pointer down and said irritably. "Give me time to think of one for heaven's sake. I have given you one strategy. Do you want me to do it all?"

Livius smiled, "Sorry Julius. You have done well."

"Besides," added the Legate, "we also have the added problem of the barbarians joining together. I fear that hanging one of the hostages, while justified, might just ignite the flames of rebellion and slow down the building of the wall."

"Then perhaps we can do two things at the same time."

"And what is that Livius?"

"Set a trap and take the war to the tribes."

"Go on!"

"Both Rufius and Marcus have reported that the Selgovae and Votadini are ripe for rebellion and yet the Brigante leader, Briac, is here in the north. If we tell our troopers that we intend to capture the Brigante leader then the spy will have to act."

"You will be risking the men in the turma that the spy has hidden within."

"True but he will have to give himself away. He will need to get a message to Briac. I think that Marcus' turma cannot have the spy within their ranks as Vibia said that she did not see him there added to which their mission to rescue the hostage would have been compromised had they had a traitor. Looking at Julius' lists there is only one of the possible traitors who is being transferred into Marcus' turma and he is replacing Sextus who has been promoted. That means Marcus just watches one man. If we use just Metellus' and Marcus' turmae as bait we can eliminate some men quite quickly. Metellus has more but that is a risk we need to take. The majority of the suspect men are in mine and Rufius' turmae. This way we narrow the search down quickly and we know where our bad apples are likely to be." He looked at all their faces and knew what he asked of them. They had to go into battle believing that one of their men was a traitor. He was pleased when they all grinned and nodded.

"I believe they will have gone back to the Votadini camp. I have been there twice now. I think that we could give them a bloody nose at least." Marcus looked at Livius. "I assume that you do not expect us to capture Briac but you want us to hurt them?"

"Exactly. The ruse is to lure out the spy but we need the mission to seem plausible. We will only tell the turmae on the morning of the mission." He paused. "Tomorrow."

Metellus grinned. "Of course, the rest of the turmae will know where we are going, that is inevitable. If someone tries to leave the fort then we will know who the spy is."

"Unless he is with your turma or mine Metellus."

"We have a handful of troopers to watch. I think we can manage that. I like the plan." The grin disappeared. "Can we get close and achieve surprise then?"

"I believe so. If we arm some of the men with bows we can cause casualties from above. There is a place above the camp where we can lure them out and then attack them from ambush. The barbarians will outnumber us but we can outrun them. If the rest of the ala is waiting close to the wall then we can bring them to battle on ground of our choosing." He remembered the caltrops. "We should take more caltrops with us so that we can slow them down as they pursue us. It worked last time. They don't wear caligae!"

Just then there was an almighty altercation outside the door. There were raised voices and then a crash as though something had been thrown to the ground. "What the…"

The officers all left the office and saw a very red-faced Appius picking himself up from the ground.

"This man manhandled me. I demand that he be punished."

The trooper said, "Sorry sir. He wouldn't listen and tried to barge past me."

"Of course I did, you buffoon. I do not obey orders from a trooper. Now punish him!"

The officers just looked at each other with the hint of a smile on their faces. "That will be all, trooper, thank you. Return to your post."

He saluted and then said to Appius, "Sorry if I hurt you sir."

"That trooper was obeying my orders. The meeting was not intended for you. I think it would be best if you returned to Eboracum as it is obvious that you cannot obey the rules of a military zone."

Appius looked shocked. "You are sending me away? I am the Governor's aide."

"Then," added Julius icily. "I suggest you go and aid him. But whatever you do, do it away from here or I will have you incarcerated."

"But, but, the Lady Vibia is here. She needs my protection."

"I think not and we will send the Lady Vibia back to Eboracum with a proper escort which can defend her effectively, rather than have you try to impress her."

"The Governor wanted you to supply me with a turma of your men to investigate the mines." His face was triumphant.

"That was before the tribes rose in revolt. I think that can wait until we have defeated this enemy. Now, which is it to be, Eboracum or a cell?"

"You have not heard the last of this, Legate!"

Livius shook his head at the arrogant young man as he stormed petulantly out of the office. "If you give me your list Julius, I will reassign the men. Marcus, would you like to tell Sextus of his promotion?"

"Thank you, sir. I wonder what his reaction will be to having a turma of twenty recruits and just ten experienced troopers."

Sextus looked nonplussed as he was given the good news. "Thank you sir but I thought you liked me."

"I do Sextus."

"Twenty fresh-faced recruits! It will be a nightmare. They'll all be killed the first time out."

"The good news is that because you have so many new men in your turma then you do not need to take them on patrol for seven days. You have that time to train them up."

"That isn't so bad then." He suddenly realised the import of Marcus' words. "Are you and the lads going out again then sir?"

"It is Marcus now, Sextus, and, yes we are. Tomorrow."

"Where to?"

Mindful of the Prefect's words he just said. "On patrol. You know how dangerous the frontier is right now; which is why, old friend, we need officers like you training your men well. We will all be needed sooner, rather than later."

When Marcus told the men that they would be out again the next day they did not ask where but they just became even more excited. "Cassius, now that Sextus has been promoted you will be assuming the post of Chosen Man. Well done." Cassius was popular and they all gathered around him to pat his back.

The signifier, Julius, came over and said, quietly, "He's a good choice sir."

"I know, Julius, but he will need help from you. You will have to watch over the younger men with him. Oh, and we have a replacement for Sextus as a trooper, Gaius Bochco from the Twelfth Turma."

119

"I think I know him, a miserable bugger but a sound trooper. I'll see to him when he arrives."

"Thanks, oh and Cassius, find out the best archers, half of the turma need bows for tomorrow. Get the equipment from the quartermaster. He knows you will be coming."

A beaming Cassius said, "Yes sir!"

The two turmae assembled early the next morning. Metellus watched with interest as Wolf inspected the new troopers with a suspicious sniff. "I hope, Decurion Aurelius, that we pass inspection?"

Marcus laughed. "He just smells you for future reference and do not underestimate that dog, Decurion Princeps. He is as much a warrior as any trooper."

Livius and the Legate came out to see them off. Rufius was watching the southern gate while two other trusted officers were watching the other two gates. Their instructions were to watch for any unauthorised departures from the fort. Marcus led them out with Felix and Wolf loping ahead of them. Marcus and Metellus had discussed the possibility of the fort being watched and their route identified. Marcus had seen a small dry valley which ran parallel with the wall when he had fled the barbarians. They would use that to hide them from the forest while Felix and Wolf scouted the edge of the trees to identify any enemy scouts.

Once they were in the hidden valley Metellus briefed the turmae while Marcus watched the suspects closely. If they showed any agitation it would be noted and if they tried to leave any message it would be seen. "Right lads, sorry about the secrecy but we are going to attack the Votadini camp and with the hostages in the fort, we didn't want word getting out. This is why you have bows." Rather than agitation all that Marcus saw was excitement. This was not to be the usual mundane patrol; this was an attack on an enemy. Marcus' turma had told the others of their mission and the other troopers had been envious. Metellus' turma, in particular, had had a boring time escorting wagons and they yearned for adventure. Seeing the Sword of Cartimandua was once again strapped to the decurion's right side gave every trooper a sense of both pride and history. The sword was going to war once more!

"Decurion, lead us off, you know the way." Metellus winked as he passed Marcus. He could watch from the rear for any abnormal behaviour.

It was slightly intimidating as they wound their way along the dry valley. They were below the forest and an ambush was always possible. Marcus knew that they should have scouts out but that would indicate their route and that had to remain secret. It was almost noon when first Wolf and then Felix appeared on the skyline. The Brigante waved to them and Marcus kicked his steed up the bank. He pointed to the east, "There are no scouts there but Wolf picked them up to the west."

That made sense; any barbarian attack would have more chance of success closer to the Selgovae warbands. "Well done, take Wolf and watch the forest. We will follow." He turned and waved north. The two turmae urged their mounts up the bank and followed Marcus. Marcus turned to Cassius. "Keep following Felix. We are heading for the forest northeast of us. I need to talk to the Decurion Princeps." He joined Metellus at the rear and they allowed the troopers to move forwards. "It looks like they are planning an attack on the gap again. Felix is taking us through the forest." He nodded at the backs of the troopers. "Seen anything suspicious yet?"

Shaking his head the Decurion Princeps said, "No, if anything they looked excited. Either our spy is a good actor or he is not here. The only one to leave was young Appius Serjanus and we sent him away anyway. He was not happy!"

Back at Cilurnum, the spy was becoming increasingly frustrated. Since Briac had left for the north he had had no communication. He wanted to further the Brigante cause but it was hard not knowing his instructions. He had seen the hostage hung and seen Briac being chased away. It was infuriating he was so close and yet he could do nothing. And then to make matters worse the Prefect's pet, the boy with the sword had rescued the Roman bitch! She would soon recognise him and he had to keep to the shadows and the barracks for he feared that he would be exposed as the man who had helped kidnap her. The Votadini were useless: all they had to do was to hold her. He hated being impotent and not being able to strike at his enemies. Sometimes he just wanted to kill them all with his bare hands. Suddenly an evil smile crossed his face. He could do something and it would strike at the heart of the Roman fort and make them fear for their lives. Before he could put his plan into operation, he heard the buccina sound assembly. Perhaps it was for the best. He could spend the time on patrol planning what he would do. The last thing he needed was to be caught. One of the troopers in his turma grinned at him. "Action at last. The whole ala is going out on patrol. It looks like we are going to take on the tribes."

The words sounded like a death knell to the spy but it hardened his resolve. He would fight with them this day but, as soon as they returned to the fort he would put his plan into action. He would do something more than pass messages on; he would take action of his own.

Marcus felt quite at home in the woods while Metellus, who had spent the past few weeks on the open road found them claustrophobic. He shook his head at the young decurion who, it seemed, had been a mere boy a short time ago and yet here he was confidently leading sixty men through the heart of the enemy country as though it was a parade in Eboracum! He now doubted that the spy was in their turmae and that meant he could concentrate on attacking the enemy and hurting them while suffering as few casualties as possible.

In the Votadini camp, Iucher was exhorting his men to revenge themselves upon the Romans. "My son will have to be the sacrifice which tears the oppressor from our lands. Our brothers the Selgovae have shown us what can be done and even now the wall to the west burns and many of the Roman legionaries lie dead. We too will fall upon the Romans. The ones who stole the girl showed us that they are cowards and thirty of them ran from but ten of us. They fear us, brothers, and tomorrow we will attack them and destroy them. Then we will join with our Selgovae comrades and rip the wall down with our bare hands. We will return the land to its people and remove all traces of the Roman!"

Briac looked in awe as the hundreds of warriors screamed their approval, banging their shields with their swords. He began to see how he might bend the Brigante to his will with a speech like that. Since he had been north of the wall he had seen how many Romans the tribes had to deal with. In the land of the Brigante, there were no legions. He had been too cautious and when he returned south of the wall he would change his tactics.

The Votadini began to prepare for war. Warriors applied the blue colouring to their bodies while others plaited their hair and daubed it with lime to make it stand up. Some of them took the offal from the deer and smeared the blood on their torsos. Weapons were sharpened and the noise of the camp reached a crescendo. Iucher had planned well; his men would move soon towards the wall and as dawn broke the next day they would attack all the way along the wall.

Suddenly a Votadini warrior pitched forwards lying with the unmistakable feathers of a Roman arrow in his back. They all looked at the body, as though it would rise of its own accord. Then more arrows fell and the warriors who were struck lay writhing on the ground. "They are above us! Kill them! Rip their hearts out!"

Briac hung back as the Votadini streamed out of the camp. He did not intend to die here fighting for another chief. He watched as they raced up the narrow trail which led to the top of the steep bluff. Even as they climbed they took casualties and, when they reached the top, Briac had a clear view as thirty javelins thrown from Romans on horses, ripped into the warriors who were eagerly trying to reach their unseen attackers. The efficiency of the Romans impressed Briac. He suspected that there were few men at the top of the bluff but they had chosen their ambush site well and only a few warriors could ascend the path at the same time. They were easily dispatched. Briac looked behind him and saw some slingers and archers. "Use your weapons!"

One of them sneered, "We cannot see the enemy Brigante."

"But you know where they are or would you have your brothers die in vain?" Briac did not know if they were stupid or just lacked leadership but, after they had looked at each other they began to loose their weapons and the missiles from the Romans diminished. Soon more warriors were reaching the top of the bluff.

At the top Metellus could see that they were taking casualties. They had stirred up the hornet's nest and now it was time for discretion. "Sound the recall!"

Soon the survivors of the attack were mounted and galloping away to the south. This time Marcus did not need to follow marked trees for they had not laid traps. He hoped that the Votadini would watch for them but it didn't matter; there were over six hundred troopers waiting to ambush them as soon as they broke cover. The dead troopers would have to be left and that pained every man who rode away from the ambush. They had succeeded but it had cost them friends and comrades. Marcus glanced ahead and was pleased to see Felix and Wolf ranging ahead. He feared for the boy on these raids for he had no horse to aid him but it was his choice and, like Gaelwyn before him, Felix was a warrior. As soon as they had cleared the ambush site Metellus roared, "Sow caltrops!" The turmae spread out into a long line and men began to drop the painful weapons behind them. They would not kill but they would maim. They would not halt the pursuit, but they would slow it down and that was the Roman plan.

This time it was not the headstrong Belenus who led the pursuit it was Iucher and he had no intention of following the Romans to his death. At the top of the rise, he looked at the handful of dead troopers. "Strip the bodies of weapons." He looked at his war chiefs gathered around him. "You two take your bands after the Romans but watch for their traps. You others follow me." He led the men to the east, towards Cilurnum. This was where the horse warriors had come from and they would return there. He would ambush them.

Chapter 14

Metellus knew he had to keep the barbarians close on their tail and he slowed down the two turmae to enable him to keep the wary warriors in sight. Marcus rode next to him at the rear, "it looks like your little tricks the last time have made them a little more cautious."

"They still follow."

"But it is not I think the whole band. The rest must be further back."

At the front of the line Felix and Wolf had broken cover. The scout was not bound by the orders given to the turmae and he could go where he would. He saw the ala arrayed before the wall and as Livius waved at him he saw the line move forwards to take up positioning the dry valley. He pointed east and the dog scampered away.

The turmae emerged from the forest and the troopers were relieved to see the sanctuary that was the wall, ahead. None of them knew of the trap set by the Prefect but they knew that they could easily make the wall before the barbarians could escape the forest. Behind them the warband closed closer to the horses and those with bows and slings began to pelt the troopers who lagged at the rear. There was a cacophony of sound as the stones and arrows pinged off the mail, helmets and the slung shields of the troopers.

When a horse fell with two arrows from its rear and a trooper clutched a bleeding leg Metellus gave the order, "Retreat!" and the two turmae rode as hard away from the barbarians as possible.

Suddenly Wolf appeared from their left followed by Felix. "The Votadini…" Those were the only words Felix uttered before he was felled by a stone. Wolf retaliated immediately and turned, teeth snarling to leap at the throat of the boy with the sling who had drawn his dagger to finish off the stunned scout.

Marcus did not hesitate. He put his heels to the flanks of his horse and, holding his spear like a lance galloped back to where Iucher and the rest of the Votadini poured over the moors. Cassius saw his decurion and followed. Marcus had no time to look to see if the ala had seen them for there were four more warriors approaching the unconscious scout. Wolf had torn the throat from the boy and, with bloody jowls, was advancing slowly on the four warriors. One of them raised his spear and Marcus thrust his own spear onto the throat of the warrior. Wolf was tearing at the sword hand of a second. Withdrawing the spear and pulling back on the reins Marcus' mount crashed his hooves down on a third barbarian as the decurion thrust his spear into the unprotected side of the last warrior. He glanced behind him where

124

Cassius had picked up the scout and was urging Marcus to follow. "Come on sir. The boy is safe and they are very close!"

Marcus could see that they were, indeed, very close as a spear flew over his head. He wheeled his horse around and raced for the defensive lines of the two turmae. The war bands from the forest had taken heart and were hurtling down the slope to attack the turma's flanks. He heard Metellus shout the order to retreat and he and Cassius followed their comrades and headed for the safety of the wall. As they crested the dry valley they saw the long reassuring lines of the rest of the ala galloping towards the exposed barbarians. The troopers left gaps through which they passed and then they reined in their exhausted mounts to watch the barbarians caught in Livius' trap.

The two opposing forces found themselves racing towards each other and they clashed with a crash of metal on metal; followed by the screams as blades and spears found flesh. The barbarians had the advantage that they were charging downhill but the weight of the horses soon forced the Votadini backwards. Stabbing with their javelins the troopers outranged the Votadini who were soon forced to begin to strike at the unprotected horses. Although the horses had no armour they reacted violently to the stabbing, scything blades and their hooves soon made the warriors at the fore fall back in fear.

Livius turned to the signifier, "Recall!"

The troopers on the flanks who had begun to charge towards the Votadini reined in and turned to form, a solid line again. Both sides hefted shields and weapons in preparation for the next assault.

Metellus had had time to reorganise his two turmae and he led them along the dry valley, out of sight of the barbarians. When he felt they had travelled far enough east he ordered them into one line. "Marcus, take the left and now might be a good time for you to use the sword eh?"

Both men knew the effect the sword could have and, allied to their sudden appearance on the barbarian flank they hoped it would make the Votadini flee. Drawing the sword, which glinted in the late afternoon sun, he held it aloft and shouted, "The Sword of Cartimandua!" The cry was taken up by the rest of the turmae.

It was though a dam had been released as the fifty warriors urged their mounts up the valley's slopes. The Votadini were so preoccupied with Livius and the ala that the sudden appearance of fifty screaming troopers took them by surprise and the two turmae crashed into the flank of the horse. The Sword of Cartimandua was a powerful sword and the first barbarian who tried to parry it found his own sword shattered in two and the decurion's sword continued its arc to rip into his shoulder, severing it like a butcher with a carcass. The young Brigante recruits were desperate to copy their decurion and they fought with a fury which belied their lack of experience. Vibius kept as close as he could to his decurion, wanting to protect the back of the man who had saved the hostage. The four of them formed an improvised wedge which began to carve through the barbarians. Iucher was fighting like a man possessed. He was fighting to revenge a son he felt was already dead and his war axe severed limbs both of troopers and horses but the cavalry were driving inexorably forward and Briac, who had hovered close to the war chief, now raced forwards to grab his arm. "Come Iucher, let us withdraw to the forest and fight another day. We have killed many Romans this day."

His face contorted with rage the Votadini war chief snarled at Briac. "But not enough!"

His bodyguards and oathsworn also added their voices. "He is right, great chief. We will join with the Selgovae and attack again."

With a roar of rage Iucher chopped his axe down to split the nearest trooper in two and then turned. "Come, my people, back to the forest."

With his bodyguard forming a shield wall the Votadini began to melt back up the hill towards the forest. Livius considered chasing them but they had but four hundred paces to go and his horses were already winded. "Sound recall!"

Troopers reined in and looked around to see which of their comrades had gone to meet the Allfather. Marcus rode back to Felix who lay in the arms of the capsarius. The orderly looked up and smiled, "He is tough this one and that," he pointed to Wolf, "is a fierce protector! He is bruised that is all."

Felix opened his eyes. "Sorry, sir. They surprised me. They were upwind of me."

"You warned us and that saved us, Felix. Next time we bring your mount eh?" Felix gave a wan smile and nodded.

"See to the wounded and despatch the wounded barbarians. Gnaeus keep watch on the barbarians."

The spy had managed to avoid killing any of his barbarian comrades. He had seen Briac and knew that he was here. He could still operate his plan. He went around the bodies taking weapons from them and secreting them in his satchel. The Romans had been clever and almost tricked the barbarians into a trap. He would not underestimate them again. It was time to prove that there were still Brigante with heart who were willing to die for freedom.

Julius Demetrius had spent the day at the new fort, Vercovicium, on the wall. The Governor's orders had been quite clear, more forts like

126

Cilurnum were needed and he and the engineers had been surveying a site close to the lake and the cliff. It would make a perfect fort for infantry and his engineers assured him that it would be almost impregnable. Julius was not certain; the barbarians had shown themselves to be remarkably resourceful hitherto. He and his legionary escort caught up with the ala as they travelled along the Stanegate back to their fort. Julius felt a pang of guilt as he saw the empty saddles and the depleted numbers. He still remembered when he had been the Prefect of the ala and he felt every casualty as much as Livius.

He joined Rufius who had formed the rearguard. "How did it go Rufius?"

"They tried to ambush us but they lost many more men than we."

"And did anyone try to run?"

"Not as far as we can tell. We will have a roll call when we return to the fort."

"It might be that we hold a parade tomorrow and ask young Vibia to identify her abductor."

"Why not tonight Legate?"

"I need to speak with her first and, besides, it is unfair on those brave men who have fought today and lost comrades."

"You are right. There is hardly a turma which has not lost numbers of brave men. What about the Sixth and the Gauls. Have they had an easier time?"

"Yes, the Selgovae, it seems have retreated to lick their wounds but the days of the overwhelming victories are long gone. The tribes are learning how to fight us."

There was a downcast air over the fort as the men groomed their horses and prepared their evening meals. It seemed, to many, that they only had the full complement of troopers for a short time. Livius could detect their depression as he wandered the fort; praising a man here, joking with another there. "Let the quartermaster know if there are any deficiencies in your equipment."

"That will cheer old Publius up, sir. He'll be even more miserable."

The Quartermaster was renowned for being a morose character. In fact he had a wicked sense of humour but he only shared that with his fellow officers. He kept a façade for the troopers but Livius knew he would be as distraught about the losses as any.

When Livius met his officers he first checked up on their state of mind. There were many young decurions amongst his officers and the first time you lost men was always hard. "You all did well today. Let me know of any who deserve phalera." He smiled as they all began at once. He held a hand up. "In writing please and give it to Julius." He

127

poured a beaker of wine, "To Marcus' Horse!" They all joined in with the toast and swallowed off the wine which the Legate himself had provided.

"I saw Briac today sir."

"Did you Marcus? I wondered if he had returned to Eboracum to cause more mischief." He suddenly seemed to remember something. "Tomorrow I want to hold a parade and praise the men directly. The only turma on patrol will be Sextus so they do not need to come in armour and helmets."

Rufius, Metellus and Marcus exchanged glances. They hated being in the know when their fellows were not but they understood the need for secrecy. On the following day they would finally know the identity of the spy and all the need for subterfuge would be gone.

The spy had finished his work quickly; his equipment was cleaned and placed on his bed, his horse was groomed- he was still the perfect trooper. He was still avoiding Vibia. With the Votadini daggers secreted about his person he made his way to the cells. He took with him a skin of wine. The cells were towards the river end of the fort and close to the bridge. They were in shadows and well away from everything but the stables. The corpse of the hanged man still swayed in the slight breeze and the sudden, jerky movements told the spy that the rats were feasting well. He knew that there were two Tungrian guards on the gate of the cells and one on the inside. He was a confident warrior and had devised a plan to eliminate both of the exterior guards. He poured a handful of wine onto his hands and spread it over his face. He took a mouthful and rolled it around his mouth before spitting it out. Satisfied with his appearance he staggered towards the cells singing a dirty ditty the soldiers sang as they rode.

The two Tungrians nodded to each other, with a grin on each of their faces, as the trooper made his unsteady way towards them. "Are you lost trooper? No horses to shag here."

The spy laughed. "No I just wanted to stick this," he held out a Votadini dagger, "into one of those bastards. My mate caught it today from another of the Votadini and I want payback!"

"Much as we might want to we can't let you in there."

"I know, here, have a drink?" He held out the wineskin.

The Tungrians eyed it greedily. They glanced around to see if there were any officers about and then they put their spears in the door jamb. "Just a quick drink eh Gaius?"

"It would be rude to refuse Julius."

As one Tungrian took the skin the spy slashed his blade across the throat of the other and then before the one with the skin could react he stabbed him in the neck. He was a strong man and he grabbed them both to lower them to the ground.

The guard inside said, "What's going on out there?"

The spy disguised his voice, "It's Gaius, and he's taken a funny turn."

"If he's been drinking again he is on a charge. I can smell it from in here."

The door opened and before the Tungrian could react the spy had pushed him backwards and stabbed him under his arm into his heart. He laid the bleeding corpse down. The keys to the cells were on a hook next to the sentry's chair and he grabbed them. There was a small opening so that the guards could check on the prisoners. The spy peered in and said, "Stand back from the doors; I am here to rescue you."

He opened one door and two of the Votadini looked at him suspiciously. "Why should a Roman help us?"

In answer the spy pointed at the corpse, "Because I am Brigante. Here," he gave them the daggers he had collected from the battlefield. When they were all armed he addressed them. "The best way out will be over the walls. Watch out for traps in the bottom and the sentries on the bridge. You can swim the river. Stay away from the bridge it is heavily garrisoned. When you get to your camp tell my chief, Briac, that his man still fights for him but I need instructions."

"Thank you Brigante we will not forget this."

"I do not do it for you. I do it to hurt the Romans. Help me to hide the bodies in the cells." When they had covered them with hay he said, "Now go, return to your forest, and I will return to my barracks so that they do not suspect me."

Iucher's son took charge and the young Votadini hugged the walls of the fort. It was dark and there was no moon, it was as though the gods of this land were aiding them. Each of the young men was determined not to be captured again. Their hanged comrade was a devastating reminder of the cruelty of the Romans. His spirit would wander lost around the river for all eternity. Above them, on the wall, the two Tungrian sentries were wrapping their cloaks around them a little tighter. Their own land was cold but here, in this northern outpost, the wind seemed to whistle from across the seas bringing icy blasts, even in summer. They could hear the revelry from the troopers celebrating their success. The Tungrians were a little envious. They might not have the risks of fighting the barbarians but they deserved a reward every bit as much as the overpaid horse warriors. It was just unfair. The two cold sentries peered across the moors, rising before them and thence to the forests. That was where they knew the Votadini were. At least they had not drawn the bridge duty where the slippery barbarians could sneak in and slit a throat.

Ironically the two Tungrians died as the handful of youths slipped up the steps and overpowered the two guards, their life blood oozing down the steps to drip and pool close to the cell so recently vacated by the barbarians. The young men wasted no time slipping over the walls and dropping silently to the top of the ditch. Mindful of the Brigante's words they peered into the bottom and saw the vicious stakes covered with faeces staring up at them. They were easily avoided and they slowly peered over the top of the ditch. They could hear the river bubbling away before them. Iucher's son led them west, away from the bridge. He did not need to explain to them his reasons, he was the son of the war chief but he knew that the current would take them towards the sea and that led under the bridge. He hoped they could all swim for any who could not and who drowned might inadvertently warn the Romans of their escape. To their left the wall rose and they could just make out the guards who were patrolling the walls. Finding a place where a bush still overhung the raging river he led them into the water. It was icy cold. The noise hid any sound they might make,

"Who cannot swim?" No one spoke. "Then in that case swim for that point over there." He pointed to a willow which overhung the dark waters. "The ones who reach the other bank first must help the others out." They nodded their agreement and Iucher's son, as befitted the son of a chief, slowly entered the water and began to swim across. He was a powerful youth and he reached the other bank first. Heeding his own words, he waited in the shallows with his arms out to grab the others who made it. The last youth, Sceagh, appeared to be struggling but the first three who had made it leapt into the water to pull him to safety. They saved his life but the sudden movement and splash in the water alerted the sharp-eyed sentry. His strident cry told the youths that they had been seen. "Quick. Into the forest. Now we run!"

The optio raced to the sentry whose shout had alerted them. He saw the movement at the other side of the river and saw the shadows scampering away. "Well done! Keep watch and I will find the centurion."

As soon as the duty centurion was summoned he took an instant decision. "Check all the walls optio and I will find the Camp Prefect." The recent sneak attacks had made everyone nervous and the centurion was quite happy to risk censure rather than losing his life.

When the optio found the two dead guards he knew that they had a problem. "Tell the centurion we have two dead guards." Almost as an afterthought the optio remembered the Votadini prisoners. He went down the steps and when he reached the bottom his worst fears were realised; the dead guards and the open door told their own story. They had hostages no longer.

Chapter 15

The Camp Prefect instantly ordered a check on every sentry. They had five dead from a half-century; that was too high a number. While the centurion checked with the bridge guards the Camp Prefect reported to the Legate and Livius. If he expected a reprimand, he did not know Julius Demetrius. "Don't feel bad about this Sextus," he looked at Livius in surprise, "it is our fault for not sharing some information with you. There is a Brigante spy in the ala. The problem is we don't know who."

Sextus Graccus was annoyed at the disclosure but he was outranked not only because Julius was a legate but he was also a close friend of the Emperor. He gritted his teeth as he spoke, "Perhaps if we had been informed then there might be five Tungrians still alive and the hostages would still be incarcerated."

"You are right but we do not know who it is and there is little point lamenting what was done or was not done. It is in the past and cannot be remedied" His face became a mask of steel. "However, we can rectify that now." He turned to Livius. "I want every trooper on parade, and no helmets. I will bring the young lady and Julius with the muster." To Sextus Graccus he added, "Tell your sentries no trooper is to be allowed out of the fort. No exceptions!"

As soon as the spy heard that they all had to report to the yard for inspection without helmets he knew that the game was up. As his turma left the barracks grumbling the spy slipped towards the stables. One of his turma said, where are you sloping off to?"

"I left something in the stable, I won't be long." He raced to the cells and found that they had not removed the bodies from where they had left them; grabbing the helmet and shield of a dead Tungrian he donned both and took the dead guard's spear. He slipped out of the gate and headed towards the bridge gate. The guards looked at him suspiciously as he approached.

"Where are you going?"

"The Camp Prefect said he needed more sentries on the far side of the bridge. The Votadini are about." He shrugged, "Typical eh?"

The two men nodded. "Aye well remember, don't let any horsemen out."

He looked at them with a realistically blank look, "Why not?"

"No idea. Perhaps one of them was caught shagging that pretty piece they rescued." He leered. "Worth a little punishment she is."

The spy strode across the bridge. He had got further than he had hoped but there would be an optio on the other side and he would be more difficult to trick. He marched purposefully along the bridge. There were eight men at the far end; they were always the most nervous of the sentries for they peered nightly into the forest. He stood to attention and faced the optio. "Sir, Camp Prefect Graccus sent me. He said there were some barbarians seen by the river." He pointed upstream. "There."

"And just what does he want me to do about it?"

The spy played dumb. "I dunno. I was just sent with a message. Can I go back now? They need me in the kitchens."

The optio grinned evilly, "No, sunshine, you can't. Hey Knuckles you and Dopey here go down the river bank and see if there are any Votadini about. Take a couple of torches with you."

The spy pretended to be outraged. "Sir! That's not fair. I just brought the message."

The huge warrior called Knuckles grabbed him. "Come on little man. Let's show you what real soldiers do!" He shook his head, "Kitchen helpers! Huh!"

The gate was opened and the rest of the tent party held their spears in a defensive half-circle as the two men left. As soon as they crossed the two ditches the gate was slammed shut and the men took their places on the wall. Knuckles led the way. "You watch the forest, kitchen boy, and I will look out for the barbarians."

The spy had to time it right. When he judged they were sufficiently far from the gate he suddenly stopped and said. "There, in the forest. I saw something."

"Don't shit yourself. It is probably a deer." As he passed the spy, the Brigante traitor dropped his spear and took out his sword. As the spear hit the ground Knuckles turned and the spy rammed his sword into his neck. He twisted the sword and the huge man fell to the ground. Pausing only to ditch the helmet and shield the spy ran into the forest as quickly as he could. They would soon search for their lost companion but by then he would be hidden deep in the depths of Votadini territory.

Julius Longinus distributed the muster lists, grumbling as he went along, "It is a good job I update these every day or this would be a complete waste of time." The officers grinned but they wondered what this was all about.

When the Legate brought out Vibia they became even more perplexed. The Legate stood before them with the young woman. "As you may know, this young lady, Vibia Dives, was kidnapped from Eboracum and taken to the camp of the Votadini. What you may not know is that a trooper from this ala, a traitor, colluded with the Votadini to do so. He also tried to poison your officers. We think that he killed two guards and helped the hostages to escape." He paused to let the significance of those words sink in. "We are now going to identify him. You will all look to the front while I pass along the lines with the young lady." He turned to Vibia and said quietly, "Just grip my hand when you see him." More loudly he said, "Decurion check your lists and make sure all your troopers are present."

Livius said, "Ten troopers in the sickbay sir."

"We will go there later if the traitor is not here."

Livius nodded to Chosen Man Gaius who had his turma list. The Prefect was tenser than anyone. He still could not believe that one of his men was a traitor. In the world of the ala you had to rely on every man as though he was your brother. He wrinkled his brow as he saw Gaius go back down the line. The other officers and sergeants were standing to the side checking their own lists and Julius was collecting them when they were completed. Vibia and the Legate were halfway through their inspection when Gaius came racing to Livius. "Sir there is a man missing."

"Who is it?"

"Scaeva."

This made no sense to Livius for Scaeva was one of the most loyal troopers; he had been awarded phalerae twice. "Are you sure? Perhaps he is in the sickbay."

"No sir, Trooper Tullus said that he went to the stable to get something he had left there."

"Legate we may have our man." He noticed Vibia shaking her head as they examined the last trooper. "Scaeva."

Julius narrowed his eyes. This could still be a trick. "Keep the men on parade. I will go to the sickbay. Livius take your Explorates and find him."

"Marcus, Rufius, Metellus, bring Felix and Wolf." The six of them ran to the stables. "Felix, we are looking for a Roman." The boy nodded and he said something to Wolf who darted into the stables. Livius knew that they could not hope to find a man quickly in such a huge building but the dog had a chance.

The dog quickly returned. "He is not here sir."

Suddenly Marcus said, "Sir, the hostages. If he released them then he could be there." They turned the corner and reached the cells. While Wolf examined the inside they looked at the bodies of the men.

"Livius, have you noticed, one of them has no helmet, his shield and his spear is missing."

"The gate!" Even as they approached the gate Livius knew that they had missed him. The guards had been told to stop all troopers. If he had the helmet and shield of a Tungrian then they would have taken him for one of their own. The guards at the gate heard their caligae pounding down the road and the five men were greeted by spear points."Where do you think you are going?" The belligerent sentry suddenly recognised Livius' rank and stood to attention. "Er sir."

"Did you let anyone out of the gate?"

Relieved that he could answer so easily he said, "Yeah one of our lads with a message from the Camp Prefect."

"Open the gate."

"Sorry, sir. Our orders are not to let anyone out of this gate…" Suddenly four swords were at their throats.

"Open the gate."

The gate swung open and they raced across. The optio was just as nervous as his sentries but he recognised the Prefect. "Yes sir?"

"Did you let anyone out tonight?"

"No sir." Livius breathed a sigh of relief. The traitor was still in the fort. "Well, apart from Knuckles and the kitchen lad the Camp Prefect sent."

Dreading the answer Livius asked, "And have they returned?"

"Not yet sir. Why is there a problem?"

"I don't think the Camp Prefect sent anyone with a message. That was the traitor who killed your guards earlier."

The optio was not afraid of taking decisions. "You four go and find them. The rest of you light more lamps and keep your eyes open."

The four men soon returned carrying the body of the auxiliary. The optio said, "Bastard!"

"We know where he is now don't we sir?"

Chapter 17

There was a great deal of tension in the fort the next day. The Tungrians were angry that so many of their men had been killed by a trooper. The excuse that he had been planted as a spy cut no ice with them and scuffles broke out all over the fort. Sextus was the subject of one such tirade and assault as he left the stables. The optio who had been Knuckles commander waited for him with three of his auxiliaries. "Another one eh lads? Are you a Brigante spy too?"

Sextus shook his head. "Look optio I am sorry for your loss but he betrayed us as much as he betrayed you. He even tried to kill the officers."

One of the auxiliaries murmured, "Fucking good thing too."

Sextus clenched his fists. "You are upset son so I will forget that but unless you want to be on a charge I would go and optio," his steely eyes stared into the smaller man's, "behave like an officer eh?"

Sextus told Marcus who told Livius. The Legate had the prefects in his office to discuss the events of the previous night. Livius apologised for being late. "Sorry sir but there is a lot of bad feeling between the men."

The Camp Prefect glared at the Tungrian Prefect who squirmed uncomfortably in his seat. Before anyone could say anything, the Legate held up his hand. "I want to draw a line under last night. On the positive side we now know who the spy is. On the negative side some brave soldiers died unnecessarily but we need to pull together gentlemen. The hostages are no longer in our custody and that means Iucher will be back and this time he will mean business. I have sent for another cohort of auxiliaries from Eboracum. When they arrive the Tungrians will go to the site of the new fort we are going to build, Vercovicium. They will help the Sixth to build it."

The Tungrian Prefect leapt to his feet, "Are we being punished for the traitor then? That seems very unfair." He glared at Livius.

"Sit down!" roared the Legate. The Prefect subsided but still showed his anger in his expression. "You are being sent there because you have a full cohort and this fort was always intended to be the base for the ala. The new fort will be your base. The ala will police itself until we receive more sentries. Any more outbursts and you, Prefect, will be on your way back to Rome! Do I make myself clear?"

The close friendship of Emperor Hadrian and the Legate was well known and the Prefect murmured a, "Yes sir, sorry sir."

"And the other reason you are being sent there is because we need to reinforce that part of the wall. With the Selgovae and the Votadini united, it is only a matter of time before they decide to attack and I assume your men would like to get a little revenge eh Prefect?"

"Yes sir."

Scaeva had never been to the Votadini camp but he had spoken with the troopers who had and he knew the route to take. He hoped that any tribesmen he met would capture him first. He hoped that they would not just kill him out of hand before he could tell them who he was. He looked Roman, but he looked like a deserter and, although few men deserted to the Votadini, he was counting on the fact that they might want to question him first. He was but five hundred paces in the Votadini forest when they appeared from nowhere with sharp swords pricking his neck.

"I am Brigante, with Briac." He blurted the words out as quickly as he could and prayed that they knew who Briac was. Fortunately, one of them had heard of the Brigante and he was taken at sword point to the camp which now had a ring of scouts a mile from the perimeter. The Votadini had learned their lesson. When he entered the camp, there was a murmur of hostility as his uniform was recognised. Scaeva wondered if their anger was too great for them to question him. Two huge warriors raced forwards to grab his arms and the Brigante began to fear for his life. Suddenly he heard a voice say, "It is him, father. That is the man who saved us and helped us to escape the Romans."

"Release him for this man is a hero. He saved the son of Iucher and we will honour him." The mood changed in an instant and the men who had been threatening to kill him now embraced him like a long-lost brother. Through the crowd, Scaeva saw Briac who nodded his approval. They had lost a spy but they had gained a powerful alliance.

The feasting went on long into the night and Scaeva, along with most of the other men of the tribe passed out at the double celebration. Had the Romans known it would have been a good night for a raid; with one blow the Votadini threat could have been ended. When he rose and had bathed in the icy stream, he joined Briac. "You have done well my brother."

"But I am no longer in the enemy camp."

Briac gave a sly smile, "It would have been difficult to pass messages and this is better. You are acclaimed a great warrior and the Votadini are now more than our allies, they are our blood brothers and that means we have more power. The chief wishes to speak with us later this morning. Prepare yourself."

When Scaeva met the chief, he was presented with a finely wrought torc and given an arm bracelet in the shape of a serpent. The chief put his arm around his shoulder. "From this day forth, this man is a brother of the Votadini and a brother to me!" The tribe roared their approval. "And now brother my chiefs and I would like you to tell us how to defeat the men you fought alongside."

The chiefs all looked eager and expectant and Scaeva knew that his words, true though they were, would disappoint them. "There are many ways to fight the Romans. You have been fighting them for many years." The chiefs punched and laughed with each other. "And you have been losing!" The joy and euphoria left their faces as he poured cold water on them. "You attack their forts. Tell me Chief Iucher, who loses more men when you attack the Romans, you or the Romans."

"We do! But my warriors die bravely."

"The Romans have more men than you can possibly imagine. This is but one part of their Empire and they are rich. Their weapons are stronger and they have armour." He could see that didn't believe his words. "Have you any of the bodies of the Romans?"

One of the bodyguards said, "Aye we have."

"Go and bring one here with his armour, his shield and his helmet."

He had aroused their curiosity and they watched as the Roman trooper, badly mutilated, was dressed and armed. "Place him against that tree." When the dead man was placed next to the tree Scaeva strapped the shield so that it covered his body. As he looked at the dead man he saw that it was Appius Nero a trooper with whom he had drunk in Eboracum. It did not bother him at all.

"You have bows?" Two men came forwards with bows. "I assume you are both good archers." They nodded proudly. "And you have killed many men?" They nodded again, "Good." He paced out fifty paces. "Now stand here and kill this Roman again."

They confidently picked out a good arrow, checked that it was true and took aim. The first arrow struck the shield and the Votadini roared. The second man aimed a little higher and the arrow pinged off the helmet to spiral into the sky. The first man looked proud of himself. "See a dead Roman again!" He and his friends thought that that was hilarious.

Scaeva walked up to the corpse and removed the shield. The arrow had penetrated the shield only. He showed it to them. "I am sorry, the Roman lives still."

He replaced the shield and told them to choose another arrow. This time he paced out twenty paces only. "Aim for the shield again!"

The two men did as they were asked and this time the tribe could see that the arrows had penetrated further. The two bowmen were not as confident this time. He took the two of them and they peered over the top of the shield. The faces of the archers fell like stones. Scaeva turned the scutum around so that the tribe could see. The arrows had penetrated the shield but had been stopped by the mail.

"And this man is a horse warrior. He has a smaller shield than the legionaries."

One of the archers asked, "Then we cannot kill them with bows?"

"Oh yes, you can kill them with bows and with slings but you need to be more accurate." He adjusted the corpse again. "This time aim for the face." They both went back the twenty paces and there was a crunch of decaying flesh and bone as one arrow penetrated the dead trooper's face. The second arrow struck the cheek guard and became embedded in the tree. There was a desultory cheer. The arrow had been so close that almost all of them could have made the shot.

"Bring me a javelin." The intrigued tribesmen brought a javelin they had retained. "You two men stand where you did for the first attempts." They did so. "Do not move, I will not hit you!" There was a gasp as he released the missile and it fell five paces short of the men. "And that is how far they can throw their weapons; more if they are on a horse."

The tribesmen all applauded the deserter. They admired skill and the soldier had shown them that he possessed great skills. Iucher clapped him on the back. "Thank you Scaeva for the demonstration but how do we defeat them?"

"You cannot beat them man for man, no matter how good a warrior you are. They are well armed and armoured. Two to one you can." He took out his dagger and pointed to his body. "Here," he pointed at his calf, "and here, the hamstring, here, under the armpit and finally," he drew the pugeo across his throat, "here. To get close you need cunning and lay ambushes and traps. When the Romans are building they cannot defend themselves and they have no shields. Loose your arrows at them and when they follow you then you set an ambush. When they bring supplies then you hide and attack the supplies. Without supplies they cannot build and, more importantly they go hungry and then they are unhappy." He pointed at Briac, "When my chief stopped their wagons the garrison at Cilurnum became unhappy and an unhappy man does not fight well. You have limited men, the Romans do not. If you die in equal numbers then they will win. You need to kill more of them than they kill of you and, as you have found out their forts are deadly." He gestured to Iucher's son. "When you escaped from the fort was it easy?"

The youth said, "No, they have traps in the pits but we could take our time and avoid them."

"No one was trying to throw a spear into him. Leave the forts and leave the walls. Defeat the Romans and they will have to leave."

Iucher nodded, "We will now talk more. I will meet with Randal and tell him of your words. Until the time is right, practise with the slings and the arrows." He pointed at the dead Roman. "There is one target and there are others, use them. I am glad that you are no longer a spy, Scaeva, for you have brought us the key to unlocking this wall."

Appius was dirty and angry by the time he rode through the gates of Eboracum. His anger had become worse on the journey south as every comment and slight was blown out of proportion until by the time he crossed the river he felt that he had been totally betrayed. The Governor had been receiving the reports from the wall and he too was now alarmed. When Appius strode into his office, his face as red and angry as when he had left the wall. Aulus Nepos wondered if the wall had been breached.

"That, Legate, is impossible and I was treated like a traitor."

"Calm down Appius and tell me what has happened. And tell me calmly," his tone grew sharper, "I do not deserve invective from you, do I?"

Realising that he could not afford to bite the hand which fed him, he apologised, "Sorry Governor." He then explained all that had happened to him. Even as he told the story he began to see that he had blown it out of proportion but the Governor became worried by the implications, if not the events.

"So the barbarians are attempting to thwart the Emperor's plans eh? There is a cohort of the Eight Augusta at Lindum. I will send for them and we can finish the wall that bit quicker. I think you and I will have to make another visit to ensure that our plans are thoroughly carried out and of course we can bring back Vibia when we return. How is she by the way?"

Appius smiled at the memory of her, "Oh she is fine and appears untroubled."

"And was she..."

"No, no," Appius shuddered at the thought, the turma rescued her within a day of her arrival and brought her back safely."

"That is one thing anyway. Rest and bathe today. I will see the decurion and we will travel with an escort of regular cavalry tomorrow."

"And I will arm myself too. I am not going to be a civilian this time."

Once the Tungrians had left the fort there was a calmer air and now that the traitor had been found there was a more harmonious atmosphere. This only developed after Livius had called the ala together to point out that one traitorous Brigante did not mean they were all to be mistrusted. Troopers like Aneurin and Scanlan had begun to stay together in cliques, afraid to mix with the others. It was a better time for all.

For Gnaeus, the absence of Appius meant he could hover around Vibia like a bee around honey and he took every opportunity to draw her out and speak with her. For Vibia's part she found the young man attractive but then the others such as Aneurin, Scanlan and Vibius also attracted her attention.

Metellus spoke to Livius about the situation. "The sooner she is gone the better. At the moment it is just harmless showing off but I would hate it to become serious."

"I agree but we cannot afford to send her back yet. When reinforcements arrive we will send a turma back for we will need more horses soon."

They had suffered more equine casualties lately and their reserve herd was dwindling. "I will send a letter to my wife then. She will need to get the new mounts broken in." Metellus noticed that the Prefect was distracted, "Was there something else sir?"

"Yes, I do not like this quiet. Once they got their hostages back I expected an onslaught but, if anything they have been quieter. It is not like the tribes."

"No, I agree. I was going to suggest a large sweep of the area north of the wall. Pairs of turma to see what the tribes are up to. We just need to keep two in reserve."

"Good idea. See to it."

That evening Aula's children met briefly to see what opportunities they had had so far. "We have not had the opportunity to visit the place by the river to find the gold. "

"And until a better opportunity presents itself the Prefect is safe. I will endeavour to ensnare him."

"I do have this!" In the open hand lay a distinctive Votadini dagger. It had been taken from the battlefield with other weapons after the ala had defeated the warbands. Many of the soldiers on the walls had such souvenirs but it gave them a chance to kill Livius and blame it on someone else.

141

"Have you managed to get close yet?"

"I am closer than I was but still too far away to affect a death. And you?"

"I tried to get close but I failed."

The pair separated; at least they were joined once more.

The legions had not wasted time while the lull in the fighting had happened. They knew that the barbarians would return and keep on returning until the wall was built and they could return south again. Centurion Lucius Massimus was in the hollow where they would be building a small fortlet. A huge cliff rose to his left and his task, or the task of his century was to lay the foundations for the wall. He was grateful for the plentiful stone which lay in large amounts. The actual quarrying had been kept to a minimum. There was even a small bay which was quite close by so that they did not have to move far for the water. All in all it was as easy a job as you got on the wall these days. He was still wary however and twenty of his soldiers stood on guard facing the moor land which rose to the north. He would trade off the work the men could do for the added security they gave. His men still had their weapons stacked in tent party groups but he insisted they wear their armour, despite the moaning and bitching when ensued.

"Listen, you moaning bastards. If those fucking barbarians come again you will be glad you have your armour on. They might be piss poor warriors but even they couldn't fail to hit you if you had no armour so stop moaning and get working."

The optio in charge of the guards smiled. Lucius was a good officer and worked as hard as the men. Unlike many centurions, he was not free with his vine staff. Something nagged at the back of his mind but he could not think what it was. He stared out again at the forest some mile and a half away. He knew that they were being watched and that worried him. He hated the idea that they could just emerge and attack at a moment's notice. He had no doubt that they would defeat them; after all, despite their overwhelming numbers more barbarians had been killed by legionaries. It had been two weeks since the last attack and that was unnerving. Suddenly he stopped staring and began to listen. Then it clicked in his mind. It was the lack of noise which was unnatural. There should have been birds in the cliffs to their right and other animals hunting in the lake but to their right was silence. Even as he stared at the cliff the fifty barbarians rose from the moors a hundred paces away. "Sir, barbarians! Two ranks." The twenty men formed two ranks and began to move towards the barbarians. He watched as they pulled back on their bows. "Shields!"

They held their shields defensively but there was no attack
suddenly, as the rest of the century tried to don helmets and scuta forty
Votadini and Selgovae rose from the water and the cliffs and began to
hurl stones from their slings at the legionaries. They were close enough
to do damage and, without shields and helmets there was a sudden
cracking as the missiles hit and broke arms, cracked heads and damaged
knees.

The optio had no choice. "Wheel right!" As the twenty men
wheeled right they exposed their backs to the archers who aimed
carefully. Their practice had paid off and two of the twenty men fell
with arrows sticking from their necks while another two had feathered
missiles embedded in their calves. By the time they had reached the
lake the slingers had disappeared and the rest of the century was armed.
As they looked north they could see the two bands disappearing back to
their homes.

"Sorry, sir!"

"Not your fault Septimus. This was well planned. Capsarius what is
the damage?"

"Three dead and eight wounded. Although none of the wounds are
serious."

Serious enough. That is three of us dead and none of them."

"So you see Legate this is a change in direction. They stayed out of
pila range and targeted the men working with slingers. We killed none
of theirs and every unit has suffered casualties. It is all along the wall."

The tribune of the Sixth who had brought the message had
witnessed one such attack and had been lucky not to have been
wounded himself. It was a savage warning to all of the commanders
along the wall. The new auxiliary Prefect was there along with Livius.
"It looks, sir, as though someone has been giving them advice!!

"Perhaps your man Scaeva?"

"Those were my thoughts, sir."

The Batavian Prefect asked, "Scaeva?"

"A deserter who knows our weapons and our tactics."

"Thank you, tribune. Tell the commanders that we will be sending
Marcus' Horse on patrol and we hope that will slow down the attacks."

The tribune shook his head, "With respect Prefect we need archers
not horsemen."

After he had left Livius said, "He is right sir."

"I know. I have sent a message to Eboracum. There is a cohort of
Syrian archers there and I think they would be of more use here."

"I agree sir but until we get them, I will arm half each turma with bows. Some are better than others but it is a start."

Julius gave a sad smile, "The days when Sergeant Macro trained them to use the bow are long gone eh Livius?"

"Sad to say, yes sir."

Chapter 16

Aneurin and Scanlan looked askance at the bows they were given. "Sir, we aren't archers."

"You are going to learn. Surely you used one when you were a boy?"

They both shook their heads. "Me neither sir?"

"You are from the south Vibius I didn't expect you to have any skill but these are Brigante and they are normally good archers." He turned to address the whole turma. "It seems our barbarian friends have learned how to aim their bows and use slingshots; they are keeping out of range of the spears and javelins we use so they will be doing the same for us. Let us give them a shock. First, we practise and learn to shoot... from the back of a horse."

He heard the collective groan and smiled. His stepbrother Macro would have had them drilled and perfect within a week. Marcus had one day before they began their patrols. Their first efforts were laughable and Marcus briefly considered letting them practise from the ground. He did not have enough time. "Just aim the bow into the air and loose on my command!"

Eventually they all managed to loose their arrows on command and they all flew, roughly the same distance. It would have to do and it would be up to Marcus to judge the best time. "Well done. Now when we come up against them you will hold two spare arrows in your left hand and loose them immediately the first has flown."

"Sir?"

"Where do we put the bow when we are not using it?"

Cassius growled, "I'll tell you precisely where I will stick it Trooper Gemellus!"

"No chosen man it is a fair question. You will all make a case which will fit behind your shield. That way the enemy will not know we have such weapons and we may achieve an element of surprise eh?" They all nodded happily having realised that it was not such a hard thing to do. Marcus wondered what they would have made of the days when he Macro and Rufius could loose arrows behind them as they retreated. "The quiver will fit on one of your saddle horns." With four such horns on the saddle the troopers had to balance the load their horses carried but Marcus knew that the quiver only weighed the same as the quiver with the javelins; they would balance. "Tomorrow we will try to surprise our Votadini friends."

As they headed out of the bridge gate Felix rode, reluctantly, on his horse now name, Drugi. He had come to love the horse although he did not enjoy riding it, Marcus had been insistent. When he scouted the signifier would tether it to his mount. Wolf, of course, ranged free and Marcus swore that he could see the hint of a grin on the beast's face. They used the hidden valley for a few miles and then Felix slid from Drugi and sprinted off after Wolf. Cassius' gruff voice murmured, "I don't know why you bother with a horse for him, sir. He is faster on foot than we are mounted!"

At the same time as Marcus and Gnaeus headed north, Sextus and Publius headed south along the Stanegate with Turmae Thirteen and Fourteen. Livius had decided that, as they had the most inexperienced troopers they should have a safer journey to their patrol point. They soon reached the site of the new Tungrian fort and headed up the road which led to the gate they were building. There was still bad feeling between the Tungrians and the troopers but the officers on both sides had been told to control their men and the journey through the construction site was merely marked by looks and gestures hidden from their officers.

As soon as they passed through what would be the northern gate of the fort Sextus halted them. He and Publius had been chosen men who had been promoted at the same time but Sextus was older. "Now lads we are going into enemy territory. The only friends we have out there are the other six turmae. Every other bugger is desperate for you jewels to be displayed around your neck. They are sneaky bastards. Don't just look in the distance, keep your eyes open for things on the ground around you. We are not going into the forest; the Sword is doing that." Marcus had earned that name by dint of wielding the mystical sword. It was also the turma to which they all aspired. "And he has the Wolf and the boy with him so we will be safe from attack in that direction." He pointed west. "Now the poor sods building near the cliff were attacked and we are going to make sure they aren't attacked again."

The two turmae headed west. The moors rolled up and down never affording the troopers the opportunity to see for more than a hundred paces or so ahead. Sextus looked to his left and the wall rising on the high land to the south. The Emperor had picked the right spot for his wall. Once it was completed, they would be able to see several miles north and patrols would be easier. Sextus knew that his troopers were good lads but they were raw; they had to learn how to become good troopers and this was not the place to learn.

The cliffs to their left rose steeply and they could see the lake which had hidden the Votadini slingers. Even though he knew that the

146

legionaries would have checked the water he led his turmae down to inspect the dark and dangerous water. If nothing else it would allow the horses a drink. He stared at the water wondering how the Votadini had hidden and then he spied, in the shallows, some reeds. He turned to four of his troopers. "Come with me and have your javelins ready." They entered the lake and began to walk around the edge. Sextus peered down into the reeds to see if he could see anything. As they approached the western end the optio on guard duty waved his arm in acknowledgement. Just as Sextus was about to wave back he saw an unnatural shape in the water. He just reacted and thrust his javelin into the Votadini slinger who lay there. As he jerked his death throes and blood erupted, the other four boys who had hidden there jumped up. The troopers behind Sextus reacted immediately, throwing their javelins into the unprotected boys. Sextus' spatha stabbed into the back of the last would be assassin.

The optio and his men raced over, weapons at the ready. Behind Sextus, he heard one of his men say, "How did he know?"

He turned, "I didn't son. I just kept my eyes open and imagined myself to be a cunning Celt. I'll say this though, they were brave boys."

It was now obvious that they were, in fact, little more than boys but it showed the three officers that the Votadini were desperate enough to throw even their children into the fray.

"Thanks, decurion."

"You are welcome. Can we leave the bodies to you lads?"

"Aye, we'll get rid of them."

Sextus led the two turmae further north but it had been a lesson well learned. He smiled as he saw his men looking about them with even more interest and attention.

Wolf and Felix found the man traps close to the entrance to the forest. Marcus dismounted to inspect them. They were shallow pits which would have pitched their riders from their horses whilst the stakes in the bottom would have lamed their mounts. "I think we will leave the forest and skirt the outside. Our job today is to deter the enemy not to risk disaster. Felix, range ahead and see if you can pick up a trail."

The two scouts disappeared and the two turmae followed keeping one eye on the edge of the forest and the other on the distant wall. They were high enough to be on a level with the wall which stood like a white scar on the green landscape. They caught a glint of light on the water of the lake as Marcus called for a halt. "Feed the horses; my turma will guard first and then yours, Gnaeus." While they ate Marcus walked along the fells to a small rock promontory. He climbed up and he saw, returning, Felix and Wolf. Further, in the distance he could see two turmae; that would be Sextus and Publius but as they were, at least, four miles ahead it was hard to tell. The promontory afforded Marcus the opportunity to see the dangers in the land. Although perfect for cavalry there were too many places where men could hide.

Felix climbed up the promontory far easier than Marcus had. "Sir, I crossed the trail of a warband. There were a hundred of them and they were heading west."

"West eh?" That means they are following the same route as Sextus. I hope he has his wits about him." He whistled for his men and the two turmae quickly mounted and galloped over bringing Marcus' horse. As he mounted he spoke to Gnaeus. "There is a warband ahead and they may be tracking Sextus."

Sextus too had decided to halt and enjoy a meal break. The wall had not reached this far yet and he decided to head for the gap known as the tree gap for the lone sapling which somehow managed to survive on the exposed ridge. He knew there was water nearby and it made sense to rest as far from danger as possible. "Publius, take charge. I need to take a dump."

Publius smiled, there was nothing worse than riding to make the bowels open. "Right. Lads, eat and feed your horses we'll be heading back soon." There was good humoured banter amongst the men for they were buoyed by their success. Five dead Votadini was a good return for them. "Titus and Livius. You two take sentry duty. A hundred paces north." The two troopers eagerly kicked their mounts forward. As recruits they were still excited by the responsibility of sentry duty and they sat peering north.

Suddenly they saw a Tungrian auxiliary racing towards the wall to the east while behind him they could see ten Votadini warriors chasing him. "Sir! Votadini and they are chasing a Tungrian."

Publius didn't waste a moment. "Mount up. We'll stick these bastards." He looked around for Sextus but his horse was still tethered to the lone tree. "Sextus, Votadini!" He kicked his horse on, "Get your javelins ready!" He peered to the east and saw that the Votadini were gradually reining in the lone auxiliary and they were so preoccupied that they had not, it appeared, seen the horsemen. "Spread out in two lines. My turma to the fore. We'll surround them."

Behind them, Sextus emerged and mounted his horse. There was something not quite right about this. What was a Tungrian doing north of the wall? He galloped after his turma. Suddenly he saw the ten barbarians turn and aim their bows at the horsemen while, at the same time, another war band rose from a hidden dell and also aimed bows at the flanks of the turmae. It was a trap. Sextus glanced ahead and had it confirmed when he could see the Tungrian no longer. He yelled, "It is a trap!" but the thunder of hooves drowned out his words.

The two flights of arrows were not the most accurate, but they did not need to be for there were more than fifty of them and many struck horses. Then there was the whirr of slingshots as stones and shot struck metal and flesh. Before Publius could react there were eight men and horses down. The Votadini continued to hurl their missiles at the horsemen who were attacked on two sides.

Sextus drew his own bow. None of the troopers had as yet done so for Publius was lying on the ground pinned by his dying horse. "Bows!" roared Sextus, loosing an arrow at maximum range to make the barbarians retreat. His arrow fell short but he saw his men take out and string their bows. It took time and his men were taking casualties all the time. The warband was becoming more confident and advancing towards the beleaguered troopers. With the wounded horses and men there were only forty troopers able to bring their bows to bear and the volley was ragged. The Votadini avoided the arrows as they descended and that emboldened them. They began to surge forward.

Sextus reached them. "I want five of you to charge that bunch over there. The rest aim and loose on my command!"

The five men charged the original ten warriors while Sextus roared, "Loose! " And forty arrows soared towards the enemy. This time they could not avoid them all and Sextus had the satisfaction of seeing barbarians fall. The enemy were so close now that all of their missiles struck home. More of the young troopers fell. Sextus had a dilemma if he withdrew he could save what was left of the two turmae but that would mean leaving the many wounded to the barbarians.

In the end, his dilemma was solved by the sudden arrival of Marcus and his two turmae. They appeared in a long line behind the barbarians. Rather than risk the bows Marcus and Gnaeus led their men to hurl their javelins into the unprotected backs of the archers and slingers. They broke and melted away in many directions. The five troopers who had been sent to disperse the original ten archers were now embroiled in hand to hand combat and Sextus led the remains of his command to their aid. By the time he had rescued his men, Marcus and Gnaeus had stabilised the situation.

"Thank the Allfather that you turned up sir! We were in the shit. A shambles!"

"Sorry, we didn't get here sooner. We picked up their trail about an hour ago. Gnaeus get the capsarii to see to the men and recapture the loose horses. Turma thirteen, sentry duty." Turning to Sextus he asked, "What happened?"

"I think they dressed one of their own in a Tungrian uniform and chased him. Publius must have thought he could rescue him." Marcus threw a quizzical look at his old chosen man, "I was having a shit!" Marcus smiled, it always happened that way. "Anyway, they were so keen to get to grips with them that they didn't see the ambush."

"Don't take it to heart, Sextus." He turned to Gnaeus. "What is the damage?"

"Ten troopers are dead sir. Another fifteen have wounds and the decurion has a broken leg. Twenty horses either dead or had to be destroyed, sir."

Sextus looked at Marcus. "Well that confirms it sir; a fucking disaster."

"Not quite Sextus. There are more than thirty dead Votadini out there and I know that some of the ones who escaped were wounded. It did not quite go their way today."

The sentry raced up to the Principia. "Sir, a column approach. It is the Governor."

"Thank you. Tell the duty centurion to call out the guard." As the auxiliary raced away the Legate turned to Julius. "We had better get the Governor's quarters sorted out Julius."

The clerk snorted. "What you mean is get your belongings out of your quarters eh sir?"

"It will make for a quieter life Julius." He strode out to the main gate and saw, to his relief, that the Governor had brought not only the cavalry detachment from the Sixth but the Hamian archers and a mixed cohort of Gauls. It looked like Nepos was at least doing something about the unrest. To his dismay, he also saw, amongst the supply wagons, the closed carriage which told him that the Governor had brought guests.

Appius Serjenus had ensured that he was wearing the most magnificent armour he could as he rode next to the decurion of cavalry. Vibia could not help but be impressed by him. He had spent the journey talking as much as he could with the decurion of cavalry. The man was, as he was a patrician and Appius felt much more comfortable discovering what it was to be a cavalryman. For his part the decurion had soon tired of the questions but, as he was the Governor's aide could do little about it. He was just pleased that they had had the extra cohorts with them. While it had slowed down their journey it had made it much safer.

"Welcome Governor Nepos. We were not expecting you back so soon and with your family I see?"

"News from the wall disturbed us," he said acidly, "and I felt I had to take personal charge again!"

Julius did not take offence at the words. He knew that Aulus Nepos was competent and that was all. He had no military experience and the only military decisions would be taken by him. His elevated title did not apply here in the military zone. "And we all look forward to your idea sir."

Flavia Nepos had insisted upon coming for she still felt a certain guilt about the girl Vibia, and Lucia was not as agreeable a companion. Her husband had been surprised at her decision but Flavia also enjoyed the attention her two companions received from the officers. She was under no illusions; it was not for her but she could bask in reflected glory. When Vibia rushed out to greet her mistress it was as though she was Flavia's daughter. This did not escape the attention of Lucia who had still to attract a husband; her sole intention.

"Did they harm you, my dear? Did those savages touch you?"

Vibia's warm smile filled her face. "No, my lady. I was rescued too quickly for that but I do not know what would have happened had I stayed there."

"Well, we shall return to Eboracum within the next few days when my husband has dealt with the problems which are here." Her tone left no one in any doubt that she thought they were an incompetent bunch and that her husband was the man to sort it out.

The Governor, his aide and the Legate were busily engrossed in the map of the wall region. The clerk came in. "Some patrols have just returned. They have been attacked."

The Legate always felt his heart sink when he heard that there were casualties. He felt each one personally. He then asked the question he dreaded having answered. "Any officers hurt?"

"One has broken his leg. Decurion Aurelius is outside. Would you like him to report to you?"

The Legate glanced at the Governor who said, "The officer who rescued my wife's companion? Yes, send him in. We might actually get a sensible answer."

Marcus felt dirty, sweaty and bloody when he entered. The three men were all smartly dressed and clean. He mentally shrugged; he was a warrior and it came with the territory. "Sir!"

151

"Glad to see you are safe." There was genuine warmth in his words. Please report, the Governor is anxious to know the state of the frontier."

Marcus took a deep breath, "Well sir. Since the deserter, Scaeva escaped the tribes have changed their tactics. They know that our javelins have a short-range and they use arrows and slings. We have been taking more casualties. In addition, they have begun to use ambushes," he looked at Julius Demetrius, "today, for example, they dressed a man in Tungrian uniform and had their men chase him. When Publius tried to rescue him he was ambushed. The bows we had managed to deter them."

"We have brought a cohort of Hamian archers with us." Appius sounded as though it was his idea.

"How many?"

"A cohort."

"A whole five hundred then? That works out at five for every mile of the frontier."

"Legate! It is more than you had and we have brought a mixed cohort of Gauls with us so we have increased the cavalry element here. I will leave the legionary cavalry here when I return south and you can detach a turma for my escort so, as you can see I am doing my part."

"Thank you, Governor."

"Now, has work started on the new forts I asked for?"

"Yes, the Tungrians are building one now but it slows down the completion of the wall."

"Yes well, I am going to upset the programme even more for I want a new fort building here." He stuck a pudgy finger at a place some fifteen miles from Vercovicium and ten miles north of the wall. "I have sent for a cohort of Dacians who are, at present on the south coast. They will be here within a month. I want the Sixth and Twentieth to build a fort here. "

Marcus and Julius looked at each other. It was a very exposed site that had been chosen. Julius could see its strategic nature. It controlled the valley which led northwards but it would be under constant attack. "A little dangerous isn't it sir?"

The Governor shrugged. "I have learned that this whole frontier is dangerous but I have also observed that, since the Selgovae attacked the marching camp and suffered heavy losses they have ceased attacking the forts. If we build a fort here and put a large garrison in it with some artillery then we can control their movements down the valley and I intend to build many more of these forts."

The Legate coughed, "Does the Emperor know about this Quintus? It will increase the cost dramatically."

Nepos waved the comment away as though it was irrelevant. "Once the frontier is secure we can begin to reap the harvest from this land. My aide has already identified copper mines to the west. That will pay for any extra forts we may have."

Chapter 17

The Legate held a feast for the Governor and his senior officers. He smiled to himself as he watched the disappointment on the faces of Flavia and Lucia as the older men walked in. The young bloods were not there. Vibia seemed quite happy to be there and she took a seat next to Livius. As soon as she did so then Lucia sat on the other side of the Prefect. Julius had to suppress a smile as he watched the horror on the face of his friend. He was trapped between two young women intent upon getting close to him. Appius, too, was annoyed that Vibia had so obviously shunned him. The Prefect was in the way.

The other officers enjoyed the two women vying for Livius' attention. They both fed him titbits and poured his wine. Livius was becoming embarrassed by the whole thing. "Thank you, ladies, but I have been feeding myself for many years and I can pour my own drinks. I am on duty in the morning and I need to take it steady."

"Just one more beaker," cooed Lucia.

"And then I will have to go."

Flavia's voice cut across the table, "A little rude Prefect, to leave us alone here."

"Hardly alone my lady but I have men in the sickbay who were wounded today and I need to see to them." He took a sip of wine. "There I have had the wine and I will return."

He almost ran from the room. By the time the cool air hit him, he felt a shiver. He decided he was becoming soft; after all these years in the north, you would have thought he would have become hardier. The stomach cramps hit him when he was approaching the sickbay and, by the time he had entered he was doubled up in pain. Marcus and Sextus were visiting Publius and they saw the pain on his face. "Doctor!"

The Greek doctor ran up to him. He opened the Prefect's mouth and smelled. "Poison. This man has been poisoned!"

Marcus looked at Sextus, "Again!"

Livius was unconscious but the Greek doctor took a small amphora and poured it down the Prefect's throat. "Luckily the smell told me what the poison was; it is a variant on the mandrake root. This is the antidote."

"Will he live?"

The Greek doctor looked at the decurion in surprise, "Of course. I am not a quack you know."

"In that case, I want him in a room on his own. Get your capsarii to take him but I want everyone to think he is dead."

Even Sextus looked surprised. "Dead, but why?"

"This is the second attempt and there is no Scaeva now. Perhaps we assumed the attack in Eboracum was Scaeva when in fact it was someone closer. This way we can keep him safe." He held his hand up. "Not a word. I will tell the Legate." They all nodded and the unconscious Prefect was spirited away. When they returned Marcus said to Sextus, "I want one of the Votadini prisoners who died brought here. He can be burned as the Prefect. Put him in a shroud doctor." The doctor sniffed as though this was beneath him. Marcus flourished a gold aureus under his nose and he smiled and nodded.

Marcus hovered close to the dining room and waited for the Legate. As he had expected, as the host, he was the last one to leave. "Could I have a word, sir?"

Julius had known Marcus since he had been born and saw, immediately, that there was something amiss. "Come to my office."

The Principia had a guard at all times as the valuables for the ala as well as the standards of the ala and cohort were kept there. It was as secure a place as one could get in a busy fort. "Sir, the Prefect has been poisoned." He held his hand up as he saw the questions rising to the Legate's lips. "He lives and he will be fine but I have hidden him in his quarters." He took a breath. "I want everyone to say that he is dead."

There was a pause. Julius smiled, "First of all I thank all the gods that he is alive but I am intrigued as to your deception."

"This is the second attempt on the Prefect's life. The first one we put down to the traitor Scaeva. This one cannot possibly be him and, unless you tell me differently, I would say that no one else was poisoned."

Julius put his hands together reflectively, as though at prayer. "True and it means that the murderer or would be murderer was in the dining room for the servants merely brought the food in and we served ourselves. Yes, you could be right Marcus but can we keep it secret?"

"I have had one of the barbarian's bodies wrapped in a shroud. We will burn him tomorrow and, hopefully, the assassin will think he or she has succeeded."

"She? It could be a woman?"

There were five people in Eboracum when the Prefect was given the poison, not counting the officers. They are all here and three of them are women."

"But you cannot suspect the Governor and his wife!"

"I can suspect anyone until I know differently. Remember sir, the background to the Prefect. His uncle was one of the last descendants of old Cunobelinus and he was a former Governor. As I recall from my father, Livius' uncle was executed for treason." Julius nodded. "Now all we need to do is work out who did it. I was not there sir. The Prefect left. What happened immediately before he did?"

"Let me see. I know that the two girls Lucia and Vibia were being very attentive. Pouring him wine and feeding him titbits..." He paused, dumbfounded, "It had to be one of those for other than them, it was the Prefect who fed and served himself."

"And Vibia has been here for some time while Lucia has only just arrived, as has Appius. They could be in this together."

"That is stretching it a little. I can believe that one of the two companions poisoned Livius although for the life of me I cannot see why but we cannot accuse them without evidence. We will have to wait until the Prefect recovers consciousness. Did the doctor know when that would be?"

"No sir. Sextus and I can watch tonight but we need someone we can trust to watch him tomorrow."

"Julius Longinus. He will watch him."

When the death of the Prefect was announced the next day, Julius Demetrius watched the faces of all those whom he and Marcus suspected of the crime. If they expected a guilty reaction they were disappointed; all of them expressed shock. The Legate had said that he died suddenly in his sleep and had been discovered in his bed. Apart from Marcus and Sextus none of the ala had any idea of the truth. Marcus took Metellus and Rufius to one side to explain to them the events of the previous night but the rest of the ala showed genuine remorse and distress that their charismatic leader had died suddenly. To the troopers, it seemed harsh that a warrior should die without violence but the ways of the gods and Nemesis were hard to fathom.

The funeral took place close to the Stanegate and the barbarian's body was burnt and the ashes placed in an urn. Surprisingly, as soon as the body was burnt the Governor became all business-like again and callously discussed the command of the ala. "Well, we shall need a new Prefect. Of course, temporarily, the Decurion Princeps can run matters but we will need someone who is a patrician." He smiled at Appius. "Perhaps you might..."

"I think it is a little soon to be discussing a replacement and, with all due respect young man, I would prefer someone who was an experienced soldier." At the back of the Legate's mind was that these two were behaving suspiciously and would bear watching as well as the girls. Perhaps there was a conspiracy as Marcus had suggested. They would have to wait until the Prefect came to in order to find out the truth.

Briac, Randal and Iucher met far to the north. They had travelled beyond the Roman horse patrols in order to guarantee secrecy. Scaeva was with them and was honoured in equal measure by the Selgovae.

"Welcome brother Scaeva. Your ideas have proved successful and, apart from one incident, the Romans have suffered more losses than we. Whenever you have something to tell us, pray interrupt."

Scaeva was a dour man and he merely nodded. Iucher stood. "The building of the wall has slowed down but it still continues and more Romans, as predicted by Scaeva, are arriving each day. Soon they will outnumber us." There was much nodding at this. In reality, they were waiting for Scaeva to come up with an idea but he was biding his time. "Briac, can the Brigante attack wagons again?"

Before he could answer Scaeva said, "They are now sending the supplies by sea and landing them on the south side of the Tinea; they have built a road to the Stanegate."

"Then Roman, tell us how we hurt them again and slow down the building of the wall. If we can achieve a victory then the other clans will join us and we will have sufficient numbers for victory."

"The Stanegate is their main road and it runs south of the wall. They have to use that to supply their forts and move men along it. They think they are safe as any attackers would have to retreat back over the wall." He gave a sly smile. "If Chief Briac were to bring Brigante north then your tribes could raid the road and when they attacked you we could lead them into a trap."

Randal too saw the solution and smiled, "So we flee the way they do not expect us to and ambush them with forces they do not know we have."

"How do we get such a large number of men across the wall?"

"That is easy, Chief Iucher and the Selgovae have already done so. The wall to the west is made of turf and it is weakly defended. Kill the guards there and slip across. The Votadini can cross near the lake for the forts are not built. The two warbands need to be close enough to each other to support and to attack simultaneously. The Romans watch the wall not the land to the south."

The chiefs all began talking at once. "Well done Scaeva that is a good plan. I will leave as soon as the meeting has finished and bring our warriors. We will make the Romans suffer this time." Scaeva looked distracted. "What concerns you Scaeva, you should be elated with what you have achieved."

"I could have returned the Sword of Cartimandua to our people. I had many chances to take it but I always planned to capture it before I left."

"Do not worry. We will get it and you can pry it from the decurion's cold, dead hand!"

It fell to Marcus to escort the engineers who were to survey the site for the new fort. It was further west than Marcus had been for some time but, with Felix as his scout, he was sure that they would avoid an ambush. Wolf and Felix had proved a doughty combination; neither might be responsible for killing many barbarians but their mere presence saved the lives of troopers. Also, with the engineers was Appius Serjenus who was keen to prove his credentials as a warrior. Marcus was determined to discover if the arrogant Roman was a murderer as well as a pompous self-opinionated bore!

The engineers, from the Second Augusta, rode uneasily on their horses. They had wanted to march but Marcus knew the Selgovae were fleet of foot and the recent ambushes meant that he wanted to be able to escape faster than they arrive. They had left before dawn travelling to the north of the wall. Felix led them through shallow valleys and woods which kept them from the skyline. Their task was not to find the enemy but to avoid them. When they reached the site, Marcus could see that someone had done their research. There were two streams which joined providing protection for two sides of the fort. The only problem which Marcus' unpractised eye could see was that the fort would not be a regularly sized Roman fort however that was the engineers' problem. He rode over to Appius. Are you staying here or coming with us?"

Appius bridled at the lack of a 'sir'. Even though he was a civilian he felt his association with the Governor merited one. When he took command of the ala he would punish this arrogant decurion who appeared to be little older than he. "Yes decurion, I would learn all that I can of serving with an auxiliary turma."

"Optio we will form a screen. Let us know if you need us."

"Don't worry decurion you will hear the hooves of our horses heading south if any of the barbarians show up."

"Felix, take Wolf and sweep north. Turma skirmish order; Cassius take the right flank, I'll take the left." Almost instantly the turma took their allotted places and Appius was curious to see them notch bows.

"I thought your ala used javelins."

He saw Appius watching Titus string his bow, "We do but, as the barbarians have learned to keep their distance, we need to use bows to keep up with them."

"Why can't you just chase them down?"

Marcus sighed, he had no time to be a schoolmaster but Metellus had told him to behave so… "You see the ground is rocky and uneven. It is not like the fells close to Stanwyck; there are not long open stretches to open the horse's legs. Here we can ride swiftly in short bursts and all that time they can hit the horses. They have begun to do that since Scaeva deserted. They can stand off and loose many arrows and stones at us. Having the bows means that we can hit them for that is our advantage. Unless they hit the horses we are safe but they have no protection."

Appius seemed almost interested and forgot his loathing of the decurion. "I had thought that the cavalry would be more glorious than the infantry; the charges, the fine swords." He looked down at Marcus'. "That is a fine sword and it seems a little too good for a decurion."

Marcus could have taken offence but he knew that the aide had been brought up with these views and it was not his fault. "I had this when I was but a trooper. It is the hereditary sword of the Brigante. It was wielded in the past by the kings and queens of my mother's tribe."

Appius looked surprised. "You are half Brigante?"

"Yes my mother is one of the last relatives of the royal family and I inherited it from my father who also served in the ala." He saw Appius nod reflectively and take it in. He glanced over and saw that one of the recruits was not keeping the line. "Lucius, keep up. You are letting your horse determine your pace." He looked back at Appius. "If you don't mind me saying I am surprised that you would wish to serve with this ala. I assume that you are a patrician and could serve with a legion if you wished."

Appius chewed his lip. He could not tell the decurion but he wanted swift promotion and glory which would give him early power. His father had told him that he had gained all his power after he had served under Agricola and defeated the northern tribes. When he had returned to Rome he had been lauded as a hero. "I had heard that Marcus' Horse has the best reputation in Britannia and the best chance of glory."

Marcus shook his head and held his hand up for the turma to rest. "Feed your horses." He turned to Appius. "Glory is a fleeting thing and only comes when many brave men die."

"But you rescued Vibia. That was glorious!"

"No that was cunning. We lied to the barbarians and we murdered them while they slept. That is not glorious. We laid traps for them. That is not glorious."

"But they were barbarians. It matters not if you lie to them." Even as he said the words Appius was beginning to see the truth. Marcus merely raised his eyebrows. "I will have to think about your words decurion. Thank you for being honest."

As they headed back to the engineers Marcus felt that Appius had changed slightly and, in some strange way, Marcus liked him a little more than he had.

When they reached the survey site the engineers had not finished and Marcus allowed his troopers to eat. "Why did the horses get fed before your men?"

"Horses are wonderfully loyal creatures and they will run all day if asked and then drop dead. A horseman without a horse is helpless. We all look after our horses much as we do our swords and our armour. They are part of us. Remember that should you ever become a horseman."

Appius, too, had been affected by their conversation but in his case it had persuaded him not to take the military route. He would, instead, use the commercial route to get power. He would use the copper mines in the west to gain money and, therefore, power.

Back at the fort, Livius had finally woken. Julius sent a medical orderly for the Legate as soon as he became conscious. It took much water to moisten the Prefect's lips sufficiently to enable conversation. As the cool water hit his stomach he was wracked by cramps. The Greek doctor, who had also been summoned, nodded his approval. "Good, that is a good sign. You will be on a liquid diet for a few days until your system is purged." He held the Prefect's head and poured a white aromatic liquid down his throat. "This will continue the healing."

The doctor left as the Legate arrived. He shook his head as Julius rose to leave. "Stay. I need another pair of ears for this. Do you know what happened to you Livius?"

"I must have been poisoned." His eyes widened in alarm. "Is everyone else…"

"No, it was just you and it was a quick-acting poison so it had to have been at the table. The doctor thinks it was the wine you drank so, the question is, who served you the wine?"

Marcus lay back with his eyes closed. "Lucia and Vibia were both being over-attentive. They were feeding me tidbits." Suddenly he contorted with pain and turned his head to vomit into a bowl by his bed.

"Get the doctor, Julius."

Julius left the sickbay and saw the doctor close by the barracks. "Doctor, the Prefect… er the patient needs…"

As the two men ran off someone saw them. A trooper strolled casually towards the Governor's quarters and began to whistle a tune. A few moments later Vibia emerged. They walked towards the stable smiling at each other as though engaged in some trivial conversation. "The Prefect lives."

"Then it will not take him long to discover that I was the one who poisoned his wine."

"You must leave."

"Yes but first I have something to do. Prepare me a horse and I will need some auxiliary armour. I will meet you in the stables soon."

When the doctor reached Livius he smiled as he examined the vomit filled bowl. "Excellent! Just as I had hoped. We have the last of the poison. See the red-tinged parts."

Julius Demetrius wrinkled his nose. "You doctors may enjoy sifting through vomit but as for me. You could have told us this might happen."

The Greek look surprised. "Do I ask you why you send men here there and everywhere to come back maimed? No! Then let me do my job. Plenty of water and he will recover. He will be weak for a few days but he will recover."

The two men were left exasperated as the doctor calmly left them. They poured water down his throat and he opened his eyes to give them a weak smile. "The last time I was as ill as that we had just wet Marcus' head!"

"Take your time Livius. You were about to tell us who gave you the wine."

"Oh yes." He closed his eyes, picturing the evening before. "It was Lucia, she handed me the wine."

"Lucia, I have just heard the Prefect lives!"

"But Vibia, we were told that he had died."

"Apparently they were wrong. Come let us drink a libation to celebrate."

"It is a little early is it not?"

Vibia leaned in, her green eyes sparkling maliciously, "I was told that the first word he spoke was, 'Lucia'."

The young companion's eyes lit up. "Oh Vibia! That is wonderful news. "She took the beaker and drank it off the joy in her eyes glinting for their last moments of life. Suddenly she did as Livius had done. Her body doubled in pain and she writhed on the floor, a white and green phlegm vomiting from her corrupted stomach. Her eyes pleaded for an answer but Vibia was already scrawling a note which she placed in the dead hand of the glassy eyed Lucia.

She met her brother at the stables. She told him quickly what had occurred. "I have laid a false trail. They will think it was Lucia."

"Then why cannot you stay?"

"You know as well as I brother, that the Prefect is a clever man. He will soon deduce that it was me. I have bought some time for myself. I will stay in Eboracum again. You will find me in the vicus. "She sadly stroked her red hair as she pushed it beneath the helmet. "I will cut my hair and change the colour. They will not know me." They embraced and she mounted the horse. "How do I look?"

"Like one of the recruits. The pass today is, *'pugeo'*."

"Thank you and take care. Do not let the barbarians kill you."

Vibia rode confidently towards the southern gate down the Via Praetoria. The sentry at the gate held up his hand. "Message for Morbium."

"And?"

"Sorry?"

"The password? Some of you troopers are dumber than your fucking horses."

"Sorry. Pugeo!"

"That's better. Have a safe journey."

With a wave of her hand, Vibia daughter of Aula rode from the frontier running from danger to even more danger but, she was free and she was alive. Her mother's plans could still come to fruition.

Chapter 18

Leaving Livius in the care of Julius the Legate sought Metellus and Rufius. He told them of his discovery. "Go to the Governor's quarters and stop any from leaving. I will, perforce, need to speak with the Governor first and apprise him of the problem."

"Are you sure it was that Lucia? She seemed like an empty headed little girl to me."

"Livius knows that she handed him the wine and he is busy trying to remember the other details. But we knew it was one or the other and we can now confront them. The Governor will have to sanction interrogation."

Metellus shuddered. The interrogators used any and all methods to get at the truth. "We will order the fort closed up too. Rufius, see to it."

The Governor and his wife were in the small dining room which they used for their lunch. Julius knew that this would be a difficult meeting. He had deliberately lied to him. They had watched the flames rising the previous day and said goodbye to the Prefect and now he would have to tell him that he lived still. He took a deep breath. "Governor Nepos, I had some good news and some grave news to impart."

Flavia stood, "I will leave you two then."

"No domina, it concerns you as well." She sat with a puzzled look upon her face. "The Prefect, Livius, whom you thought dead, lives. He was poisoned."

"But the funeral…"

"A deception to protect the Prefect. We now believe that the poisoning attempt in Eboracum was made by the same person who tried to kill him at the dinner. We needed him to recover enough to tell us who poisoned him."

Flavia put her hand to her mouth, "But we were at that dinner! We too could have…"

Julius held up a hand. "The doctor and Livius believe he was given poisoned wine."

"But we all drank the same wine!"

"Yes, Governor which is how we know who it was. The poison was put into his beaker only. He said that Lucia, your companion, handed him the beaker but it could have been either or both of them who put the poison in the wine."

"Impossible!" Flavia stood up, red-faced and angry. "We will see the girls and get to the bottom of this immediately!"

"This is just what I had in mind. Shall we all go?" Julius would leave the thorny matter of the interrogators until later.

Lady Flavia tapped on the door of the girls' quarters. "Lucia, Vibia? May we come in?"

There was no reply and, when the Governor gave a subtle nod Julius opened the door. There lay Lucia with the note in her hand, her body already contorted and stiff. Flavia fainted and Julius caught her. "Metellus send for the doctor." Aulus Nepos threw a look at Julius who shrugged. "I wanted no-one fleeing."

By the time Flavia came to the note had been read. "Well, this seems quite clear. Apparently, she wanted Livius so much that she poisoned him to stop anyone else having him."

The doctor looked up, a sceptical look on his face. "Excuse me Legate but I had some cause to treat the young lady." He pulled a face. "She always seemed to have minor disorders whenever she came here. It strikes me that she had neither the wit nor the means to acquire this poison. She was a pleasant girl but I have sat on seats with more brains and guile. Now the other one, she could have done it for she was intelligent and knowledgeable. When she was returned from the Votadini I found her to be made of sterner stuff than many troopers." He shrugged, "Of course that is just the opinion of an old doctor."

Metellus and Rufius both nodded. "I have to say, sir, that we agree."

"Let us not jump to conclusions. Search the fort and find her. I am a little concerned that she is not here. Where is she?"

When she could not be found there was a worry that she too might be found dead and then Rufius took it upon himself to question the sentries at the gates. It was almost dusk when he returned. Flavia had gone to her bed, drugged by the doctor. Quintus and Julius were at a loss to explain it all. Rufius strode into the office and his dark face told the story. "It seems our Vibia rode out of the main gate this morning dressed as a trooper. She had the password and she rode south."

"So she has escaped but that still begs the question why did she try to kill the Prefect? She did not appear to be Brigante. Was she paid? Is there some plot here of which we know little?"

Quintus shook his head. "These things are heard of in far off Rome but I had not expected them here in my own home, on the frontier." He glanced up at the Legate. "It is obvious that we cannot remain here, besides which you now know my plans and I am happy that you will see them through to their conclusion. I require two turmae from you as an escort with one of your two senior decurions in command. They can search for Vibia when we are safely ensconced in Eboracum."

Although Julius could ill do without Rufius it was a small price to pay to get the fort and the frontier back to normality. "Very well. I will tell Rufius he is to escort you."

Rufius was less than pleased with the news. "Sir, we will be escorting a closed carriage and my place is here on the frontier. Without the Prefect we are shorthanded as it is."

"Which is why you will take the Prefect's turma and you can train up the chosen man on the way to Eboracum. It is time the Prefect stuck to administration for a while."

"Very well we will leave in the morning." He threw a dark look in the direction of the Governor's quarters. "Early!!"

Appius was extremely tired as the turma returned, after dark, to the fort. The sentries were particularly vigilant which irritated the aide but intrigued the decurion. "What on earth is the matter with you? I am the Governor's aide and you have all seen me enough to recognise me."

"Take it easy, Appius. I would rather they were this keen and we were safe wouldn't you?"

The aide gave a grudging nod. He was desperate for the bath house and a good meal. He had to admit he had seen a whole new side to the military in his day beyond the frontier. He had emptied his bowels on at least three occasions. Marcus had smiled and told him that was normal on the first patrol where you saw a blue painted face behind every rock. As they dismounted the aide put out his arm, "Thank you decurion. I have much to think on."

Marcus shook his head as the Roman abandoned his horse. The decurion led the two mounts to the stalls. "Never mind boy, he did appreciate the ride you gave him although he did not show it."

Marcus was surprised to see Rufius and the two turmae already there, making the stables quite crowded. "How was it today Marcus? Did you manage to avoid punching the young patrician?"

"He's not so bad when you give him a chance and get by the arrogance but what is going on?" Rufius took him to one side and gave him an account of the day's events. "Vibia?" he shook his head. "Mind you I should have suspected something when we rescued her. She had more resilience than I would have expected. Do you think she was in league with the Votadini and Brigante?"

"After this day nothing would surprise me but I do not think so. The tribes would have behaved differently once we had rescued her otherwise. And remember we only discovered Scaeva because of her."

"I suppose you are right. So you ride tomorrow?"

"Yes I don't expect to be back for a week which makes you second in command until Livius is up and about again. Metellus will need all the help he can get."

If Marcus was surprised then Appius Serjenus was devastated. The shock of the poisoning of the Prefect and the death of Lucia was nothing compared with the knowledge that he had been courting a murderer! He had had a lucky escape and the journey back to Eboracum seemed to him to be a sign from the gods that his future lay in what passed for civilisation.

Flavia was still heavily drugged as the two turmae and the carriage set off south. Aulus Nepos was pleased that, the death apart, he had ensured that his plans and his grand vision for the frontier would go through. Walking back to the principia the Legate and Metellus were discussing just what they would actually do now that the Governor had departed.

"First of all, Metellus I think that it is impractical to build a stone fort where he wants to. I want the thing up quickly so that your troopers can get back to protecting the frontier. We shall build in turf and wood. That way we can let the Dacians build it themselves while you watch them. For the rest we will finish the wall and the existing forts first and then we will make them look pretty and think about building the extra ones."

"I hear he want forts in the heart of the Selgovae and Votadini land?"

"He does."

"That is a recipe for disaster. I thought the Emperor wanted a wall which marked the end of Roman domination."

"Yes, Metellus and so did I." He rubbed his hands. "Now that he has gone let us concentrate on getting supplies up the Stanegate. I want a big push. Get your ala, all of them, north of the wall, especially near the site of the new Dacian fort and chase the barbarians from morning until night. Your turmae can bunk with the legions. I can't see them objecting." Metellus pulled a face. "And if they do it matters not; that is an order."

Marcus led Gnaeus out again the next day, with Sextus as the third turma. As he had surveyed the site Metellus felt he was better prepared, and as he said quietly, better experienced than the other officers. "Stay with the Sixth. It shouldn't be a problem. They think highly of you."

"I'll sweeten it with some venison or wild pig. Felix appears to be missing his hunting."

"Wild pig?"

"I might have to help him with that."

166

They rode down the Stanegate to make better time although soon the military road which was being built closer to the wall would shorten the journey still further. "When we get there I will take half the turmae to the northern forest. That will be you, Gnaeus with me. Sextus take the other half and patrol the area to the west of the site. When we are sure the forest is clear of scouts Felix and I will engage in a little hunting."

Sextus sniffed, "The privileges of ranks, sir!"

Marcus gave him an innocent look. "And you Sextus could you guarantee game?"

The whole ala knew that Marcus was a skilled huntsman. "No sir. Enjoy yourself!"

There were many valleys in the forest and dells where the game liked to gather. Once Marcus had checked that the main trails were free from Votadini he and his two scouts dismounted and, taking two javelins with him, they descended the side of one of the shallow valleys. They were both experienced enough to move downwind of any game; Wolf just disappeared into the undergrowth. He returned and lay down next to Felix. Felix mimed, 'deer' and Marcus nodded. Felix strung his bow and Marcus stood to one side. This one would be Felix's kill and Marcus would pick up any secondary game which the dog flushed. Felix sent the dog away and they waited in the undergrowth. They would only have a tiny opportunity to make a kill but they were both confident hunters.

They heard the noise of something coming towards them through the undergrowth and they both tensed. When Felix wrinkled his nose, he realised that the boy was sniffing to smell the prey. Suddenly he loosed a shaft and quickly loaded a second. A huge stag, the feathers still visible in its neck, lurched drunkenly towards them and Marcus thrust his javelin into its chest ending its final fight. The second arrow flew over the stag and the hind fell to her death.

"Well done Felix, two fine hits."

"You were quick decurion. Drugi said that you were a good hunter; he was right."

As they hoisted the doe on the javelin to carry her up the slope Marcus felt a certain pride that Drugi thought he was a good hunter. He had never been told that by the former slave but the compliment was all the greater for its source. Gnaeus beamed when he saw the deer. "Take four men, there is a stag at the bottom."

Felix waved Wolf away. "The dog will take you. Follow him."

They reached Sextus without incident. "There are signs that the tribes have been watching the wall but the numbers were too small to worry about."

"Well, that is good news. Let us see our friends in the Sixth and find out if we can use their camp for the night."

All three officers knew that fresh meat would gain them entry to any camp along the wall. Marcus also knew that they would have been welcome for who they were. Marcus' Horse had a reputation for being solid fighters who would stand their ground as well as the legions and Marcus himself, had the reputation of being a temporary standard-bearer for the eagle of the Ninth in the last days of that legion. The legions did not forget gestures like that.

After they had eaten Marcus produced a jug of wine he had taken from the fort. As they enjoyed a meagre beaker each he asked about the wall and its progress.

"It is going better now and that worries me. The barbarians are best when they are doing something. You know then what they are up to. I like not this inactivity. It reeks to me of planning and cunning. Still, as long as the supplies keep coming we are happy. I hear we will have new neighbours soon?"

"Aye, a thousand-strong cohort of Dacians will be north of the wall."

"They might be hard men but I do not envy them that task. I would not like to be beyond the wall surrounded by those bollock collectors!"

"We will ride close to their settlements tomorrow and see what they are up to. I will send you a message with my report."

"That is good of you but is that not dangerous?"

"I was an Explorate and that was my life for some years besides I have the two best scouts with me." He pointed to the boy and the dog both of whom were sleeping.

"He is just a boy."

"A boy who survived a barbarian massacre and a boy who is far tougher than you can imagine. He was one of those I took with me into the barbarian encampment. I will back him."

The centurion put his hands out. "Don't get me wrong, I am just saying that appearances can be deceptive."

The troopers were also happy, having eaten well and being protected by the well made camp of the vexillation, but Vibius had been quiet. "What is the matter Vibius you look like you have lost an aureus and found a denari?"

"It is Lucia, Aneurin, I think our Vibius was sweet on her."

Suddenly Vibius turned around and snapped. "Shut up you stupid barbarian. You know nothing about me."

Scanlan put a muscular arm and hand on Vibius' shoulder. "Watch who you are calling a barbarian Vibius. Some people might take offence. I would hate to have to teach you a lesson."

"And you, barbarian, can fuck off as well!"

Scanlan smiled and twisted Vibius' arm so that he was underneath the Brigante who pulled out his pugeo and pricked the neck of the older trooper. "Now I did warn you Vibius."

"What's going on here?"

Scanlan rolled off, "Nothing Chosen Man. I was just teaching Vibius here a few moves which might come in handy."

"Is that right trooper?"

"Er yes, chosen man. Thank you Scanlan." There was a smile on his face but it was belied by the hatred in his eyes.

"Well get some rest. We will be on patrol all day tomorrow too."

As Cassius moved off Aneurin and Scanlan tried to make light of the incident but Vibius was having none of it. "Just leave me alone eh? You made your point; you are both better at street fighting than me. I get it."

Aneurin was shocked. "What is up with him? I thought we were mates."

"Maybe you were right and maybe he was sweet on that girl who got killed. He'll be better in the morning."

Cassius rode next to Marcus the next day as they headed for the settlements along the valleys. As Chosen Man he was the link between the officers and the men. He explained what had occurred. "Are you worried Cassius?"

"No sir. But there just seems something funny. I like Aneurin and Scanlan; they are good lads and, well what you see is them but that Vibius, I thought he was the same but he isn't, he is, well deeper."

Marcus understood Cassius. Macro, his step brother had also been deep with many layers and career soldiers found them difficult to fathom. Perhaps Vibius was like Macro and would show qualities as yet hidden. He was certainly brave, as he had shown when winning his phalera for his rescue, but perhaps there was more and the death of Lucia had affected him. "Just keep your eye on them Cassius. We can't afford to train up recruits and then lose them because they fall out. We have to make a fighting unit here."

"Don't worry sir. I'll sort 'em!"

Not all of the Selgovae and Votadini settlements were belligerent. None of them liked Rome, that was true, but many just wanted to get on

169

with herding their animals and existing. Marcus knew that many of the villages close to the new fort were peaceful in nature. He halted the turmae a mile from the first one and, taking Gnaeus and Felix with him, he rode towards the first one. It was a handful of huts by the river. The river provided food even in winter and they were prosperous. As the two of them rode in with Felix and Wolf ahead Marcus was looking for signs which would tell him the mood of the people.

Dogs in the village began barking when Wolf appeared. His ears went down and he growled a deep growl which sent them packing. Felix whistled for him to return and he did so. The looks the three of them received were not welcoming but there was no sign of aggression either.

Marcus dismounted when the headman approached. Marcus bowed his head to show respect. He held a bag of salt in his hand. "Greetings, headman. Please take this gift from Rome as a sign of our friendship." The old man kept his hands by his side. "There is nought tied to this gift." He placed it by the side of the hut. "It is here as a present." The old man gave a slight nod of acceptance and the bag was whisked away by an old woman. "How is the fishing?"

"It is good."

"And the hunting?"

"Not so good."

"Ah, we had a good hunt and the next time I visit I will bring some venison for you."

"Why are you here Roman?"

"I am here because Rome wants nothing from you, just your friendship." He took out the sword. "I swear this by the sword."

Every man on the frontier knew the sword and had heard its many stories. "I believe you Roman for you would not swear otherwise but tell me this, if you only wish friendship then why do you build the wall and why the forts?"

"You know, old man. Your young men raid our lands and the wall is to make sure they do not." He glanced around. "I can see that there are no young men here."

"They tend the cattle and the sheep."

His eyes betrayed the lie but Marcus nodded. "I am sorry to have missed them. Should your people need anything then send to the fort and ask for the sword to come forth and I will return."

"Alone?"

"If you wish it."

"Then may the Allfather watch over you."

Chapter 19

"And so sir it was the same story in every village we visited. There were no young men, just the old and the lame. We received the same excuse from all of them, the young men were with the herds."

"But you don't believe them?"

"No sir. We saw young girls and boys tending the animals. They are planning something."

"Well done, Marcus. The problem is what are they planning?" He rubbed his chin.

Livius was seated in the corner of the office, although still not fully recovered he was keen to rejoin the planning and the strategy meetings. "But you saw no sign of large numbers of men?"

"No sir and we scouted the forests. Felix even went close to the camp we raided but it was deserted. It is as though they have disappeared."

Livius turned to the Legate. "I think we need prisoners again."

"I agree."

"I will send Metellus along with Marcus on this next patrol with four turmae. The rest I will send to patrol the Stanegate."

Julius was curious. He never doubted Livius' strategies but this one seemed unusual. "Any particular reason Livius?"

"If there is trouble then we can reach that trouble far quicker from the Stanegate than north of the wall. In addition we will need to escort the Hamians and the Dacians when they arrive and, with their wagons, the Stanegate is the best option."

"Good. Although I had planned on keeping the new cohorts here and at Vercovicium until we have a better idea of what they are up to."

Metellus was glad to be away from the fort. He, like Rufius and Marcus, still missed the free days of being an Explorate. This was the next best thing. As they rode across the river Metellus headed north east. Marcus knew the decurion princeps too well to ask why they were riding in that direction but he was curious. After a few miles Metellus laughed. "You have grown up young Marcus. There would have been a time when you would have plagued me with questions about the direction of this patrol."

"Perhaps my time as a slave mellowed me sir."

"It probably did. Anyway you said the camp in the forest was empty and the nearest place I could think of was the east of the old road. It has access to plenty of game and fish and they know that, as that area is quiet, it does not require as many patrols."

Marcus laughed, "So it is a guess then sir?"

"Aye, a guess backed up by the noses of those two scouts of yours. Word is they can find a barbarian who is a couple of miles away."

"A slight exaggeration but about right sir."

"Good, then we will send them off when we reach the old fort."

Marcus wrinkled his brow. "We have used that many times sir. Do you not think they will become suspicious?"

"No Marcus, it is easily defended and we can escape easily too. We will use that and leave Sextus, Gnaeus and one turma there while we explore a little closer to the enemy. When, of course, they have found them."

When they left the old fort, the recruits from Marcus' turma were unhappy to be left behind. Marcus and Metellus chose the thirty troopers whom they thought they could depend upon. Everyone was an experienced trooper and both chosen men were taken. Vibius, in particular seemed put out and, as the elite turma left he rode over to Sextus, who had been left in charge. "Sir, why wasn't I chosen?"

Sextus was not the man to use flowery words or dress up bad news. He took a chew on some dried meat and said, "Cause, compared with the ones he did take, you are fucking useless."

Vibius was affronted. "Did I not show my bravery outside the walls?"

"Which shows what a dick head you are, son. This is not about being brave. This is about being sneaky and knowing the land. Do you know the land where they are going?"

"No sir."

"There and now having wasted too much spit on you already go down to the river and get a bucket of water for the horses."

He looked confused, "A bucket decurion?"

Sextus spread his arms in exasperation. "See, you know fuck all! Under that tree over there is a leather bucket. The patrols who use this leave one there and there is a stone water trough that you can fill. So fill it!"

Felix found the trail of the Votadini hunters soon after leaving the fort. He waved to show that he was scouting and was away for a short time. He ran back, with an attendant Wolf, to the two officers. "Five men went along the trail, I think they were hunting. There is a camp a mile ahead. They came from there."

"Cassius, Julius." The two chosen men rode over. "There are five men hunting in that direction. Go with Felix and ambush them. We want prisoners. At least three."

"Sir." Julius paused. "And where will you and the decurion be… sir?" It was a weighted question. Chosen men were renowned for having a maternal nature.

Metellus grinned, "Well we will be lying here in the sun, enjoying some olives and an amphora of wine Julius. Happy?"

"Not really sir as I am fairly certain that you will be scouting the enemy camp." He looked aggrieved. "I just need to know in case I have to rescue you. It would help to know where you are."

"Don't worry Chosen Man, Felix and Wolf will find us if we get lost."

"Thank you, Decurion Aurelius." The chosen man wagged an admonishing finger at Metellus, "a little courtesy does not hurt, sir."

As Marcus and Metellus left for the camp Metellus said, "I thought I just had the one wife. It seems I have two!"

They soon found the trail which wound down a shallow valley lined with scrubby trees and bushes. Although it was dangerous to travel in daylight along such a visible route they needed to spy out the enemy and be able to make a cogent and useful report for the Legate. The tendril of smoke rising from the hill top ahead told them that the camp was close. They left the trail and tied their horses to a tree in a dell. They drew their swords and set off. Marcus held up his hand to stop Metellus and he sniffed. Metellus looked at him curiously but said nothing. When he was satisfied Marcus walked on, followed by the decurion princeps. Marcus stopped every few paces to sniff. Eventually, he went on all fours and slithered forwards. Metellus copied him and they found themselves at the tree line looking at an improvised camp. This one had an enclosure of stakes and a gate. There were sentries watching towards the woods; had they ridden or walked they would have been seen. The camp was huge; far bigger than the one seen and visited by Marcus. Inside they could see men practising with bows and swords and they could hear the clang and bang of a smith. This was a tribe preparing for war. They were both counting the warriors that they could see and, after a few moments, they backed out and slithered along the trail to the point they had last stood.

When they reached their horses Metellus said, "Well there is no doubt about it they are preparing for war and, from the look of the men practising with bows they aim to use the same tactic they tried against the legion."

They kicked their horses on. "I made it at least a thousand men that I could see."

"I made it the same and this is just one camp. I didn't recognise any of the leaders we saw."

"No. A worrying thought."

"By the way what was with the sniffing?"

"Oh, a little trick I picked up from Felix. The Votadini smell differently to us and when you sniff you are quiet so you hear more. He may be a boy but I have learned much from him."

They returned the place they had left the turma. Neither officer was worried about the outcome of their ambush. If their thirty men and two scouts could not capture a couple of Votadini then it was time to take the pension and head for the farm. The two decurions, both recently married, discussed their home lives and how lucky they were to have such understanding wives.

"I would we were based closer to home Metellus."

"As would I. I expect when the wall is completed then we may well be moved." He looked seriously at Marcus. "The problem may come if they choose to move Marcus' Horse overseas."

Marcus had not thought of that. "Would they, could they do that?"

Metellus shrugged. He and Livius had discussed it at length. "We are a famous, some may say infamous ala. Who knows? There may be a problem abroad, such as the Batavian uprising in the year of the four Emperors, and Marcus' Horse may be the best answer to that problem. Once the land south of the wall is peaceful then we could be moved. For me it matters not. I could take my pension. To be honest I was thinking of doing so when the wall is completed anyway. The life of the ala is for younger men such as you and Rufius. I yearn for a comfortable life with my wife."

Their conversation was ended by the return of their men with three Votadini tethered to their horses. Metellus nodded his approval. "Where are the rest?"

"Three are dead," said Julius evasively.

"Where are the rest?" Metellus' tone was terse.

"Two escaped; there was a rock and a gully. They leapt and we could not follow." There was a pause. "Sorry decurion."

Metellus held up a hand and smiled. "I know you will have done your best Julius but it means we have to move swiftly." He pointed behind him. "There are over a thousand warriors less than two miles away. We need to move. Sling those three over the saddles of the three lightest riders and we will use the spare horses at the fort."

There was an urgency about them as they rode swiftly away. Marcus rode at the rear with Felix and Wolf for company. The dog would be their best warning of approaching barbarians but they made it to the fort safely. Whilst they prepared the spare horses Marcus and Metellus questioned the three prisoners.

174

"Why are you preparing for war?"

"Because you are Romans and you have despoiled our land and soon you will all be dead."

Metellus was the most intelligent of all the officers in the ala and he attacked the problem obliquely. Direct questioning would get them nowhere. "We have pour wall and our fort. What can a few Votadini do to hurt the might of Rome? You are puny!"

A second prisoner spat, "And that is all you know Roman. We have the Selgovae and Brigante as our brothers. We are not puny and we will have more men than you."

"The Brigante are far away and have no arms. It is you and the Selgovae and the wall will stop you."

The three prisoners exchanged a sly and furtive look of joy. "When the Brigante come you will not see them. They will be the knife in the night and your families will feel their blades first."

"Get them on the horses and tie them tightly." Metellus turned to Marcus. "That sounds like a threat of an uprising in the south while we are fighting in the north."

"You are right. The Legate and Eboracum need warning. Should we send riders?"

"Yes. You have the best horses. Choose two riders; one to go to the Legate and the other to warn Morbium and the Governor."

"Two volunteers." As expected Aneurin, Vibius and Scanlan put up their hands. Perhaps this was the opportunity to begin to heal the rift. He would choose one Brigante and Vibius. Perhaps they would bond again."

"Scanlan. Ride to the fort and warn the Legate that the Brigante may be planning to rise while we fight in the north. Vibius, give the same message to the Prefect at Morbium and the Governor."

They both grinned and poor Aneurin look crestfallen. "Yes sir!"

The two messengers had the advantage that they could ride a more direct route than the turmae who, needs must, stayed to the road and headed for the wall. It was close to dark as they wound their way down the well-worn trail which led to their bridge. Marcus called over Felix. "Any sign of Votadini?"

He shook his head, "Nothing recent."

"That is strange sir. They should have scouts watching us."

"Not if they are planning something somewhere else. This confirms what those captives told us. It gives us the edge Marcus. For the first time we can do something to pre-empt their attack."

It was dark when the messenger reached Iucher, Randal and Scaeva at their huge camp in the high hills some miles from the new fort. "Chief Iucher. We have had a disaster. The Romans have captured three of our hunters."

"And you are worried that they will tell the Romans of our plans?"

The man bowed his head in obeisance. "Yes my chief."

Iucher shrugged, "It must be the Allfather's will. Do not worry. We will still win."

When the man had gone Randal turned to Scaeva, grinning like a child. "Your plan works Brigante. The information we fed to our men will now be spread as the truth."

Iucher frowned and scowled, "I like it not. My men are brave and they deserve the truth."

Scaeva was calmness personified. In his mind any sacrifice was worthwhile to rid the land of the Romans. "They would have been captured whether we gave them the correct information or not. Would you rather they had been captured and told the Romans of our real plan to attack the Stanegate? This improves our chances of success considerably. Even now my brother Briac is bringing our army north through secret ways ready to attack at the same time as us. It may not be as large an army as yours but it does have the advantage of being invisible."

Vibia had made Eboracum successfully. She had even managed to increase her money by offering to escort a merchant who was heading for Eboracum and thought she was a Roman trooper. His body would not be found for some time if ever; after she had slit his throat and taken his money she had hurled his body down a gully. Now with a change of clothes, money and a spare horse she was ready to embark on the final part of the plan to recover the gold. Her brother would join her when he could and she was disappointed that they had not killed their uncle; but they had tried and, when they were rich, they could pay an assassin to carry out their wishes.

She halted a few miles from the mighty fortress and changed her clothes. At the same time she picked the plenteous elderberries which abounded close by. The merchant's cloak had a hood which hid both her hair and her face. She needed to arrive in Eboracum and disappear almost as quickly. She found the most disreputable inn in the vicus that she could. For a couple of denarii, she was able to stable her horses and receive a tiny room. From the look on the owner's face she was under no illusions, when he thought his guest was asleep he would slip along and after murdering the occupant would receive far more than the paltry

176

denarii. Once in the room she began to cut off her lovely hair. A pragmatic woman she knew it would grow again. Once that was done she used the knife to remove the fruit from the elderberries and dropped it into a bowl. She was careful to avoid getting the stain on her hands. She took off her shoes and crushed the berries with her feet which quickly became a purple black colour. Finally, she poured in some water to make a liquid. It was pure guesswork on her part but she hoped that the dye would change the colour of her hair. She had no idea what colour it would become but it would not be the distinctive red. Putting the bowl on the floor and an old cloth she had taken from the merchant around her neck she immersed her head into the liquid. She kept turning her head to ensure the maximum coverage. She was careful when she stood to avoid getting the liquid on any other part of her body and stood. She had no mirror and could not judge the colour but she would do that soon enough. She rubbed it dry and then, after dressing, slipped out of the inn when it was busy.

As she rode away she wondered what the inn keeper would make of the bowl of elderberries and the puddles on his floor. She headed for the fort. Close by, in the most expensive part of the vicus was the mansio. She had chosen to play a youth, travelling north to see his father who was stationed on the wall. She had paid attention and knew the names of some of the senior officers. She was taking the chance that someone might know of the officer's family but she was prepared for that saying that her father had had a secret lover. She hoped she would not have to use the full story and that they would not be inquisitive.

Although she kept the hood up she knew that they would see her hair this time as the mansio was better lit than the inn. She asked for a room for a week and stabling. There appeared to be no interest in either her name or her business. They were used to frequent traffic travelling the road. She was in a much better position than the last time she had been in the fortress. Thanks to her brother she now had an idea of where the gold lay and thanks to her light fingers she had acquired much gold and jewellery, stolen when she had fled the fort. Now all that she needed was her brother and they could find the gold and start the new life their mother had wished for them.

When Julius Demetrius received the report he summoned all the commanders from the wall and the adjacent forts for a conference. For the prefects of the Hamians and the Dacians, this was a chance to meet their new colleagues. "I have decided not to send our new cohorts beyond the wall yet, in light of this disturbing development. We now know that when the Brigante rise there will be an attack from the north.

We need to keep a constant patrol along the Stanegate and the wall. Priority will now be given to completing the military way which will run south of the wall. I want to be able to move cohorts quickly to any point which comes under attack. I have no doubt that we will defeat the tribes but the Brigante may well enjoy some success in the south for there is but one cohort in Eboracum to face them. However, we will cross that particular bridge when we come to it."

When Vibius rode exhausted into Eboracum he reported directly to the Governor. He was rather less phlegmatic than his legate in the north. He summoned Rufius. "It seems we may have a rebellion here amongst the Brigante. You have the only auxiliary cavalry. I need you to find these Brigante."

Rufius gave him a wry look. He had been looking forward to a swift return north and the prospect of hunting down a Brigante army did not appeal. "And if I find them, sir, then what?"

"Then you tell me and the Legate and the Legate can bring the army down and defeat them."

"Who told us this sir?"

"Why, one of your troopers," He turned to Appius who had been in the corner waiting patiently. "Bring in the trooper."

Vibius came in and smiled when he recognised Rufius. "So trooper what exactly did you discover? I assume it was Decurion Aurelius who found this information?"

"Yes sir. He was with the Decurion Princeps. The Votadini we captured said that the Selgovae and the Votadini would attack when the Brigante rebelled."

"With due respect Governor that places a different complexion on things. If the Legate brings the army south then the tribes will attack and we will lose the frontier. "

"We can recapture it!"

Rufius saw, in an instant, that Governor Nepos was no soldier. They would have no chance of recapturing the frontier which they only held with their fingertips. He would need to get a message to the Legate. "Very well sir I will leave in the morning but if you could put all the forts on alert it would help."

"I warned Morbium when I passed through sir."

"Well done Vibius. If you come with me I have a task for you."

Once they were outside he said, "Take a room on the mansio tonight and return in the morning to the Legate. I will send Gnaeus to the mansio with the message you are to take." He handed some coins to the trooper. Vibius looked as though he would refuse. He handed him a small wax tablet. "Ask for a receipt and I will claim it back."

Vibius was pleased with the task. It meant that Rufius thought well of him. Perhaps he would ask for a transfer when he returned to the fort. It was now obvious that Marcus thought more of the other two young recruits than of him. When he reached the mansio the official at the desk gave him a curious look but thought better of it. He took the money and gave the wax tablet to the man who wrote the figures down and marked the wax with his stamp. "There are few guests at the moment and I am sure the bath house is available. You have paid for the use of the facilities."

As Vibius went to his room he reflected that the official's attitude was symptomatic of this part of the world. Baths were seen as a luxury rather than an everyday necessity. He decided he would take the opportunity to bathe and, after putting his weapons and armour in his room, he headed for the bath house. He spent a luxurious hour in the bath house which, while not the most opulent, had all the features, save a slave with a strigil, that you could wish. He wondered where he would eat, as he went back to his room. He had just turned the corner towards his room when he came face to face with Vibia; although changed she was still recognisable. She too recognised him. They embraced. "Sister!"

"Brother!"

Chapter 20

"Gnaeus, take this message to Vibius in the mansio. Tell him to leave before dawn. It is imperative that this reaches the Legate as soon as possible." Rufius had explained the Governor's thinking and why he thought it was erroneous. Since arriving in Eboracum he had used his contacts in the vicus to ascertain the mood of the populace and, in the decurion's opinion, there was no unrest; in fact it was the opposite for the increase in commerce meant profits and jobs for all. Rufius knew that once they began collecting their taxes in earnest this might change but that was the future.

Gnaeus took the letter. He had enjoyed his promotion and did not mind performing a task which could, in all honesty, have been performed by a trooper but he appreciated the trust Rufius p[laced in him.

"Where is the room of Trooper Gemellus?"

The bored official pointed towards the corridor. Gnaeus was thinking of his meal later in the evening for he and his chosen man were going to enjoy a night in The Saddle. As he stepped around the corner he thought he was seeing double, there was Vibius and, with a much altered appearance, was Vibia. The changes she had wrought had made her look more like her brother. Gnaeus took a step towards her, the memory of the murder forgotten. "Vibia."

She turned to him with a loving smile upon her face and her arms open. As he closed with her the decurion saw the hate fill her eyes just as the pugeo sliced under his arm. He slumped to the ground in a pool of blood as the twins ran from the scene. Pausing only to gather their belongings they both ran through the atrium leaving a shocked official wondering what had just happened. He ran down the corridor and found Gnaeus in a pool of blood. He quickly balled a towel which Vibius had dropped and pushed it against the wound. "I will get help!"

Gnaeus tried to speak but the official was gone. He ran to the entrance of the mansio which faced the main gate and shouted, "Help! There is a soldier and he has been stabbed!"

The optio had seen Gnaeus leave. He turned to the sentry, "Send for a capsarius and the decurion from Marcus' Horse. When you have done that put the fort on full alert."

The optio was the first to reach Gnaeus whose life blood was leaking across the mosaic floor of the mansio. The optio pressed the towel close to the wound to staunch the bleeding but Gnaeus shook his head and beckoned the optio closer. He knew his life was measured in moments and he had to tell someone of the twins he had seen.

The decurion and the capsarius arrived at the same time but the shake of the optio's head told them that they were too late. The capsarius examined the body and he shook his head.

Rufius took the optio and joined the official. "Tell me, what happened and where is Trooper Gemellus?"

When he said the name the optio looked up in surprise. Before he could say anything the official said. "He took off with the other guest just before I found..." unable to say the words he pointed down the corridor.

"Did he say anything?"

The official shook his head but the optio said, "He spoke to me and it is funny because he said twins too. He said it was a Vibia who had stabbed him and Vibius was her... then he died but I am guessing brother."

Suddenly Rufius saw it too. They were obviously not identical twins but they had much in common with each other. The problem was she was always dressed as a woman while Vibius was a trooper. Rufius and the others had seen what they expected to see. "Which way did they run, mansionarius?"

"I do not know but they both had horses."

The optio and Rufius went directly to the stables where the stable boy was cleaning out three of the stalls. "Did someone just leave?"

He grinned and held out a coin. "Aye. Two guests and they paid me to help them pack." He shook his head. "It comes with the stabling but," he tossed the coin. "You know what they say about a fool and their money eh sir?"

"Which way did they go?"

"West sir!"

Rufius looked to the west where the sun was already dipping behind the distant hills. There would be little point following them until the morning and then the trail would be cold. He swore to himself that he would have them both and they would pay the price for the murders of two innocents; Livia and Gnaeus deserved more than to be betrayed by someone they trusted.

The two fugitives had ridden hard for five miles west and then headed south to join the main road. They had escaped by the skin of their teeth but they had found each other. "Nemesis brought us together brother for you know where the gold is and we can now retrieve it. "

181

"Yes, but we need somewhere for the night. There is another mansion ten miles away. We will stay there."

"Is there not a risk?"

"A slight one. If they find that we have been there then they will assume that we fled south. We will, in fact, be heading east and north to the bend in the river." He looked at her. "That was a good disguise."

She put her hand to the muddy black looking hair. "Unfortunately, it is washing out each day but it will last a little while longer. I have spare clothes if you need them." As they rode south she explained about the merchant and the money and Vibius, not for the first time admired his sister's resilience and intelligence.

After Rufius had retrieved the letter he sought out Flavius, his chosen man. "Tomorrow we ride to find these murderers but I need our most reliable trooper to ride to the Legate."

"That would be Decius. He will deliver it."

"Good. Give him this missive and a pass to leave before dawn. It is imperative that this letter reaches the Legate tomorrow."

"It will be done."

Rufius then went to see Aulus Nepos. The family and Appius were eating. The servant looked down his nose at the decurion who smelled of horses and dressed like a plebeian. "The family are at dinner sir."

Rufius was in no mood for officious servants. "And the Governor will need to hear this so move your arse before I push you out of the way!"

The servant looked into the glaring eyes and backed into the room saying. "A decurion to see you sir, apparently it is urgent."

The sentry on the door grinned as Rufius winked as he walked by. "Sir I am sorry to interrupt your meal but I have urgent news."

"It had better be urgent to disturb our meal decurion. Could it not have waited until the morning?"

"Not really sir. Vibia Dives was in Eboracum and she has killed one of my decurion and she has fled the city with her twin brother who also served in the ala!"

Had Vesuvius erupted there could not have been a greater effect. Rufius hid his smile as Flavia Nepos' mouth dropped open and the normally urbane aide was at a loss for words. Aulus Nepos was the first to recover. "Oh. And what have you done about it?"

"They have fled the city but we will pursue them in the morning."

"Which puts paid to the pursuit of the Brigante?"

"If I am honest sir, I am not certain that there is unrest in this part of the province. From my investigations, any rebellion will be closer to the border rather than in this area but I will keep my turmae here in case I am wrong."

Even the Governor knew when he had been outwitted. With a cohort of the Sixth in the fort he knew that he was safe and if there were an attack then he had the garrisons of Cataractonium and Morbium close at hand. "Very well decurion but keep me informed. It is disturbing to have so many traitors in one ala!"

Rufius ignored the criticism. Only two bad apples in the barrel that was Marcus' Horse spoke volumes for the rest.

The next day the two turmae were determined to revenge themselves on those who had killed the popular, young decurion. Rufius divided the turmae into four and sent them in four directions. He took the southerly road. He used his Explorate training to do so. He assumed that, having fled from the north, they would not wish to fly into danger. East led nowhere but had to be checked and west and south were the best options. He sensed, more than anything that they would have travelled south and when he had been a scout, his feelings had never let him down.

Rufius rode as far as the mansio. Although the pair had travelled at night the mansio would have had security in the form of night watchmen who would have heard any travellers who were heading south. Rufius wanted to eliminate that as a direction. His own view was that they had gone west but the south was the most logical escape route and he had to check it. When they reached the mansion, he was amazed to find that the couple had stayed there. It annoyed and piques him; had he followed south he might have caught them. Ifs and buts did not catch the beast. The mansionarius did not know which direction they had taken and his look told Rufius that he thought it a stupid question. Once visitors left the mansio then his work was done!

"Were there any other travellers here last night?"

The mansionarius was happier with that question and could answer easily. Rufius discovered that the other travellers had all been in wagons which helped him in his next task. "Spread out in a circle. I need hoof prints so do not use your horses. Walk!"

His men knew better than to cross their legendary leader and they, carefully, traversed the land around the mansio, covering every angle. Eventually, a trooper shouted. "Here sir. There are tracks of more than one horse and they are travelling there." He pointed northeast.

Rufius ran over and knelt on the ground. "Well done trooper. Three horses; one with little weight on it. Good. Saddle up!"

Vibia and Vibius had made good time and found the bend in the river. They took out the letter,

My Dearest Aula,

If you have received this letter then I am dead. For that I am sorry- I loved life but I am sorry that you did not share in my victory as much as I would have hoped.

I hope that I have killed my brother but if I have not, then swear that you will do so. In return I can offer you that which you prize the most, Gold!

Before I left Eboracum, I buried a box of gold. It is at the place that they ambushed us. It is buried beneath a dead elm tree which is ten paces from the river where the bend is the most acute. I hope you get the gold and, if you do, reward Marcus' Horse with the pain they deserve.

Your husband,

Decius Lucullus Sallustius

They rode their horses to the river bank. "Follow me." Vibius headed upstream for a few paces and then allowed the current to carry them a hundred paces downstream. He had chosen a spot where the current would bring them back to the bank. Once ashore they tethered their horses and let them stand on the shingle bank. "You go upstream and I will do down. Give a shout if you find an elm tree."

Vibia nodded to her brother and rode along the heavily overgrown river. Would the box still be here after all these years? Perhaps this quest was doomed to failure, like their attempt on the Prefect's life but they would at least have tried. Their father had died not knowing that he had twins; they owed it to his memory to do all they could to retrieve the treasure. Suddenly she saw the elm tree; it looked like any other dead elm, lying at an ungainly angle close to the river but some voice in her head told her that this was her father's legacy. "I have the tree!"

By the time Vibius had reached her she had tethered her horse and was searching for the box. The problem they both had, as her brother helped her was that they had no idea of the size of the box. In addition, it was perfectly possible that someone had already discovered it and was enjoying the fruits of their father's success. Suddenly Vibius said, "I have a box!" His fingers had found the edge of something hard. He took out his pugeo and began to dig in the ground around the edge.

"Use your sword!"

184

Handing his dagger to his sister he began to dig and soon the two of them had discovered a box, the edges of which were well defined. "It is massive." The box was as long as Vibius' arm and almost as wide. He stood. "We will never get this on the back of our horses."

"And if they search for us we need to be free of Britannia, we need a boat."

They both looked around as though one would be waiting there for them. "You must go to Eboracum and hire one. Here," he handed her all the money he had. "You ride to Eboracum and I will continue to excavate the gold." She threw him a doubt filled look. "You look nothing like the lovely Vibia but they will know me for the sentries have seen me many times. Take all the horses and sell them. Leave the three saddle bags here and I will fill them with the gold or the treasure; whatever is in the box. You need a small boat with a crew of one or two. When we are safe we will dispose of them." Both children had inherited their father's and their mother's ruthless streak.

"Very well but stay safe brother."

Rufius led the pursuing Romans, trusting none save himself. Had Felix been with them, Metellus or Marcus, he might have deferred but the instincts of fifteen years serving the ala meant he could not afford mistakes. He saw that they were heading for the river. The fact that they were well south of Eboracum disturbed him but there was something familiar about this land and he could not quite put his finger on it. The trail occasionally deviated, as though they were trying to throw him off the scent and he had to follow the blind alleys for he did not want to lose them. Finally, as the afternoon drifted towards night he smelled the river. It was close. "Be alert. I want two lines behind me. Cover fifty paces each side of me and watch for the two of them or sign."

He reached the river and saw the hoof prints enter. Had they crossed the river? It was not wide at this point and then he remembered why it was familiar. The boats taking Decius Sallustius had left from this point. He spun around, much to the consternation of the troopers. This was the place where the ship carrying the gold had closed with the shore. The question was, why had the twins come there? Homage? Or something else? There was nothing else for it, they would have to cross the river and explore the opposite bank.

"Turmae, we are going to cross the river. Stay close and head upstream, the current will take you downstream but trust to your horses. They can swim, even if you cannot!"

They all managed to cross safely save Agrippa who floundered in the shallows and had to be plucked from the waters by his jeering comrades. "Examine the bank for two hundred paces in each direction. Find hoof prints. "He paused, "Not ours."

Vibius stopped his work. He had been busy emptying the gold from the box into the saddlebags. Two were full and he was on the last one when he heard the noise in the water on the opposite bank. He froze and lay in the water. How had they tracked him? He was just grateful for the fact that his sister and the horses were not there. He might be able to escape detection. He lay back and glanced up at the sky. It was getting dark and his sister could not be here before morning. He would be patient. He lay still and waited for the dark to engulf him and give him the protection of night.

Rufius hated to give up the chase but his men had found nothing. He rode up the small ridge. "Make camp here."

The troopers looked appalled. A lone voice called, "A proper camp with a ditch and everything?"

Flavius' voice rapped out, "No you fucking moron. With a wall five paces high and ditch deep enough to bury you in. Get on with it!"

Rufius walked over to his chosen man. "Have we any fishermen amongst the men?"

"Lepidus is half Batavian; they say they are almost fish themselves."

"See if he can catch some fish. It may make up for the extra work."

The men were a little happier when Lepidus proved to be a competent fisherman and they dined on fish roasted on an open fire. Rufius was not worried about attack; he just didn't want anyone surprising him.

"Sir? This place. You know it?"

"Yes Flavius. A few years ago there was a rebellion and the Prefect's brother led it. He stole a fortune in gold and this was the place he left this land with his treasure."

Flavius' jaw was visibly open. "The Prefect?" There was awe in his voice. "What happened?"

"The Prefect, the Decurion Princeps and me went to Gaul. We recaptured the gold after the Prefect killed his brother."

There was a reflective silence as Flavius took that news in. "Then why have Vibius and that girl come here?"

"I have no idea. There must be a connection to the Prefect's brother but I can make neither head nor tail of it. I have lost them Flavius. Tomorrow we will head back to Eboracum. At least Agrippa won't have to swim this time. We can use the road. Over there."

186

Vibia easily sold the horses for the Roman army was paying high prices for any beast and she made more than she had expected. She made sure that her two daggers were handy for she was about to go to the wharfs; it would be a dangerous place but the resourceful woman was confident that she would be safe. Her beguiling smile and elfin eyes made her look like an innocent abroad but, as Lucia and Gnaeus had discovered, she was a cold blooded killer who could wield a deadly blade.

She wandered down the quays, ignoring the larger ships which were moored there. Even the small ones had a crew of four and she needed something with a crew of one or two. In her mind she was already assessing how to dispose of them once she and her brother had the gold. She reached the last boat and had identified four or five which might suit her purpose. She waited in the shadows of the warehouses which lined the river watching both the boats and the people to find the ones she wanted. She watched curiously as a youth, she took him to be approaching manhood was furtively watching the boats too. He had not seen Vibia watching him. He looked around and, assuming no-one was watching, darted into one boat and retrieved what looked like an amphora of wine. Amused she stored that piece of information. No crews had approached the boats and darkness was falling on the river. Eventually, she saw an older man come to the boat where the boy had stolen the amphora. He descended into the boat and was looking around for something. When she heard a curse she knew what he sought.

She left her hiding place and headed back to the busier area closer to the vicus and fort. The man's boat looked to be ideal. It had a small sail and was big enough to accommodate four people. The simple tiller and the narrow width indicated to Vibia that it be both nimble and easy to handle. She would seek out the sailor away from the quay and, either engage his services or his boat. When she neared the bustling end of the quay where merchants and sailors were completing last minute deals at the end of the day, she saw the youth who had stolen the amphora. The discarded, empty jug lay some distance from him and his ferrety eyes were scanning the crowds for his next victim.

The sailor wandered up and greeted another sailor as his eye spied the empty jug. He strode up to it and grabbed it; looking around fiercely to find the culprit. Vibia waited until he was satisfied that the perpetrator had left and approached him. "Sir. Do you have a boat?" She lowered her voice to continue with the illusion that she was a boy.

"Aye young man. What is it to you?"

"I would like to hire it and you for a short voyage down the river to pick up my brother." She had learned, with her lies, to keep them close to the truth and easy to remember.

"Hmn. How far down the river?"

"Just five miles, perhaps six."

"And why no walk to meet your brother?" The sailor was rightly suspicious and, although the youth appeared to be harmless, he had learned through bitter experience that appearances could be deceptive.

"We have a box we wish to bring back to Eboracum."

"How big is the box?"

"I can lift it."

"And how much are you willing to pay?" She held out four denarii. "Ten."

"Sir you are trying to rob me. Six."

"Eight and that is my final offer." She nodded. "It is too late to leave this night."

"I want to leave as early as possible."

"There is a tide just before dawn."

"I may also be bringing a servant."

"You didn't say that before."

Her voice hardened. "That was when the price was four, for double the price I assume I can have a servant."

The man had already charged her far more than the going rate and he shrugged his shoulders. "When we get the box and your brother, I will decide how many we bring back. I am not overloading my boat for you, young man. Not for eight denarii. I will meet you here before dawn and I want half now." He held out his hand and she counted the coins. She would not get those back for he headed directly for the tavern.

When he had gone, she watched the furtive youth who was trying to get aboard one of the bigger ships. She smiled at the effrontery of him. He was persistent. She could see that he was hoping to take advantage of lax security with most of the crews in the taverns but he was unlucky. The men on guard cuffed him and sent him on his way. She had to find somewhere safe to hide and she headed to the vicus. She would wait in the stables where she had sold the horses. She was suddenly aware that she was being followed and she knew who it was. She slipped her hand beneath her cloak and slid the pugeo from its sheath. She saw the narrow alley between two small huts and slipped between them. She heard the slight footfall and tensed for the next movement. The furtive youth had obviously thought that Vibia was a smaller youth than he and he planted his hand on Vibia's right shoulder. She was expecting something and she reached over with her left hand as she dropped her right shoulder and the surprised youth flew into the air to land with a thump which winded him. When he opened his eyes, there was a sharp pugeo pricking his neck.

"A little careless, aren't we?"

The youth's eyes opened wide in terror. As he looked into Vibia's cold green eyes he saw real evil and he was afraid. "Please don't hurt me!"

She laughed and the coldness of it frightened him even more. "If I wanted to hurt you then you would be dead. No, I may have some use for a thief. It all depends upon your answers to my next questions."

He nodded, eager to please. "I will do anything I swear!"

"Good. Can you sail a small boat?" He nodded eagerly. "How would you like to work for me?"

He nodded and then a frown appeared, "What for? Why do you need me to help you?"

She pushed a little harder on the knife and a tiny tendril of blood trickled down his throat. "I am the one asking the questions and if you want to live then you need to answer them. I will ask you again. Do you want to work for me?"

He squeaked a, "Yes."

She stood and he put his hand to his throat looking with fascination at the blood. The man you stole the jug from." He looked up with shock on his face. "Yes, I watched you. The man, do you know him?"

"Aye, they call him the old one. He used to captain larger ships but he was shipwrecked once and now just plies the river."

"Is he honest?"

"As honest as any." He was about to ask why but remembered, in time, about questions.

"I have hired him to take me down the river in the morning. You will come with us as my servant. When the time is right, I will ask you to do something for me."

"What?" The knife was in her hand and pointed at his nose before he could blink. She cocked her head to one side. "It doesn't matter. I will do whatever you ask."

"Good and what is your name?"

"Arden."

"Good. Well Arden, you may call me master. Now where do you normally sleep?" The shrug told her he was homeless which suited her. "We will sleep in the stable nearby and, before you get any ideas I am a light sleeper and if you run I will find you and kill you. Do you understand?"

He smiled as he said, "Yes master." He had no intention of running. The lonely life of a quay rat was hard and this youth looked as though he could handle himself. He would stay with him just to see if his lot could be improved.

They were both waiting at the boat when the Old One arrived. He looked suspiciously at Vibia. "How did you know this was my boat?"

Arden came out of the shadows. "I described you and my servant told me."

"What that thief? If he is your servant, I should sleep with one eye open. He'd take the coins off a corpse would that one."

Vibia shrugged. "That is my problem, not yours, is it not?"

"Your funeral. Get aboard and sit in the middle. Don't move around."

Vibia sat in the middle with Arden in front of her. The Old One was competent enough and he untied the boat from the metal ring and pushed them away. Vibia noticed then his knotted arms. This was a powerful man. It would not do to underestimate him. She would watch and wait. Once they had picked up her brother then they could decide what to do about the Old One.

Chapter 21

Vibius had spent a cold and uncomfortable night. He had seen the Romans build their camp eight hundred paces downstream on the opposite bank. Once he was sure that they were settled for the night he finished emptying the gold. The three saddle bags were filled and the rest he had put in his satchel, now worn on his baldric. He saw the first glimmer of light on the horizon and he slowly made his way closer to the bank. Once he saw Vibia he could waste no time getting aboard but he would avoid the icy waters for as long as possible. He saw a faint white movement on the river. It was a boat. He could make out the white faces but not who they were. He chewed his lip. What should he do? Then he deduced it was unlikely to be the Romans; it was either his sister or another innocent traveller on the river. He stood and raised his arm. When he saw the arm raised in return, he knew it was Vibia. They were going to succeed; they had done half the task they had promised their mother; they had their father's gold!

The sail dropped and the boat nudged closer to the bank. Vibius picked up one of the bags and stepped into the shallows; they came up to his waist. He saw two crew on board but, most importantly, he saw the smiling face of his sister.

The old man on the tiller said, "I thought you said a box?"

"It is three bags. Here is the first."

As soon as he handed it over and it thudded to the thwarts the old man said. "Are they all as heavy as that?" Vibius ignored him and went back for the second. "If they are then the servant stays. They are too fucking heavy."

He did not notice the evil look flash on Vibia's face nor did he see her slip the dagger to Arden and give a slight nod. "Wait until they are all aboard Old One and then make your decision."

When the second one thudded down he began to become quite agitated. "No, get the thief off now or leave your brother."

As he made his way back Vibius noticed with some alarm that the noise was loud enough to be heard from the Roman camp and, equally worrying, dawn was breaking. He hurried back to the boat and slung the last bags over. This time the boat sank a little deeper into the water.

As Vibius began to pull himself up the Old one tried to push him back. "No I said just one. Either the boy stays or your brother. "

He was now shouting and Vibius could see movement at the Roman camp. He looked at Vibia. "The ala, they are over there!"

She nodded and said to Arden, "Now!" The two of them stabbed simultaneously with their daggers. Even had he been expecting it he could have done little but, with a strangled scream he fell with a huge splash into the river. "Quick, get the sail set and I will help him aboard."

Arden might have been a thief but he was quick thinking and he had the sail hoisted in two tugs of the sheets. The wind caught it and they began to move, with the current and the slight breeze, downstream. Vibia hauled Vibius on board but, even as he slumped to the bottom he spluttered, "Keep to the right bank. There are Romans there!"

In the Roman camp the sentries had woken Rufius when they heard the commotion. They had witnessed the murder and the body of the sailor drifted by, the crimson tail marking its passage. By the time Rufius had reached the riverbank the boat was level with them and he could see both Vibia and Vibius. "To arms! It is the deserter and the murderer! To horse!"

Vibius struggled to the stern where he grabbed the tiller. The boat dipped and the side almost dipped below the river level. "The two of you! Stay in the middle or we'll be in the water. You… boy… whatever your name is. Keep the sail trimmed or whatever sailors do with it."

Vibius kept as low as he could, almost crouching below the side of the boat. He had to keep looking up to check that they were not going to hit the bank. "Vibia, watch the bow and tell me if we are going to strike anything."

The troopers quickly mounted, "Flavius, take ten men and cross the river. I want them either taken or dead!" Flavius marked off his men and they plunged into the river. "The rest of you follow me. Have your bows ready!"

To Rufius' dismay, the boat began to pick up speed as both the wind and the current picked up. He strung an arrow to his bow and tried a ranging shot. The arrow arced and struck the water ahead of the boat. "Loose arrows!" The rest of the turma were neither as accurate nor as strong as Rufius but two arrows struck the boat while others fell on either side. Glancing across the river he saw that Flavius and his men had reached the other side but were further behind. He saw Vibius, for he could now see him clearly, turn and see Flavius. The tiller went over and the boat headed for the middle of the river which brought him closer to Rufius and his men. Unfortunately, the boat was now moving faster than the horses could travel and they were escaping.

"Keep loosing arrows! We may get lucky!" Rufius took out another arrow and this time aimed, if he could hit Vibius on the tiller then they might have a chance. He held his breath and loosed. The arrow arced high; the rest of the turmae were peppering the boat and sails but none had struck. Rufius' arrow plunged down and struck Vibius in the neck. As his life blood erupted over the boat the arrow pinned his body to the boat and it carried on down the middle of the river which now entered a straight phase. They were escaping. Even as they watched the boat went beyond arrow range, even for Rufius.

On the boat Vibia was watching ahead and she suddenly saw that they were in the middle with no obstacles before them. The sail stopped her seeing her brother and she crawl back to speak with him. As soon as she ducked under the sail she saw that he was dead. His glassy eyes started at her and seemed to mock them both. Arden had been too busy trimming the sails to see the tragedy. Vibia saw Rufius and his bow and she looked to heaven. "Brother I swear I will have revenge, not only on Livius our uncle but on Rufius who took your life." She went to the stern and snapped the feathers from the arrow then she napped the arrow in tow and said, "Forgive me brother but I need to be able to steer." She gently moved the corpse into the middle of the boat and then said to Arden. "Keep a sharp lookout. We are heading for the sea!"

If Arden was shocked by her words, he said nothing as he had looked into the green eyes and felt himself frightened beyond belief. He had left one lonely life on the street and who knew where he would end up; one thing was certain, he was now the slave to Vibia, daughter of Aula and Decius, and she was a killer. Vibia stared over her shoulder at the troopers who had, once again, thwarted her in her plans.

Rufius had seen his arrow strike the deserter and knew that he had killed him. It did not make Rufius feel any happier about allowing Vibia to escape. He saw her leaning over the stern of the boat and felt those eyes boring into him. She was a dangerous woman and he would not underestimate her. He had tried to capture or kill both and he had not succeeded. He was left with a bad taste in his mouth as he ordered his turmae back to camp. They would destroy the camp and return to Eboracum. Their job was only half finished.

The Governor did not seem bothered by the escape of the murderess; he was still worrying about the possible uprising of the Brigante. He had already summoned reinforcements from the south and, when Rufius reported, he still demanded that the two turmae seek the Brigante rebels.

Rufius knew that it was a waste of time but he saw a way to allow the rest of the army to remain on the frontier. "Governor Nepos, I will take my turmae on patrol and sweep further out each day. If we do not find the rebels within three days then there is no immediate danger to the fort and the vale."

Quintus looked at the map. The land of the Brigante was huge. It was the largest tribal area in Britannia. What the decurion said made sense. "Very well but I want you back here in four days to report and then you can go further out."

Rufius sighed, "It was a waste of time but at least the other fourteen turmae would not be wasting their time. "And if I might put your mind at rest Governor. The Brigante have never managed to capture a fortress like Eboracum. The best they ever managed was a sneak attack on a marching camp and even then the cohort killed more of them than they lost. If you use ballistae on the walls then you will be safe within this fortress."

Both Appius and the Governor took some solace from the decurion's words. Neither were warriors and Rufius left their company desperate for fresh air and troopers who knew how to fight and to die.

Briac and his Brigante were already well to the north of the Dunum. They had slipped northwards in warbands of a hundred warriors. Between Vinovia, in the east, and Bravoniacum, in the west, lay forty miles of rough and open country through which the Brigante could flood. Warriors had travelled from the furthest corners of the land of the Brigante. Every young warrior who was eager to prove himself a man had left his farm, his village, his family to join the army of Briac. Briac promised a final defeat for the Romans and the young wanted to be part of it. The fathers and uncles; the older ones did not join the exodus for they remembered the previous uprisings which had seen the Brigante suffer. Their meeting point was south of the Stanegate and north of the wall Scaeva and the chiefs planned their attack to coincide with the arrival of the hidden army.

Meanwhile, Iucher and Randal had been slowly feeding their men across the turf wall at the western side of the wall. The auxiliaries were still in a state of shock following the earlier raids and were fearful of the dark beyond the wall. The land to the south of the Stanegate now had many warbands waiting in eager anticipation of the attacks. The two chiefs wanted as many men south of the wall when the attack started while the remainder of their armies lurked close to the gap, ready to flood the land once the soldiers marched to meet the new threat. The priests of the tribes had made offerings to the gods for aid against the invader and the gods had smiled on them. The autumn rains began early. The Stanegate was passable but the new military road and the construction site became a sticky morass which sucked caligae into its depths and armour rusted as you watched. It was a miserable time for auxiliaries and legionaries alike.

Iucher and Randal took it as a sign that the Mother and the gods were on their side. Patrols beyond the road ceased as the horsemen of the ala huddled beneath their cloaks trying to keep dry, an impossible task. The barbarians benefited from shelters they threw up, invisible to the Romans who found it hard to peer through the rain which appeared to come down continuously.

Livius and the other officers were also devastated when news of Gnaeus death reached them. He had been popular with all of the ala but Marcus felt particularly close to him, having mentored and coached him to reach his elevated rank and now he was murdered, killed by the woman who had fooled them all. What galled Marcus was that he had risked his young troopers to rescue her. At the back of it all was the knowledge that Vibius, too, had deceived them. Scanlan took it as Nemesis but Aneurin took it as a personal slight. He had been, for a time, the closest to Vibius and felt he was a friend. The news which reached them from Eboracum made Aneurin, the youngest of the troopers, doubt everything in his world. Marcus saw the young Brigante drift deeper into depression.

"Cassius what can we do about Aneurin? He is not the trooper he was."

"He'll snap out of it, trust me."

"No Cassius, we cannot afford to ignore these things. Good troopers are hard to come by and Aneurin has the making of a good one."

Cassius was a plain speaking soldier. All this talk of feelings and emotions was beyond him but it was Marcus Aurelius who had asked him and he had to think of something. "I'll ask Scanlan to have a word. He seems to get on with the lad and is a bit more sensible if you know what I mean."

Scanlan appreciated the task he had been given, it showed him what his officers thought of him and Scanlan aimed to be a decurion some time. He too had noticed Aneurin and his moods; he rode next to him as yet another wave of rain drove in from the east. "Filthy this weather eh Aneurin?"

His dull flat voice told Scanlan his mood. "The whole place is filthy. I don't know why we hang on to it. What is the point?"

Scanlan looked askance at Aneurin. His tone became sharper. "I do not believe you Aneurin. Do you hate your family so much? Do you hate the decurion?"

His mouth opened and he looked briefly like a fish taken from a river trying to gulp in air. "No! If course not! What a horrible thing to say! I would do anything for the decurion and the sword!"

"Well that is the point isn't it? If we weren't here defending this bit of land, which, I agree, is filthy and apiece of shit not worth dying for but," he paused and pointed to the south, "down there are our people and the decurion's people. They are living in peace and do you know why? Because we are willing to fight to keep the barbarians at bay. I, for one, am happy to be fighting here for that means my family is safe and my land is free from war."

There was silence save for the slop of the hooves in the puddles and the whoosh of the sleet filled wind. Scanlan glanced at Aneurin. He could almost see the thought processes at work. The grin returned, for the first time since Vibius had left. "You are right! Sorry, Scanlan. What was I thinking?"

"That is your trouble Aneurin you think too much, don't. It does you no good in the end. Just follow orders and you will be fine but I think you need to apologise to the decurion. He has been worried about you."

"Me! I didn't know he even saw me."

"There you go again. Of course, he does. He watches us all. That sword he carries is more than a powerful weapon it is a symbol of the Brigante and that, old son, is you and me!"

The messenger reached Scaeva and the chiefs at dusk on a day where the sun had barely lightened the day. "Chief Briac is in position and is ready."

Scaeva had now become the unofficial leader of the group. All of his predictions and plans had borne fruit and it saved Iucher and Randal from arguing over trivialities. "Tomorrow morning we attack the Romans along the length of this wall. Remember, when they respond we must do as they expect us to and flee south. Briac is waiting at the narrow valley near the Allyn River. The Romans will follow you and when you turn at the head of the valley they will think they have you. That is when Briac will launch his attack from the hills." He looked sternly at each of them. He had only been a trooper for a couple of years but he had taken on all the discipline of the Romans, something the tribes did not have. "They must obey orders or we are lost!"

"They will."

It was as though the very earth and skies were on the side of the barbarians as the day dawned, or it would have dawned were it not for the thick clinging fog and low cloud which meant you could only see someone four paces from you. The icy chill permeated their armour and their cloaks. The soldiers going to work on the wall that day were in no mood to work.

The Batavians were still in their armour, although bareheaded, when the Votadini struck. The muddy bog in which they worked made it hard to shift the cobbles. When the arrows struck, they appeared to come from nowhere. The archers were blind but they loosed so many that they knew they would have struck men. The Batavians were disorientated; the arrows appeared to come, not from the north, where the Votadini lived but the south, the Stanegate. The hesitation caused more casualties as the Votadini swordsmen plunged in to hack the auxiliaries before they had time to organise.

The picture was repeated along the wall. The legionaries were the first to recover but they too took heavily casualties. The wagons on the road were massacred as the barbarians appeared like wraiths alongside them to drag the drivers from their seats and ruthlessly butcher them. They took the draught animals from the traces and drove them away then they upturned all of the wagons making the road impassable in places. As instructed they withdrew to the woods to await the Roman response.

One of the horsemen who was at the rear of the wagons which had left Coriosopitum managed to escape and he fled back to Cilurnum. He was the first to deliver the news. Julius Demetrius immediately ordered Livius to take the whole ala and find out what was going on.

"Sir, this may be something bigger than a raid on the wagons."

"What do you mean Livius?"

"All the intelligence we had was that the tribes were planning something big. They have been quiet for too long. Luckily we didn't send this ala back to Eboracum but they may think we have gone."

"You may be right. I will follow with the Hamians and I will pick up the Dacians at Vercovicium. We will meet you south of the new fort."

When Livius and the ala reached the wagons they could see the devastation. "Sextus ride to Vercovicium and warn the Dacians that they are to march when the Legate arrives. Marcus, take Felix and scout the gap. Find out where they have fled."

He turned to Metellus. "We will keep the rest of the men together. This looks like a big warband."

"Sir."

"Yes, Marcus?"

"Felix has found out where they went."

"That was fast." He looked north, although the fog still hid all.

"No sir. They went south. There are no tracks to the north."

Livius was nonplussed. "Well done. Follow the tracks." He turned to his decurion princeps. "Metellus, send a rider back to the Legate tell

197

him the barbarians have fled south. And send out scouts. In this fog we could easily miss them."

They rode with weapons at the ready all thoughts of the cold gone. Livius kept them in a column of fours ready to deploy at any moment.

The trooper, Sextus, rode towards them. "Sir! They are attacking Vercovicium."

"Ala wheel right. Turma frontage!"

The ala rode off in twelve lines. The land between the Stanegate and the wall was treeless and, if they were careful they could avoid the few dips and hollows. They would, however, have the maximum number of spears and javelins to bring to bear. They could hear the fighting long before they could see anything but the Votadini who were engaged with the Tungrians had no warning either and the thirty troopers crashed into their rear ranks. Metellus and his turma overlapped and the barbarians were caught between the Tungrians, with the newly arrived Dacians and the troopers. They fled but, to Livius' amazement, they did not flee northwards but west and south, taking his horsemen by surprise.

Gaius Culpinus, the Prefect of the Tungrians took his helmet from his bloodied head and extended his arm. "Thank you, Livius. That was well timed. We were losing too many men."

"Any idea where they came from?"

He pointed to the Stanegate, "South! They took us completely by surprise."

"The Legate is coming along with the Hamian archers and he is going to take your Dacians as well."

"Don't worry about us. We will improve the defences and sod the building!"

"Metellus take four turmae and ride to the Sixth, find out what has happened there. I will ride along the Stanegate and make for Vindolanda." Vindolanda was only a construction site but there were Gauls there and they might also need help.

Marcus was taking no chances as he followed the Votadini south and east. It was undulating land, with scrubby bushes and copses. The dells and hollows made perfect ambush country. Felix and Wolf were good but even they only had a certain amount of luck. They rode in a loose formation. Marcus had seen them begin to use arrows and a tight formation, whilst effective in many ways, it was not while being attacked by arrows. It also afforded him a wider frontage and they could see further although with the fog that was not very far.

Felix returned, like a ghost from the mist. "They are moving quickly decurion. They are running."

"Cassius, does this make sense to you? They successfully attack a wagon train. They are not disturbed and then they run, not north for home, but south, away from their tribal lands."

"No sir. But I don't like it. If they were Roman then it would make sense. We would do this to lead them into a trap."

Suddenly it all became clear to Marcus. "And of course they now have a Roman."

Cassius looked confused for a moment then he said, "Scaeva!"

"Lucius, ride to the Prefect. He will be on the Stanegate heading west. Tell him I think that they are leading us into a trap."

Livius reached Vindolanda and saw the pitiful remains of the four centuries who had been building it. He sent out his skirmishers and then tended to the wounded. Lucius reached him at the same time as Metellus and the Legate. The Legate listened to all the reports. "The Sixth and the Twentieth were attacked, from the south again sir and the Batavians, further west, well they suffered badly again."

"Thank you Metellus. And this news from Marcus. What do you make of that?"

"He is a bright lad, always has been and it makes sense. The tribes normally run for home and when they do they run fast."

"Right." He looked down at the Gauls, "Centurion, take your men and go to Vercovicium. You can bolster the garrison there until this is over. Livius, send a rider to the Sixth. I want the whole cohort here."

As the rider galloped off and the Gauls began to tramp through the fog north Livius said, "It will take them some time to reach us, sir."

Julius smiled, "I know what you are thinking Livius that the Governor will have my head if I am wrong. Well it is an old head but think about it. If Marcus is correct and this is an ambush then we are merely keeping our enemies waiting. If they are intent on raiding the land of the Brigante, which they could be, then they have a long way to go before they can do any serious damage and you could catch them and, if they are intent on returning north then we still block their route. We will try to have as many men as possible." He waved a hand at the Syrian archers and Dacians. "I do not think they can know about our reinforcements, perhaps they may get a shock when they do."

Centurion Quintus Broccus led the cohort to the gathering. Marcus could see that they had lost men but they had the determined look of soldiers who mean business. Julius briefed him and the small army set off south. Marcus, with his Brigante scouts was the point of the weapons and he and his turma were five hundred paces in the van of the rest of the ala. The Hamians followed then the legion and finally, the Dacians brought up the rear. They were a good cohort, according to the

199

Legate but, as yet, untried. The Syrian archers could hide amongst the legionaries if trouble occurred. Everything now depended upon Marcus and his men finding the enemy.

Chapter 22

Felix and Wolf did not ride down the old Roman road, even though the main trail went there; Felix might be young but he was not stupid and he knew that the tribes did not follow regular lines of march. They wandered all over the route and Wolf was happily following the Votadini who had massacred the wagon drivers. The land rose steeply and the valley twisted and turned as it wound its way south. Rather than hurrying Felix slowed and that saved his life. He was above the half built road and negotiating a steep slope; Wolf was above him sniffing out a Votadini smell. The archer, who had hidden in the rocks had spied the scout and wanted an easy target. The growl from Wolf made Felix drop to the ground and the arrow flew harmlessly over his head. He was up in an instant and had notched an arrow and aimed at the rock he thought the archer had loosed from. Sure enough the head popped up and the arrow took him in the middle of his forehead. Felix used speed to race to the dead man. Wolf growled at the dead body. From the vantage point, Felix had a good view of the thousands of barbarians who were filling the end of the valley some thousand paces ahead.

"We can return now Wolf. I hope the decurion has a plan to defeat them for there look to be many."

"Sir, Felix, on the left."

"Halt."

"Sir the main army looks to be at the head of the valley. There are many more than there are Romans."

The doubt in the boy's voice made Marcus smile. "It is a good job that we are better then. Titus, ride to the decurion and give him the information. Tell him I will scout the large hill to the east."

The hill in question was like a large dome, an upturned jug. "Cassius, take half the men and go the right. I will take Felix to the left."

There were some bushes and trees around the top but, to Marcus' eye, there didn't appear to be any gullies or cliffs. He realised he had the recruits with him. "Keep your weapons ready and your eyes peeled."

Livius sent a messenger back to the Legate and then took the ala forward at the trot. He could see the valley narrowing knew that the trap Marcus had suspected was ahead. They had led the Romans on to their spears. As soon as the valley turned left he could see them; there were thousands of them arrayed in many ranks along the terraces of the hills. Even at a thousand paces he could see the archers and the spear men.

Scaeva had advised them well. The only advantages the Romans would have were their discipline and their shields for few of the tribesmen had them. He held his hand up and halted the thirteen turmae in a long line, filling the whole valley. When they attacked, the frontage the legionaries would have would be less than this. It would be a tight killing zone.

Julius Demetrius had made his plans as soon as he realised what they faced. The Sixth strode up with the first century flanked by the second and third with the fourth and fifth in reserve. They were eight hundred of the finest warriors Rome had but they would be fighting over four times that number. Half of the Dacians were on the left flank with the other half on the right and the five hundred Syrian archers were between the two ranks of the Sixth.

Livius waited until he heard the command for the cavalry to withdraw. His ala fed through gaps left for them by the legionaries. The troopers nodded to the men of the sixth that they knew. Livius nodded to Centurion Broccus. "There seem to be a lot of them Quintus."

"It doesn't matter how many there are, they can only fight us one to one. They may have picked this place because they can't be outflanked by you horse boys but it suits us more. It might take us a little longer but we will grind them down. Believe me!"

Livius shuddered, when Quintus said grind down, that was precisely what they meant. They were like the mill stones turning the lumps of corn into a fine powder; but this powder would be the bones of men. Julius nodded to him. "Put half your men on each flank."

"Metellus take half on the right. And I will watch the left. Keep your eyes on the hills. They may have men there."

As the buccina sounded the three double centuries and the Hamians moved forwards. The jeering and cheering of the tribes diminished to be replaced by a whoosh of arrows. He watched as the legionaries held up their shields but most were not needed as the enemy arrows fell short. The legion halted and presented their shields to the enemy. Then the Syrian archers pulled back on their bows and five hundred arrows plunged into the unarmoured men in the front rank. Almost before the first had struck a second wave flew and a third. It was as though someone had punched a hole in the enemy's centre. The three centuries moved forwards and the reserve centuries joined them. Once the five centuries had overtaken them the Syrians moved forwards and stopped eighty paces closer to the enemy. The Votadini and Selgovae archers and slings kept sending missiles towards the Romans who contemptuously blocked them with their shields. The Syrians now showed that they could aim as well as any and the archers in the second ranks were targeted.

Julius could see that the centre was now weak and he ordered the Dacians forwards to take the pressure off the legion's flanks. This would take time but they would finally defeat the tribes. Just then a rider galloped down the hill waving and shouting at Livius. Julius could see and hear the commotion. He wondered what disaster it heralded.

"Sir! The Brigante! They are attacking. There are thousands of them."

Livius and Julius looked up at the hill, they saw thousands of Brigante pouring over the top of the hill and running down in a mass. They would strike the left flank of the Roman line and, simply, bowl it over. "Ride to the Dacians and tell them to halt and face the enemy. You," he gestured to another aide, "bring the Dacians from the right as quickly as you can and the rest of the ala." There was little point in halting the Sixth, they were committed but he could save the Syrians. He had run out of aides. He kicked his horse forwards and shouted to the Prefect of the Hamians. "Withdraw to me. We are being attacked from the left."

Livius had moments to come up with a plan. He knew that Marcus would not sit idly by and watch the attack. That meant he had six turmae to try to halt ten times that number. "Wheel left! We are going to charge them! Follow the Wolf!" With the Wolf Standard to the fore the two hundred men galloped uphill to the charging Brigante. Livius held his javelin overhand and, aiming at a chief with a torc he hurled it; striking the man and pinning him to the hillside. His second javelin he held like a long sword and he stabbed left and right at every Brigante who crossed his path. Although they killed many, more evaded the charge and carried on down the hill. The ala was also taking casualties. Scaeva had advised well and axes hacked into horse's legs allowing others to stab and kill the riders.

Marcus had managed to reunite his turma. He had been saved from surprise by Felix who had seen the horde moments before they would have seen him. It had allowed him to send a message to the general but it had left Cassius and half the turma in the path of the horde. Marcus had led his fifteen men around the hill and they managed to save Cassius and five others before they too were killed by the warband. He looked down the hill and saw the vain attempt of the Prefect to halt the charge. It was like a grandstand view. He saw the Sixth Legion punching their way through the tribes and the Dacians preparing to receive the bulk of the warband. Metellus and his turmae were also charging the Brigante. There was only one thing Marcus could do, use the Sword of Cartimandua and charge the enemy.

"Form one line. Draw swords" There was a hissing sound as all the blades were held aloft. "Today the Sword of Cartimandua goes to war. The Sword of Cartimandua!"

As he had expected the oath was taken up by the turma and some of the Brigante looked around. Marcus kicked his horse on and they plunged down the hill side at a suicidally fast pace. With Cassius on his left he leaned forwards the shining sword sparkling in his hand. He sliced down one side of his mount and then swung on the left. Soon he was in the rhythm and men were falling to the razor-sharp blade. He risked a glance up and saw that the ala was now engaged in hand to hand combat and the Dacians, although reinforced by their comrades were struggling to hold their line. The battle was no longer a wide one, it was the width of this turma as Marcus and the men of the Second Turma, Marcus' horse had a magnificent charge into two thousand Brigante.

Suddenly one warrior, braver than the rest, turned and stabbed his spear into the ground in front of Marcus' mount. Horse and rider were catapulted into the air. Marcus relaxed and rolled his shoulder. Although the wind was knocked out of him he rolled and came up on his feet just as a huge warrior with a double handed war axe roared up to him swinging the powerful weapon. He must have expected Marcus to panic but instead he half turned his body and slid the blade under one arm and out of the other side. The warrior died with a surprised expression on his face. Marcus had no time for self-congratulation as another three warriors turned to fight him. The practice, all those years ago with his step brother, came to his aid. He parried one with his shield. Stabbed a second with his sword and spun around to stab the third in the back. The first warrior was lying on the floor and Marcus jabbed the sharp edge of the shield onto his windpipe.

Momentarily alone he looked down at the battlefield. The Dacians had held and the Syrians were emptying their quivers into the ranks packed before the eastern warriors. In the main battle the Sixth legion was still surrounded but there were far fewer barbarians than there had been. Just then an arrow flew down the hill over Marcus' head. Marcus looked and saw the Brigante fall to the ground, his head pierced by Felix's arrow. Wolf held a horse's reins in his teeth. "Thought you might need a horse sir."

"Thank you Felix. I owe you and Wolf."

"Are we winning sir?"

"Not yet but we will." He threw himself into the saddle and saw the knot of troopers surrounded by the Brigante. It was Livius and Metellus and they too were unhorsed. "The Sword of Cartimandua!" He covered the hundred and fifty paces quickly and, leaning forwards stabbed one warrior in the back and then allowed his new mount to crash through three others. His sword flashed death and another warrior fell with his throat slashed. Just then an axe took his horse in the neck and once again Marcus found himself afoot but this time the leather strap on his shield broke and he found that he was shieldless.

"Now I shall have the mighty sword which belongs to my people and a new day will dawn for the Brigante people."

"Scaeva!" The deserter faced him. He had a Roman shield and a sword but, on his head, he had a cavalry mask hiding his features but Marcus knew his voice. "You will die today traitor and you will die by the sword."

"Let's see how you do against a warrior with armour and shield! Especially as you have no shield yourself." He slashed forwards with his spatha and Marcus barely had time to deflect the blow. Sparks flew as metal struck metal. At the same time Scaeva punched with the boss of his shield and Marcus felt ribs crack as he fell to the ground. He barely had time to roll away from the sword which stabbed down and scored his mail shirt. He remembered that Scaeva had been a good swordsman and he had made the final of the ala tournament one year. This would not be easy.

As they circled around each other Marcus found it hard to fight a man whose eyes were hidden by a mask and then he suddenly relaxed. He knew how he would win. He fought easier with the confidence of knowledge. As Scaeva swung in again Marcus merely spun away so that Scaeva struck empty space. He then continued around and slashed across the back of the deserter's armour. The mail stopped total penetration but a tendril of blood and an angry shout told him that he had struck. Marcus then spun the other way as Scaeva tried to turn. The turn left a slight gap and Marcus stabbed forwards. The sword sliced across the bare shield arm and blood gushed from it. Marcus dropped to his knees as the deserter tried to take off his head and, as he did so he stabbed forwards connecting with Scaeva's thigh. Marcus stepped back and to his left.

Suddenly Scaeva ripped the cavalry mask from his face. "Tricks! Is that all you have decurion? Tricks?"

"Not tricks traitor, skill." He dipped his left shoulder and, weakened by the loss of blood Scaeva tried to turn an already weakened leg. He did not make the turn and the sword of Cartimandua plunged into the throat of the Brigante rebel and he fell dead at Marcus' feet.

Cassius reined up next to Marcus as Felix and Wolf joined them. "I tried to get to you." He pointed at the bodies around them, "but I was held up." He looked down at Scaeva's body. "Why did he wear the mask?"

"Don't you remember Cassius, he won it as a prize at the games we had. I guess he thought it would make him more frightening. Instead it restricted his vision. Those things aren't meant to be used in battle." He suddenly remembered Livius and Metellus. "The Prefect..."

"They are safe." He pointed to where the remains of the ala were reforming. "And as soon as the Legate can reorganise the Dacians it will be all over." He shook his head. "It is a shame those Syrians ran out of arrows. They could have killed them all on their own."

There were pitifully few horses left for the unhorsed troopers but they found one for Marcus and he joined Livius and Metellus. Both men had been wounded. "We saw your reckless charge. Reminded me of Macro!"

"As did your combat with Scaeva. Now if Briac is among the dead then we will have done a good day's work and the losses would have been worth it."

An aide galloped up, "Sir the Legate's compliments and could you and your ala be ready to purse the enemy. It looks like they are going to break."

"Yes. Tell the Legate we will do our best."

Metellus shook his head. "We have not a chance in a thousand. They will just climb the hills and find the rockiest way back to the north."

"I know but we can make their life difficult can we not and remember the more we kill now the fewer we chase through the winter."

"Don't you believe it. They have nothing better to do all winter; they will be breeding like hares. Fifteen years from now you will be fighting their sons."

They hunted the survivors for fifteen days. The ala, much depleted, was split into pairs and the thirty odd troopers scoured the land. Marcus and Felix led their men through the land of the Brigante but they never managed to find Briac who disappeared. They returned, weary to the fort at Cilurnum to find Rufius and the others already there and tending to armour and weapons in need of repair and horses and men requiring tending.

Livius, now recovered from his sword thrust greeted Marcus. "Did you find Briac?"

There was little hope in his voice for he knew that, if he had, then Marcus would have had him tethered to his horse. "No sir. It is my fault. Felix found one small band of five men who split off from the main warband and headed over the high pass near Glanibanta to the coast. I did not have enough men to follow and I kept after the main band. I suspect he was with the small group."

"You did well Marcus. The fifty you captured were all good fighters and your action means they have fewer warriors available for their next rebellion."

"You think they will rebel again?"

"I am certain of it. They came very close this time. Had your turma not stumbled upon the ambush then they would have had complete surprise and the army would have been routed. We defeated them, but it was a close-run thing. We failed to capture Iucher and Randal. They will be north of the wall again, plotting their next incursion. But," he smiled and patted Marcus on the shoulder, "at least they will not have the deserter to aid them."

"Speaking of deserters what about Vibius?"

"Rufius slew him but his sister escaped and I do not think that one will have forgotten us."

"Why did they hate us so much?"

Livius was quiet, he had spent many nights pondering the same problem. His dreams had been filled with Vibia's face and finally, waking cold and shaking with fear he had seen the connection. "I think they were the children of Aula and Decius."

"Your brother?"

"Yes Marcus, my brother. Their ages would coincide with the time Aula and Decius were together after she left my uncle. It all came together when Rufius mentioned where they hid before leaving Britannia; it was the spot their father had taken the gold to Gaul. I can only assume he hid some there."

"Which means she now has the money to help her pay for her revenge?"

"Yes Marcus, but at least we know what she looks like. For my part I have no wish to kill my last living relative. I hope that she takes the money and lives well, far from here."

"But you do not think that she will."

"No Marcus, she has inherited too much from my brother and his woman. There is hate in her heart and only my death will rid her of it."

Epilogue

Appius Serjanus had his wish. He had been given a turma of auxiliaries, newly arrived in the province, and a cohort of foot to explore the possibility of extracting copper and gold from the land of the lakes. He had learned his lesson; the military way was not for him but he had seen that he could fool Aulus Nepos who cared only for glorious monuments to himself. So long as Appius sent favourable reports on a regular basis he would not care what Appius was up to. The decurion and centurion he had with him were not the men of Marcus' Horse and he had them in the palm of his hand. He gave them an easy time and ingratiated himself well into their company. They thought him a rich fool and he happily played that part.

The tiny fishing boat bobbed about on the water. Briac had barely escaped Britannia with his life and he knew that his own land was too hot for him. Stealing the boat and killing the fishermen had been easy and he now approached the island of Manavia. He hoped that the cult which had flourished there, the cult of the mother, still existed somewhere. Although the Romans had invaded he knew that this was no Mona, this was bigger and he had heard that there still existed a small group of women who worked their magic against Rome. As his boat approached the beach close to the burned-out settlement he was desperate to find them and unite them in a crusade against Rome.

Londinium had been rebuilt since the slaughter of Boudicca and the people there saw themselves as the new centre of Britannia, outstripping the old capital of Camulodunum. This time they had built a mighty wall to surround the city in the unlikely event that the natives, once again became restless. The procurator welcomed new settlers to his burgeoning town. Especially if they had money for the people had to pay healthy taxes for the privilege of living in such a fine, new city. Vibia Dives, now Flavia Gemellus, fitted very well into the procurator's plans. She had arrived with her servant and money enough to have a town house built which dwarfed the others which were already there. She proved to be a kind and witty dinner companion who entertained well and showed favour to those others in the city who were the movers and shakers of the putative commercial centre. She even began a successful business importing amphorae of wine from Gaul, a new source which was proving popular. Soon her warehouses along the river were packed with goods sent to every part of the province. The procurator used her as an example to all the other business men of what they should be doing especially when she began to employ her own, well trained guards to protect her warehouses. As she had told the procurator, they would be available to the city should trouble need to be quelled. Yes, Flavia Gemellus was a paragon of business acumen and an ideal citizen.

Had any of them looked into her green and evil eyes they would have shuddered but Flavia only showed the rest what she wanted them to see. Her heart and her mind were her own and revenge was writ large upon it. She would return and deal with those who had taken her family from her. She had fooled them once and would do so again. Her brother and father would be avenged.

The End

Historical Background

Aulus Nepos was the Governor of Britannia for a short time and it was his decision to enlarge Hadrian's original ideas. That proved expensive and his tenure was a mere three years. He was responsible for Housesteads and the other forts on the wall as well as those built north of the wall.

The Dacians were stationed at Bewcastle north of the all and the Syrian archers did arrive at about the time the novel was set. South Shields became Arbeia or Arab Town, when the Hamians and the river boatmen from the Euphrates and Tigris arrived in the province making the north east quite a cosmopolitan place.

The Selgovae, Votadini and Brigante kept on revolting right up until the reign of Antoninus Pius who built the Antonine Wall to subjugate those tribes. It never quite worked out and eventually Hadrian's Wall became the northern frontier and the Brigante finally accepted Roman rule.

The building of the two walls was the last work of the legions in Britannia and the defence of the wall was left to the auxiliaries who were sent to the northern frontier to guard it. The wall itself was built largely as described. Where there was plenty of local stone, in the east and the middle then it was made of stone. In the west it was made of turf which is why the best sections to explore are in the centre of the wall.

Marcus' Horse will return in another chapter of life in Northern Britannia during the second century but not for a while. I have other projects which are calling me.

Griff Hosker February 2013

People and places in the book.

Fictitious characters and places are in *italics*.

Ambrinus -Gallic Prefect

Aneurin-Recruit

Appius Serjanus-Governor's aide

Aulus Platorius Nepos-Governor of Britannia

Briac-Brigante warrior

Capsarius(pl) capsarii-medical orderly

Cilurnum-Chesters (on Hadrian's Wall)

Claudius Culpinus-Senior centurion vexillation of the 6th

Coriosopitum-Corbridge

Felix-Brigante Scout

Flavia Nepos-Wife of the Governor

Gaius Culpinus-Tungrian Prefect

Iucher-Votadini warrior

Julius Demetrius-Legate

Julius Longinus-Ala Clerk

Livius-Chosen Man

Livius Lucullus Sallustius-Prefect Marcus' Horse

Lucia Scaura-Flavia's companion

Lucius Garbo-First Spear XXth Valeria

Macro-Marcus' son

mansio-State inn for travellers

mansionarius-The official in charge of a mansio

Marcus Gaius Aurelius-Decurion Marcus' Horse.

Nemesis-Roman Fate

Pons Aelius-Newcastle

Quaestor-Roman official or tax collector

Quintus Licinius Brocchus-First Spear 6th Legion

Randal-Selgovae warrior

Scaeva-Brigante spy

Scanlan-Recruit

sesquiplicarius-Corporal

Sextus-Marcus' chosen man, later a decurion

signifier-The soldier who carries the standard

Titus Plauca-Camp Prefect Eboracum
tonsor-Roman barber
Trierarch-Captain of a Roman warship
Vercovicium-Housesteads (Hadrian's Wall)
Via Claudia-Watling Street (A5)
Via Hades-Road to Hell (A1)
Via Nero-Dere Street (Al)-Eboracum North
Vibia Dives-Flavia's companion
Vibius Gemellus-Recruit
Vicus (pl)vici-Roman settlement close to a fort

Other books by Griff Hosker

If you enjoyed reading this book, then why not read another one by the author?

Ancient History

The Sword of Cartimandua Series
(Germania and Britannia 50 A.D. – 128 A.D.)
Ulpius Felix- Roman Warrior (prequel)
The Sword of Cartimandua
The Horse Warriors
Invasion Caledonia
Roman Retreat
Revolt of the Red Witch
Druid's Gold
Trajan's Hunters
The Last Frontier
Hero of Rome
Roman Hawk
Roman Treachery
Roman Wall
Roman Courage

The Wolf Warrior series
(Britain in the late 6th Century)
Saxon Dawn
Saxon Revenge
Saxon England
Saxon Blood
Saxon Slayer
Saxon Slaughter
Saxon Bane
Saxon Fall: Rise of the Warlord
Saxon Throne
Saxon Sword

Medieval History

The Dragon Heart Series

Viking Slave
Viking Warrior
Viking Jarl
Viking Kingdom
Viking Wolf
Viking War
Viking Sword
Viking Wrath
Viking Raid
Viking Legend
Viking Vengeance
Viking Dragon
Viking Treasure
Viking Enemy
Viking Witch
Viking Blood
Viking Weregeld
Viking Storm
Viking Warband
Viking Shadow
Viking Legacy
Viking Clan
Viking Bravery

The Norman Genesis Series
Hrolf the Viking
Horseman
The Battle for a Home
Revenge of the Franks
The Land of the Northmen
Ragnvald Hrolfsson
Brothers in Blood
Lord of Rouen
Drekar in the Seine
Duke of Normandy
The Duke and the King

New World Series
Blood on the Blade
Across the Seas
The Savage Wilderness
The Bear and the Wolf

The Vengeance Trail

The Reconquista Chronicles
Castilian Knight
El Campeador
The Lord of Valencia

The Aelfraed Series
(Britain and Byzantium 1050 A.D. - 1085 A.D.)
Housecarl
Outlaw
Varangian

**The Anarchy Series England
1120-1180**
English Knight
Knight of the Empress
Northern Knight
Baron of the North
Earl
King Henry's Champion
The King is Dead
Warlord of the North
Enemy at the Gate
The Fallen Crown
Warlord's War
Kingmaker
Henry II
Crusader
The Welsh Marches
Irish War
Poisonous Plots
The Princes' Revolt
Earl Marshal

**Border Knight
1182-1300**
Sword for Hire
Return of the Knight
Baron's War
Magna Carta
215

Welsh Wars
Henry III
The Bloody Border
Baron's Crusade
Sentinel of the North
War in the West

Sir John Hawkwood Series
France and Italy 1339- 1387
Crécy: The Age of the Archer

Lord Edward's Archer
Lord Edward's Archer
King in Waiting
An Archer's Crusade (November 2020)

Struggle for a Crown
1360- 1485
Blood on the Crown
To Murder A King
The Throne
King Henry IV
The Road to Agincourt
St Crispin's Day

Tales from the Sword

Modern History

The Napoleonic Horseman Series
Chasseur à Cheval
Napoleon's Guard
British Light Dragoon
Soldier Spy
1808: The Road to Coruña
Talavera
The Lines of Torres Vedras
Bloody Badajoz
The Road to France

The Lucky Jack American Civil War series

Rebel Raiders
Confederate Rangers
The Road to Gettysburg

The British Ace Series
1914
1915 Fokker Scourge
1916 Angels over the Somme
1917 Eagles Fall
1918 We will remember them
From Arctic Snow to Desert Sand
Wings over Persia

Combined Operations series
1940-1945
Commando
Raider
Behind Enemy Lines
Dieppe
Toehold in Europe
Sword Beach
Breakout
The Battle for Antwerp
King Tiger
Beyond the Rhine
Korea
Korean Winter

Other Books
Great Granny's Ghost (Aimed at 9-14-year-old young people)

For more information on all of the books then please visit the author's web site at www.griffhosker.com where there is a link to contact him or visit his Facebook page: GriffHosker at Sword Books